Room
and
Board

Also by Miriam Parker

THE SHORTEST WAY HOME

Room and Board

A Novel

MIRIAM PARKER

DUTTON

DUTTON

An imprint of Penguin Random House LLC
penguinrandomhouse.com

DUTTON and the D colophon are registered trademarks of
Penguin Random House LLC.

LIBRARY OF CONGRESS CATALOGING-IN-PUBLICATION DATA

Names: Parker, Miriam (Miriam Rebecca), author.
Title: Room and board: a novel / Miriam Parker.
Description: [New York] : Dutton, [2022]
Identifiers: LCCN 2021050001 (print) |
LCCN 2021050002 (ebook) |
ISBN 9781524744502 (paperback) | ISBN 9781524744496 (ebook)
Subjects: LCGFT: Novels.
Classification: LCC PS3616.A74546 R66 2022 (print) |
LCC PS3616.A74546 (ebook) |
DDC 813/.6—dc23/eng/20151015
LC record available at https://lccn.loc.gov/2021050001
LC ebook record available at https://lccn.loc.gov/2021050002

Printed in the United States of America
1st Printing

BOOK DESIGN BY TIFFANY ESTREICHER

*To my love, Ben Olson, without whom this
book could not have been written*

Give me a girl at an impressionable age and she is mine for life.

—Muriel Spark, *The Prime of Miss Jean Brodie*

PROLOGUE

Homecoming 1996

They felt electrified. Proud. On top of the world. Or, at the very least, the school clock tower.

Miranda tied one side; Gillian tied the other. Aiden stood back and watched, a grin on his face. They had accomplished one of the most epic feats in school history and they had done it together: the annual senior prank. The stealing of the senior banner was a Glen Ellen Academy tradition and they had taken it to the next level.

"*As cool as I am,*" Gillian sang, her arms out and spinning.

"I thought you knew that already," Miranda said, as they broke into song.

"*I will not be afraid of women,*" they belted together. "*I will not be afraid of women.*"

Miranda took Gillian's hand and they spun until they were dizzy.

Gillian threw her head back and laughed. Then she closed her eyes and tried to burn the feeling onto her brain—this was the moment from high school she wanted to remember. The best day. Surrounded by her two best friends, doing the thing they had always planned to do. "I knew that you'd be able to wrap your arms around the pole to hang the banner on that little hook," Gillian said, her arm slung around Miranda's waist.

"That was the key move," Aiden added, beaming.

"It all was building to this," Gillian said. "All our time here at the Gem."

"The three of us," Aiden said.

"Just the three of us, we can make it if we try, just the three of us," Miranda sang, slightly off-key, but they all knew what she was doing.

"You and you and I," Gillian finished.

They had stolen the banner from the gym and carried it up all 364 stairs of the clock tower and hung it over the clock. Usually the banner ended up in the front hall of one of the dorms or on the headmaster's porch. But Aiden and Miranda and Gillian aimed higher. The clock tower had never been done before.

Getting the banner was easy—the custodian left the gym unlocked on the Friday before homecoming—but Gillian and Miranda still stood guard outside the gym door. When Aiden came out with the banner, carefully rolled and tied, they did their group handshake and laughed together. "It's really happening," Miranda said.

They had talked and planned for years about this night— hanging the banner on the clock tower was Aiden's idea, but he couldn't do it by himself, so the three friends had joined forces. They had scoped out the entrance to the tower, the weight of the banner, the possible ways to put it up; they had settled on a combination of tying and tacking. They had even practiced running stairs together to make sure they were fit enough to get in and get out of the tower.

"We're like the Reservoir Dogs," Aiden had said as they rehearsed.

"Except we all have our ears," Gillian said.

When the task was done, they ran down the stairs and out onto the campus. They stood back and admired what they had done. The banner wasn't entirely centered, but it did cover part of the clock and seemed secured to the posts on either side.

"We did it," Miranda said. "I love us."

"I love us too," Gillian said.

"I love us three," Aiden said.

Aiden snapped a photo with his disposable camera and put it in his pocket. It was the best high school could ever be.

He had made copies of the photo and given them to Miranda and Gillian in little frames for Christmas that year. Gillian couldn't bring herself to throw away the frame, even though she also couldn't bear to look at the photo anymore. She kept a shot of herself holding a client's Grammy Award in the front of the frame now, but she always knew that the other image was lingering behind. It was the first thing she packed when she left New York City to return to Glen Ellen Academy.

ONE

Driving through the gates of Glen Ellen Academy was like returning to the childhood home she'd never known she missed. To get there, the cab wound up through the hills of Glen Ellen, past Jack London's estate turned parkland. The road forked off and snaked through an ill-kempt vineyard. But behind the rows of grapevines was hidden a neatly manicured campus, introduced by an understated sign bearing the words GLEN ELLEN ACADEMY in a sans serif font, small but strong. The cab passed under a brick archway, by a stately clock tower, and continued on toward eight brick buildings situated around a quad that made up the small private school Gillian Brodie had attended for high school. They hadn't been the happiest years of her life, but they weren't the worst. This past year had been the literal worst. And for some reason—probably mostly because of timing and her reliable series of donations over the years—she had been invited back to the school. Not to give an inspiring speech about her career as a publicist to the stars (which was what she had always hoped they would do), but as a dorm mother to a bunch of teenage girls. Oh, how she had fallen. Though also, how grateful she was to be taken in.

"It's right up here," she said to the driver, who inched around the quad. This road would soon be closed off to cars, but they were allowed during move-in and move-out weeks. This quad would also soon be filled with students—children who didn't know what the world was like before September 11. It was history the way JFK's assassination and the Vietnam War and the 1970s gas crisis were to Gillian. By returning to Glen Ellen, she felt she was revisiting both the happiest and the most traumatic parts of her own personal history—if there was a history to be written about her at all.

The quad was even more stunning than it had been when she was in school, more than twenty years ago. It was crisscrossed with curving brick paths—the founders of Glen Ellen Academy, Winston and Millicent Royce, hadn't believed in walking in straight lines—which were surrounded by flower beds and well-pruned vegetable gardens. It was possible sometimes to pick a cucumber or a pepper from along a path. In Gillian's day you would report a "Veg Collection" on the dorm bulletin board, but probably that kind of update went on your InstaStories now. The gardens seemed more curated now though, more pruned. Maybe there was a chief gardener who made sure the campus was well-manicured, or maybe it was just cleaned up for the sake of the arriving families. There were new trellises climbing with grapes, as well as cedars and dogwoods scattered about, making perfect little picnic or reading spots. Seeing the quad brought back so many memories—of happy moments like her second-day-of-school picnic, though also painful ones—but seeing it empty of people was a first. She guessed being "faculty" had its privileges.

Freshman year, she and her roommate, Miranda, had instituted a "second-day-of-school picnic," where they pocketed food from the dining hall and took it outside to eat on a checkered blanket. The blanket was one of the few luxuries Gillian had brought with her, and it had inspired Miranda. "If they see us having fun out here, they'll want to be our friends," she had said as they stuffed sloppily made sandwiches into their backpacks. Gillian had thought that Miranda was a genius—by making up a tradition, they put themselves in the center of the school's social life. And having it happen at the beginning of the year meant that it was an event guaranteed to be documented on dorm bulletin boards, in the yearbook, and in the printed promotional materials the school sent out to prospective students. The first year, it was only the two of them on a picnic blanket, but the second year, dozens of students joined—a picnic blanket became a necessary item on the school packing list. By senior year, it had become a girls' dorm ritual. Miranda and her picnic basket graced the cover of the 1996 Glen Ellen Academy catalog. Gillian wondered if it still happened, and if it didn't, if she could rekindle the custom.

The cab came to a stop right in front of Vallejo, the six-story red brick dormitory with a green roof that Gillian would call home for the next nine months. She took a deep breath as she stepped out into the fresh Sonoma air. The smell of cut grass and newly picked grapes, with a slight aroma of cow wafting through occasionally—she hadn't thought about this scent in years, but it brought back all of her feelings about school: the terror she'd felt when she'd first arrived, a total fish out of water; the happiness she'd felt when she had a group of friends; and the eventual sadness that had developed by the time she'd graduated. All of those memories appeared with one inhalation. She took in the scene while the driver piled her luggage on the curb before driving off.

There was nobody here to meet her. She pulled out her phone to see what the arrival instructions had been. The email said that she should just go in—the front door would be open, as would the door to her room. Her set of keys— including the master key to all the rooms in the dorm—would be in her suite. So different from New York City, filled with lockboxes, dead bolts, and entry codes. She stood there surrounded by all of her portable possessions, which were cradled in Louis Vuitton luggage that had been left behind by a former client. Gillian had appropriated the set, as she had so many of their cast-offs. She picked up a suitcase in each hand, sighing. Back when she had traveled for business all the time, someone else had always been moving her luggage around. But now that phase of her life was over. It was bittersweet; the job had been simultaneously fun and hard, though the perks had been pretty fabulous. She headed through the front door of Vallejo and looked around for a cart. There was nothing to be found. She left her bags next to the elevator and went back through the lobby to shuttle the rest inside.

When she returned outside, standing next to her assortment of suitcases was a tall girl dressed head to toe in Lululemon, with a long blond ponytail streaming from the top of her head. She was taking a photo of the pile with her phone. "Hello?" Gillian prompted.

"Oh, hi," the girl said. She put her phone in her back waist pocket and held her hand out to shake Gillian's. "I'm Bunny Winthrop. Senior class president. Class officers get to move in three days early. You must be our new dorm mom. Our last one was, like, fifty thousand years old, so you're already better. Also, nice luggage."

"Thanks," Gillian said. "And yes, I'm your new dorm mom, Gillian Brodie. Coming back to my alma mater is making me feel fifty thousand years old. But I'm not really."

"Well, you certainly don't look fifty thousand. So, you're a Gem alum? How cool."

"You still call it the Gem?" Gillian said.

"Yeah, it's kind of a dumb name, but everyone uses it."

"Do you know why?" Gillian asked.

"I've always wondered!" Bunny said. "But I was too lazy to find out."

"It's because the founders' granddaughter couldn't say 'Glen Ellen Academy' and she called it 'Gem' and they loved it. So they started calling it the Gem and used the name for the newspaper and on T-shirts and things."

The shirt that said, I'M A GEM—TRULY OUTRAGEOUS was the most popular one when Gillian was in high school. But she felt that trying to explain that to Bunny would be uninteresting.

"Wow," Bunny said. "I can't believe you went here. I'll have to look you up in the yearbook. We digitized them all for our junior class project."

"Please don't," Gillian said.

Bunny was already searching on her phone. "Oh, you were cute in high school. This is going to be great. Can I help you with these?" She picked up Gillian's biggest suitcase and walked toward the dormitory door. Gillian grabbed the last two and followed behind, marveling that it had taken about thirteen seconds for Bunny to find out Gillian's high school status.

When she got to the elevator, Bunny was already inside with the other bags, holding the door with one hand, still scrolling through her phone with the other. "So you went to Yale and then you worked for Ken Sunshine—one of the most famous publicists of all time—and then started your own PR firm, all before the age of thirty?"

"I did," Gillian said, taken aback.

"Oh," Bunny said, her face suddenly all concern. "Looks like you've had kind of a bad year."

"I wouldn't be here if I had had a good year." Gillian gritted her teeth. She knew that there was information about her online, but she hadn't quite realized how accessible it would be to the students at school.

"Good point," Bunny said. "Well, then, I guess I'm glad you had a bad year, but wow, sorry."

"It wasn't the best," Gillian said.

"I can't believe you worked with all of those people," Bunny said, waving her phone in Gillian's face. "Brendan Reid, Walter Quinn. God."

Gillian shrugged.

"Is all of this accurate?" Bunny asked.

"Sadly, it is." Gillian hung her head.

"Not sad at all. It's amazing. Remind me never to get on your bad side."

"That would be wise," Gillian said, thinking about how she was going to have to discipline these girls even though they would know so much about her and some of it was pretty embarrassing.

Within five minutes, Bunny had downloaded Gillian's entire life, analyzed it, and deemed Gillian to be acceptable—if not fear-inspiring. It was the kind of analysis that record labels paid focus group researchers top dollar for but a seventeen-year-old could do instantaneously. Gillian had spent a few weeks telling herself that what had happened in New York was over, and yet here she was, barreling right back into it via a Google search. Not just the past of her adulthood, but also the past of high school. High school was a different kind of pain—of heartache and loneliness and insecurity rather than public humiliation and grandstanding. Sadly, Gillian had experienced all.

The elevator opened and Gillian and Bunny bucket-brigaded her suitcases to the suite at the far corner of the top floor. Memories of her own trips to the dorm mother's suite flooded back. She had found herself in Louise's room many times with tears running down her face, but the one that stood out was the night during her senior year when the gossip was flying, when everyone had turned on her and the whiteboards on each door all displayed G's with X's through them. High school: the original cancel culture. That night, Louise had said, "I know this feels horrible now, but it's going to get better. You're going to have a great life and this will only motivate you to be better than they are." Louise was kind of right—it did get better, although not until after she left the Gem.

"Your room is at the end of the hallway," Bunny said. "It's nice. They cleaned it since the last dorm mom lived here. But the furniture she picked out might still be there. She had terrible taste."

It was like nothing had really changed at all. The girls were still mean. The carpets looked the same. Gillian wondered if they had purposefully chosen the same pattern as had been there before—a purple background covered in twisting green vines—or if it had never been replaced. She had spent so many hours lounging in these hallways, the vines were etched in her brain. Regardless, the vibe was the same. Heavy wood doors with old-fashioned numbers on them connected by dark wood chair rails lined the dark hall. Photos of crusty old Gem alumnae in between each room. Some rooms had little plaques next to them engraved with obscure names, indicating that people nobody remembered anymore had lived in those rooms. Gillian herself had lived in room 308 of Vallejo, but she was sure she didn't have a plaque.

On her first day of school, she had shown up with her mom's old plastic suitcase that didn't even have wheels on it and a faded Acer desktop computer. She and her mother had moved her stuff, piece by piece—the giant monitor, the tower, the keyboard—into the dorm and onto her desk. When Miranda, who came from generations of wealth, had walked into their shared room and unpacked her fancy laptop covered in stickers, she had laughed out loud at Gillian's desk setup. "Where did you get that thing?" she asked. Gillian had been crawling under the desk to find the power outlet.

"Oh, it was my grandfather's," Gillian said, her face turning red. She had felt lucky to have the machine up until that moment.

"I can tell," Miranda said. Then she opened the closet where Gillian's two "nice" dresses and three pairs of jeans hung. The jeans were new, one pair from Banana Republic and one from the Gap and one a designer pair of Mavi's from Burlington Coat Factory. The Mavi's were the nicest pairs of jeans she had ever owned, bought on high discount. "Are you not done unpacking?" Miranda asked.

"No, that's all I brought," Gillian said.

"Oh," Miranda said, looking a bit befuddled, but then realizing her luck. "Can I have some space in your closet? Mine's overflowing." She opened her closet, which was filled to the brim with every color of shirt and dress, each in its own individual dry cleaner bag, which meant that she had spent a fortune not only on her wardrobe, but also on dry-cleaning each piece of it. Gillian had only had one thing dry-cleaned ever, the dress she wore to her uncle's wedding: a hand-me-down that needed alterations before she wore it. Gillian and her mother had gone together to the dry cleaner to have it taken in and cleaned. Gillian had saved the plastic bag and hanger it had come back on as it had felt like such a special thing.

"I just . . ." Gillian stammered, looking back at her empty closet. She had never felt more humiliated in her entire life.

But Miranda was sweet: "Don't worry, this is a win-win. I need more space and you need more clothes. You can borrow my things. I think we're about the same size. You already wear your jeans a little long, so it should be fine."

Gillian had known that she would be coming to a place where everyone had more than she did and nothing she could do to "keep up" would be sufficient. The funny thing was that in the end, Miranda wore Gillian's jeans more than Gillian wore Miranda's. They were more comfortable, it turned out. It was random that they had been paired together as roommates, but as they spent more and more time together, they came to feel it had been a good match on the part of the housing committee. They had the same taste in music and both secretly loved math class. Gillian looked down at her own present-day jeans, a limited-edition embroidered pair of Amo jeans she had gotten at an "influencer trunk show," and her Golden Goose sneakers and a three-quarter-sleeve T-shirt from the Row that probably was worth more than her entire high school wardrobe. She wondered how much of what she owned now and even how she lived, acted, and looked was a reaction to Miranda's response to her boarding school wardrobe on that first day.

Bunny opened the door of Gillian's suite, dropped the suitcases she was carrying next to the door, and flopped down on the couch. "I'm glad you're here. I've been in town for a few days. I've been staying at the hotel down the hill, but I knew there was new-hire orientation today, so I thought I'd come up and meet you."

"When can you check into your room?" Gillian asked, noting that Bunny had told her that class officers got to arrive early, which was obviously not true.

"Thursday is the official move-in day. But my parents had reservations at Le Club 55 in Saint-Tropez, so they had to go to Europe. It's okay. I don't mind being here early, except it's a little lonely." She didn't seem remorseful about her lie, or even really aware of it.

Gillian looked around. Her room—suite, actually—was furnished with slightly shabby commercial-grade couches and bookshelves—a step up from what you might find in a dormitory common room, but only in that they hadn't had one million Mountain Dews spilled on them. Very different from the Design Within Reach she had left behind in her West Village apartment. "Well, I guess we're the only ones here for now," Gillian said. What was she supposed to say? And she could tell it would be good to have Bunny as an ally, even if the girl wasn't always truthful.

"We should have dinner together," Bunny said. "My treat."

Alarm bells went off in Gillian's head. She couldn't let a student take her out to dinner. Seemed like an ethics violation waiting to happen. "We should probably go dutch," Gillian said. "But I'm up for it." She was still trying to figure Bunny out—she seemed more grown-up than other teens she had met. Or at least she was trying to be. Bunny shrugged and nodded. Gillian took it as a tacit acceptance.

"Well, I guess I'll unpack . . ." Gillian said it as an invitation for Bunny to leave. But Bunny didn't get the hint. She hooked her leg over the back of the couch, pulled her phone out, and started smiling at it.

Gillian went into her bedroom, dragging behind her the largest suitcase, which contained, she hoped, a set of sheets. The bedroom was less shabby than the living room. The mattress seemed newish and the closet was large, with plenty of storage. There were advantages to leaving New York, she guessed, and closet space was one of them. So was the view— the large picture window looked out across the campus; the sixth floor was right at the top of the tree line, so she saw the quad's treetops, the campus clock tower in the distance, and mountains behind that. In New York, if she craned her neck, she'd had a view of a sad-looking maple from her bedroom and someone else's living room from her own, although she did have a beautiful view of downtown Manhattan from her bathroom. The scents of the Italian restaurant downstairs would waft up through the air shaft. It was a good Italian restaurant, but being that generally she wasn't eating carbs, the smells of sauce and bread didn't really help matters. Now she opened the window to let in the fresh Sonoma air and the warm breeze. It was a perfect day here, as it so often was. She hadn't appreciated the weather when she was in high school, but after more than ten years in the ups and downs of New York weather and scents, she loved it. Another sign of growing older, she guessed. Appreciation for mild temperatures and fresh smells.

As she started unpacking, Gillian thought back to her last days in New York, some of the worst of her life. The ones Bunny had found out about via a quick search. Back then, she had been avoiding her in-box, the contents all too painful—accusations of being a misogynist sympathizer, accusations of being a quitter, accusations of being a feminist, accusations of hating women—people had lots of opinions. But she peeked one day, mostly to see if any of her clients had reached out, and she happened to land on the email from Helene Waxman, the president of the board of the Glen Ellen Academy, asking her if she would be interested in making the school her home for the next year. She quoted a salary that was much less than Gillian currently made but seemed reasonable for a job where she just lived with a bunch of teenagers, and stated that it also included "room and board"—the same stipulation as the scholarship she had gotten more than twenty years earlier to attend the school in the first place.

Gillian almost started crying she was so relieved. She hadn't thought of her alma mater as a refuge—in fact, its place in her mind was one where she had been shamed, rejected, brokenhearted—but she had stayed connected to it in loose ways. She had given donations to the scholarship fund she had been a beneficiary of, and since she'd started her own company, she had always taken on Gem students as summer interns if they had reached out to her. She had even let one crash on her sofa for a few weeks. Helene Waxman was married to one of the top Hollywood agents at CAA and had read about her situation in *The Hollywood Reporter*. She had been a few years behind Gillian at Glen Ellen and had recognized her name. She wrote that she'd heard that Gillian was in a bit of a jam and that she would be honored to have her as a dorm mother if she would accept the position. She mentioned as well that Headmaster Stuart Kent had remembered Gillian from her time at school, so when Helene had suggested her, he'd immediately agreed. Normally Gillian would have run through all the pros and cons in her head, but in her heart, she knew that she had no options, so she just responded "Yes!" and signed up for VRBO to list her Manhattan apartment as a long-term rental. She found a tenant, put her most precious things in storage, and headed to California with five Louis Vuitton suitcases.

The first of those suitcases was almost empty when Bunny walked in carrying another one. "What's in here?" she asked. It was the small one that Gillian had packed her toiletries in. At least she still had an excellent assortment of rich-lady skin

care that she had acquired back when she had a lot of disposable income and not a lot of disposable time.

"Makeup. Skin care, you know."

"Can I look?" Bunny asked.

"Sure," Gillian said. "But why don't we go get something
to eat. I'm starving."

"All of the campus places are closed, so we'll have to go
to town. And we don't have a car." Bunny began taking
items out of the toiletry case. A jar of Crème de la Mer eye
cream, Clé de Peau concealer, a sample of the Re-Nutriv Re-
Creation skin cream, La Prairie Platinum Elixir. "Oh, this
stuff is nice."

"Most of it came out of client gift bags."

"You're such a New Yorker," Bunny said. "With all your
perks."

"Perks always have their costs—don't forget that. I'll get a
Lyft so we can go into town."

"We should go to the Glen Ellen Inn. I have a tab there
that my parents pay."

"Sounds good," Gillian said. "But remember, we're going
dutch." She took out her phone and called a car to come pick
them up. This wasn't how she had expected her first hours on
campus to go, but she was a dorm mom now; she figured she
was supposed to hang out with her charges. As they waited
for the car, she tried to push away the feeling of alienation
she associated so closely with high school—that feeling of
being outside looking in—but she had to get used to the fact
that now she was part of the inner workings of the school.
Besides, these teens would be different—they weren't her
classmates; they were her students. And yet, not unlike

during high school, she was both terrified of them and also wanted to impress them. The only difference now was that she was the adult, and regardless of what they actually thought of her, they would all be looking at her. So she had to get over her insecurities and act like a role model.

TWO

....

The cab dropped them off at the unassuming little yellow building with a maroon roof and awning on the main street of downtown Glen Ellen. A tiny town that was basically just a few storefronts on the elbow of Arnold Drive—a kind of secondary link between downtown Sonoma and Santa Rosa. The scenic route, as Gillian's mother would have called it. There was one inn, a small gourmet market, and one freestanding restaurant. The Glen Ellen Inn happened to also have a restaurant inside and this was clearly Bunny's regular haunt. They walked in through the main door and the hostess immediately recognized Bunny. She gave her a big smile and a wave.

"Hi, Bunny," the hostess said.

"Hi, Francesca," Bunny said. "I was up at school today and I found our new dorm mom, Gillian. I wanted to show her my home away from home."

"Welcome," Francesca said to Gillian. She then led them through the empty dining room to the outdoor patio. There were small square tables with metal barrel chairs surrounding a rocky garden. They sat across from each other and looked out at the little center section filled with gravel and healthy succulents arranged in a circular pattern around the edges. California was so good for succulents. The restaurant had opened at five and they were the first ones in the door.

Gillian ordered an Arnold Palmer—her favorite nonalcoholic drink—but Bunny asked for a glass of rosé. Gillian looked at her askance, "Are you sure about that?"

"My parents let me," Bunny said.

Gillian wasn't Bunny's parent or guardian, or even her teacher, just the person who was charged with keeping her in her assigned room at night. That said, she didn't want drinking going on in her residence hall—or at the very least she didn't want to know about it, even though she was sure all the kids drank. "Well, on my watch you can't."

Bunny sighed, "Fine, I'll have an Arnold Palmer also."

Gillian had been a wine cooler aficionado in high school—Miranda had her older sister's expired driver's license and they were able to buy bottles at the Village Market, a little grocery store in town. She was sure that teenage tastes were more sophisticated now—at the very least they had alcoholic seltzer, which had to be better than Bartles & Jaymes, and besides, they were in the heart of wine country. Some of these girls had probably been drinking pinot noir since childhood. Still, she was proud of herself for putting her foot down. She needed to show these girls who was in charge.

As they quietly sipped their nonalcoholic drinks, Gillian felt like she had won her first battle. There was a bottle each of Tito's and Hendrick's, plus a six-pack of her favorite tonic water, in her packed luggage; she would dip into them when she had some time alone. She had planned to relax in her apartment on her first night, but clearly that plan had been revised by Bunny Winthrop.

"I'm surprised that your parents let you drink," Gillian said with a bit of a disapproving tone in her voice. Drinking had been just such a *thing* when Gillian was a teenager—so forbidden by adults and so desired by teenagers, but they would never have considered drinking with or in front of an adult.

"My parents don't give a shit about what I do," Bunny said defiantly.

"I can't imagine that's true," Gillian said.

"Well, right now they're in Saint-Tropez eating caviar and sipping champagne on a yacht and I'm staying in this hotel because school doesn't start for three days. I spent my entire childhood being watched by nannies and au pairs while they went to parties all over the world. They're professional party guests. And I'm just an inconvenience. So, if anything is true, it's that they don't care what I do as long as I don't bother them about it." She said all of this in a defensive way, like she was trying to prove to herself that she believed it.

This was a part of boarding school that Gillian had forgotten about: for her, acceptance had been a crowning achievement, but for others, it was just another phase of high-class parental neglect. It had been something that Miranda had bonded with her boyfriend, Aiden, over. Miranda's father was an ambassador to countries where Americans generally weren't welcomed, and Aiden's parents were partners in an international law firm that required enormous amounts of travel. Both had similar sob stories about being raised by hired help. To Gillian, a scholarship student raised by a single mother, it sounded sort of romantic. But ever since she had grown apart from her mother—starting during her days at the Gem and exacerbated by her move to the East Coast, where she'd thrown herself completely into her career—Gillian had come to understand that parental absence wasn't romantic; it was sad. Now she was feeling protective of the girl she had just so recently branded as a con artist. Bunny had been lying to Gillian about her special access to campus, so Gillian wasn't sure how much to trust her on all other fronts. That said, she could tell that if she had Bunny's allegiance, the other girls would like her too.

"It sounds like they trust you," Gillian said, trying to think of the bright side of parents like Bunny's.

"Whatever," Bunny said. "They're selfish. The only good thing about being their child is I have a model of how I don't want to be as an adult."

This was a fascinating take for Gillian. One she hadn't expected. "What will you do differently?" She was honestly curious.

"I'm going to focus on authentic relationships, on making the world better, on ideas, not possessions."

"Those all seem like good goals."

"I just don't want to be an asshole."

"And you think your parents are . . ."

"Assholes? Yes. All they think about is fun and meeting rich people. Social climbers through and through. They are boring and shallow."

Gillian sighed, wanting to change the subject—there was so much going on with Bunny that she didn't know how to respond. She took a deep breath and tried for an easier topic. "Well, what are you looking forward to this year?"

"Lots of things. Seeing my friends, winning state in volleyball, turning eighteen so I can officially be free of my parents. You know, typical teenage stuff." She stuck out her tongue as if trying to show that she knew that being a typical teenager was boring but that she ultimately was okay with her own basicness.

"You play volleyball?"

"When you're as tall as me, you have to play basketball or volleyball, so I chose volleyball. What was your sport?"

"I kind of loitered around the field hockey team, but I was never really good enough to play."

Bunny shrugged as if she didn't know what it was like not to be good at sports. Gillian remembered that, like many schools, the Gem had an athletic requirement. She had chosen field hockey because Miranda had played. Miranda, like Bunny, was tall and graceful. Gillian could imagine that all kinds of athletics came easily to her. On the other hand, Gillian's short legs and uncoordinated gait never quite worked on the hockey field, but she was an enthusiastic practice and sideline cheerleader at games.

"We can't all be good at everything," Bunny said. "You went to Yale, so you must have been good at the school part. I'm not great at that. Mostly because I don't try very hard."

Gillian shook her head; she was still surprised when Bunny knew things about her that she hadn't told her. "There wasn't much else to do back then. So, I did my homework. But homework isn't the most important thing. Since I graduated from high school, my grades have never mattered once, although I guess they do for some people, like if you want to go to medical school or law school. But for me, nobody cares what grades I got at Yale—just that I went there. And even that doesn't really matter. Just gave the newspapers another thing to skewer me about."

Gillian clamped her mouth shut. She needed to keep things professional with her charges, and she didn't want to encourage further googling on Bunny's part.

"True," Bunny said. "I wish more grown-ups knew that. Not that my parents care about my grades. But they don't want me to flunk out, so it's a delicate balance. I work as hard as I need to and no more."

"Well, I think you should try a little bit harder," Gillian said. "Just to play devil's advocate."

"Whatever," Bunny said, but Gillian could tell that she wanted an adult to push her to work harder.

Gillian looked around the restaurant and thought about Aiden Lloyd—how could being in this town not remind her of him? It had been a complicated situation—they were all friends, and then it changed when he became Miranda's boyfriend during their senior year, although Gillian still couldn't help having a crush on him. He was cute and sweet and there was something about being the third wheel in their relationship that had made her feel close to him, and there was that one weekend . . . She shook her head. She had to stop thinking about it. It was the past, after all.

"What does it feel like to be back?" Bunny asked. "I would never come back here voluntarily."

"I didn't think I ever would either," Gillian said. "But life takes turns you don't expect. And you know what? It feels weirdly like a relief. I don't really have a home to go back to, so this is as close to home as I have. I feel lucky that Ms. Waxman reached out to me when she did. Otherwise, I'd still be in New York, going broke and struggling to figure out what to do. This is like a reset."

"You sound like a self-help book," Bunny said.

"One thing I've learned about being an adult is that sometimes a self-help book isn't so bad. Sometimes it's okay to seek a little help."

"That's depressing," Bunny said. "I don't think I want to be an adult if that's what it's like. But I also don't want to be a kid anymore."

"Well, being an adult can't be all cocktails and shimmery things. There's also taxes and responsibilities."

"Unless you're my parents. They've managed to be adults without any responsibilities, including their own daughter."

"Maybe one day you won't have responsibilities either," Gillian said, thinking about her former classmates that Bunny's parents reminded her of. Based on recent Instagram evidence, many of them seemed to just work out all day long and attend parties and fundraisers all night. Gillian knew that Instagram was a curated experience, but the photos were consistent enough to verify the lifestyle. They had specific causes they championed—political candidates, environmental issues, rare diseases whose researchers and patients were in dire need of support. Occasionally, one would host a party for a change of pace—fundraising for their most preferred candidate or climate disaster or rare disease. The parties were so ubiquitous that Gillian wondered who organized the annual calendar—how did they arrange it so that every night there was something different to do, some different cause to support or birthday to celebrate. It was like one giant dinner-go-round. Each evening an assortment of the same set of rich people did one thing or another. Only occasionally were there competing galas. Maybe the participants were being paid to attend (the mildly famous ones), although more likely they were paying to attend (the ones who just had trust funds or rich spouses or both).

What did she know about being ultrarich? Certainly the celebrities she worked for were paid to attend parties, but that was to make the adult Bunny Winthrops of the world look more glam and to get them to fork over more money to save the long-footed potoroo or find a cure for Noonan syndrome. Regardless, it was nice to have beautiful homes in multiple cities and private jets—but a lot of the rich people she knew were bored and lonely.

"Anyway, I guess eventually I'll be an adult whether I want to or not, and when I am, I won't be irresponsible and flighty like they are," Bunny said. "I'm going to have my own business. Something real like selling solar panels, not something stupid like a skin-care line. Anyone can have a skin-care line."

Gillian laughed at this observation. The server, who was older and had that perfect bored look on her face, like she knew what you were going to order before you ordered it, returned and took out her pad to indicate that it was time for them to make their choices.

"I'll have the filet, medium rare, with prawns," Bunny said. A perfect rich-kid order; Gillian hadn't learned to order with that much confidence until she was well into her twenties.

"Fish tacos for me," Gillian said. Though she knew how to order fancily, after many years of being the publicist for celebrities who didn't eat or who ordered strange things, she had grown into her own tastes and knew what she wanted on the menu, even if it wasn't the fanciest or the healthiest thing.

She had left total disgrace behind this morning in New York City and here she was in Sonoma, dining with a trust-fund kid. It was amazing how all teenagers, even ones as sophisticated as Bunny Winthrop, just wanted to be loved by their parents. Gillian had been loved by her own mother, but life as the daughter of a single mother wasn't easy.

Gillian's mother worked long and frustrating hours as a real estate agent—always busy at night and on the weekends. And as Gillian got to junior high school, it seemed more and more that she was the one taking care of her mother. Making dinner, doing laundry, confirming that the phone and electric bills were paid. Her mother became more of a friend than an authority figure. So, when the possibility of boarding school came up—via a plucky guidance counselor and a full ride—they both jumped at the chance to get Gillian out of the house. Gillian got a scholarship, and her mother got her freedom. Glen Ellen Academy was only a couple of hours from their Sacramento home, but it felt like a far enough divide to relieve them of their burdens to each other. Their relationship actually got much better after Gillian left the house—Gillian started to value the fact that her mother had interests other than her daughter. And her mother liked that Gillian had gotten to know some rich kids at school, thus creating some valuable real estate referrals for her.

Bunny took a long sip of her Arnold Palmer and a deep breath. "So," she said, dramatically. "A crazy thing happened last year that everyone's still kind of freaking out about."

"What?" Gillian asked. She was honestly curious to learn about the lives of these high school students.

"Well, these twins in our class, we've always called them the Eccentrics, but their names are Farrah and Freddy. They've always been the weirdest kids at school, super nerdy and only friends with each other. They kind of scurry around and don't make eye contact."

"Okay," Gillian said, remembering how hard it was to be young. Even in the age of the internet, where individuality was theoretically valued, everyone fell into a category.

"Anyway, at the end of last year, a song they wrote and sang got super popular with the kids at school. They posted a video on their private Instagram and we all follow each other, so we all listened to it."

"Oh," Gillian said.

"It was called 'Let's Hang Out.' And everyone at school has heard it. The DJ played it at the prom last year."

"I've never heard it," Gillian said.

"It's just a Gem thing. But it's so annoying. I guess while we were all taking selfies and swapping dresses, they were working on their piano and guitar skills. And now they're, like, the most popular band at school."

A PR strategy for the twins started running through Gillian's head. Then she pushed the thought to the back of her mind. She wasn't a publicist anymore. Her one identity, gone—a small pang of regret echoed in her mind. Who was she if she wasn't a publicist?

"Well, I'm worried that now everyone loves them here. It's my senior year and we have all of these plans—my friends Julia and Rainbow and me—and we don't want the twins to ruin them with their new status."

"I'm sure it'll be fine," Gillian said, although of course that's the last thing a teenager wants to hear. If it was going to be fine, she wouldn't have been telling the story.

"What if they become popular? What if they run home-coming? What if just everyone wants to hang out with them, and all of our plans are ruined? Ugh, it'll just be . . . the worst."

"I'm sure it's hard for them too," Gillian said—thinking back to her own experience. "They're not used to being in the limelight. I'm sure they don't want to do that stuff now if they didn't want to do it before. Maybe you can help them and think of them more like fun people to know than enemies."

"I feel like you're on their side," Bunny said.

"I just feel like I know what they're going through—a change of social status can be hard on people."

"But what if they get more popular? Like people outside of school know who they are. They could go viral," Bunny said.

"I just don't think that you should worry about this," Gillian said. "Maybe you should try to be kinder to them."

"I don't feel like being kind," Bunny said.

"Just try it for one minute," Gillian said.

"Their songs *are* good," Bunny said.

"Exactly. Just a tiny bit of generosity."

"Ugh," Bunny said and crossed her arms.

Gillian didn't know if she had gotten through to her, but she had tried. Gillian looked around at the other tables starting to fill up with people in their thirties and forties, sipping wine and eating appetizers. This place was going to be a god-send for her, she could already tell. She was going to need to escape campus, and this was close enough to be convenient, yet far enough away to be a perfect home bar. In the West Village she'd had WXOU, a divey old-timey bar where she could always go and have a drink and escape from the world. She knew most of the bartenders and the regulars. Sometimes she would talk to someone and sometimes she would just read a book or look at her emails. She'd even watched whole episodes of dumb shows like *The Real Housewives* with her headphones on in there. Nobody ever bothered her. She never saw anyone from her work world there; it was like living a parallel life. An oasis of normal in a world of insanity.

She missed her WXOU world—Dennis, the bartender, who knew exactly what kind of red wine to pour her (he ordered bottles of tempranillo specially for her and opened them fresh for her when she walked in), and the regulars: Keith, the interior designer who got her discounts on all of her furniture, using his "decorator's discount"; Harold, the stockbroker, who always had a broken heart; and "Lady Roxanna," a classic old-timey West Villager who claimed to be a poet but whose most distinguishing characteristics were her gravelly voice, her brightly dyed almost neon-pink hair, and her liver of steel. Nobody ever figured out where Lady Roxanna got the money to maintain her West Village apartment and her love of faux fur. But she always had a glass of vodka in her hand and a story about what New York used to be like on her lips. Gillian loved these people because they weren't like her clients—they were authentically themselves and they were giving as opposed to needing. Her clients were always needing something. Her friends at the bar always seemed to be offering something.

"Maybe it's what the twins always wanted," Bunny said. "To become accidentally famous."

"You can't worry about it until it happens," Gillian said. One of her favorite pieces of advice to her nervous clients.

"I just want to be prepared," Bunny said. "Julia, Rainbow, and I have been texting about it for the past month on our group thread. We want our senior year to be perfect."

"I think the only thing you can do is just enter the school year with the best of intentions," Gillian said, thinking back to her own senior year, when she had resolved not to be jealous of Miranda before school started.

Their food arrived and they were both quiet for a few moments as they ate happily. Gillian's fish tacos were delicious—a nice balance of guacamole and a tangy aioli along with grilled fish. She smiled; this felt like a uniquely California meal and made her happy that she had left New York.

New York could suffocate you with its intensity and its claustrophobia. It could slowly eat away at you, bit by bit, until you had been devoured by it. Nothing about living in New York was relaxing. Yes, you could pay for peace at a super-expensive luxury spa or in the back of an SUV going to the airport at four in the morning, but the cost of these things often canceled out any attempts to de-stress. The only places she could really relax were WXOU and Northern California.

She had always associated Northern California with serenity. The relaxation-focused, self-care economy of today's California was more about expensive yoga pants and essential oils than the batik-and-crystal economy of Gillian's youth, but Gillian liked all of it. The commitment to calm was inspiring to her. Her mother now lived in an over-fifty community in Sacramento with her third husband, whom she had married after Gillian graduated from Yale. There had been a second husband at one point also, but Gillian had barely met him—they had been married briefly when Gillian was in high school when she rarely came home. The third husband, Robert, was a divorce lawyer (he had been the lawyer on her mom's second divorce, which Gillian had chosen not to ask too many questions about) who treated her mother well. Robert had a daughter named Carrie who lived nearby in Chico, and she was also a real estate agent, so Gillian's mother felt a kinship with her. Gillian was sure that they talked about what a strange life her daughter had, a Yale student, then a publicist shuttling between New York and Los Angeles. Gillian was like a foreigner to them—they who had never left a hundred-mile vicinity of Sacramento. And how could she explain to them what her life was like?

"I'm glad to be here," Gillian said to Bunny, apropos of nothing. Bunny had been contentedly scrolling through Instagram as she ate.

"Well, it sounds like you kind of needed a change," Bunny said. "And I guess if we have to have a dorm mother, I'm glad it's you. You seem chill. I already told Rainbow and Julia about you and they're excited. They'll be here tomorrow."

"I thought the dorms didn't open until Thursday," Gillian said.

"They don't—the dorms, I mean. We're going to rent the fanciest suite at this hotel using my parents' credit card and have a little pre-school retreat together."

"Sounds good," Gillian said. At least Bunny would be out of her hair and she could relax with a vodka tonic in peace in her own home. "It's nice to reconnect after a long summer."

"Oh, we basically spent the entire summer together. But I

haven't seen them in, like, three weeks. So, there's a lot to catch up on."

"I'm sure there is." Gillian nodded, already dreaming about being alone after this dinner. "I should probably get back."

Bunny waved for the check. Gillian tried not to shake her head. "I know, I know. But they expect to pay for things," Bunny said. "Just remember that money can't buy happiness."

Although it could buy a lot; that was one thing Gillian had learned from her celebrity clients.

"True, true," Gillian said. "But you also can't pay for my dinner." She handed her card to the server. "As I said before, we're going dutch."

THREE

....

Gillian called a Lyft. When it pulled up, she said, "It was fun getting to know you, Bunny. I'll see you on campus."

"Thanks for being our mom," Bunny said. She gave Gillian an awkward hug. Gillian had temporarily forgotten that Bunny was a teenager. It was like she swung between super sophisticated and super young. Maybe that was the truest expression of being in high school—it was a liminal state between childhood and adulthood.

Gillian got into the car and waved good-bye to her charge, trying not to worry about her spending a night alone in a hotel. Back in her room, she realized how tired she was. She had woken up that morning in New York City and here she was in California, twenty hours later. It was okay to be tired. To be exhausted, really. Gillian splashed some water on her face in the bathroom and then went into her bedroom to apply what she called her "express" evening skin-care routine—toner, serum, eye cream, moisturizer. There was another routine that took longer, but it was too late for that.

She got into bed. Her room had a beautiful view of the

Gem clock tower, the oldest part of the campus. She remembered how in senior year for homecoming, she and Miranda and Aiden had climbed to the top of the clock tower (364 steps, a number she would never forget) and hung their graduation banner over the western face of the clock. They were convinced that they were the first to choose that location. At the very least, in their years at the Gem, they had never seen it done. Gillian had been so excited at their triumph, but it made her heart ache when she looked over and saw Miranda and Aiden nose to nose, smiling at each other. Even now, the yearning hadn't quite gone away. Gillian felt for Bunny and her friends, remembering how hard those first experiences of love and infatuation were, how strong the feelings could be. How the pain of being a teenager can shape the future. Now that she was in her late thirties, she felt more capable of shutting off her feelings, or at the very least avoiding them. Nevertheless, being here was bringing everything back.

Not just her feelings about what had happened to her in high school, but what had just happened to her in her career. As a publicist, she had always been behind the scenes. But when she closed her business, the eye of the internet turned, if only briefly, toward her. She had declared that she would rather be out of a job than represent liars, and she had taken heat for it. But instead of hiding, she had decided she needed to project a brave face on her personal social media. She didn't have oodles of followers, but they were her clients, her contacts, producers and writers—it was a small yet exclusive list—people she considered friends, until she realized they were only friends until they didn't need her anymore. Not cocky—she wasn't going to post photos of herself somewhere fancy and remote, like Portofino or Monaco or on a flying trapeze or with a dozen beautiful people. But she did show a photo of a beautiful latte and a copy of a bright yellow book with flowers on the cover that she had gotten in a gift bag at a party, with the hashtag #selfcare. She also posted a picture of a friend's French bulldog wearing a baseball cap, a cute café table with a full glass of rosé on it, and a knitted scarf draped over a velvet chair, even though it was summer, with the hashtag #lookingforwardtofall. Her supporters had commented supportive things. Haters had commented hateful things. But it was what she wanted to convey to the world: *I'm going to be okay.* She wasn't entirely sure she believed her own hype, but she had followed through as much as possible on her own crisis management strategy. That night in Glen Ellen, she fell asleep hopeful that her new life would be better than her old one.

The next morning, she felt refreshed after a night of good sleep. But she didn't have time for messing around. She had to take a shower, get dressed, and go to an orientation meeting for dorm parents and other student advisers. She still hadn't fully unpacked, so she put on the outfit she had been wearing the day before, sprayed some perfume on herself, and walked over to the clock tower building. Her first stop was Headmaster Kent's office—not to see him, but to say hello to his longtime assistant, Gloria Rhodes. Gillian had always had a fondness for Gloria, one of the few people at the Gem she felt had understood her. Her mother had always taught her to be respectful of everyone on every staff. And when Gillian had met Gloria, sitting behind the desk outside the headmaster's office, she'd known she should be polite to her.

It had started casually—Gillian would say hi when she walked by the headmaster's office and Gloria would politely smile in return. But as the days and months rolled on, Gillian would stop in to chat with Gloria. She generally had no business in the headmaster's office, but Gloria had a dish of candy on her desk and was always ready with an engaging story—everything from a backed-up toilet flooding the boys' locker room to the girl who had to quit school because her dog had cancer and she couldn't bear to be away from him. Gillian would tell Gloria about her problems—her unrequited crush on Aiden, her frustrations with her mom, and her general feeling of being an outsider at school. The things Gillian couldn't talk about with other kids at the Gem, even Miranda. And it was an added bonus that by hanging around the headmaster's office, she got to know him just well enough to cement herself in his mind.

When she first walked into the office, she was surprised that Gloria looked almost the same: perfect posture in her seat, dressed formally in a silk blouse with a tie at the neck. She even had the exact same corona of hair around her head that she had when Gillian was in high school, just now it was white instead of brown. Her face seemed not to have aged, although a pair of reading glasses was now perched on her nose. She looked a bit confused when Gillian greeted her, but then Gillian could almost see her sorting through the years and years of students in her brain.

"It's Gillian Brodie," Gillian said, holding out her hand. "I'm here as a dorm mother now, and I wanted to say hello."

"Wow," Gloria said. "Gillian Brodie. You're a sight for sore eyes. It's great to see you. You're even prettier than you were in high school."

"I have an epic skin-care routine," Gillian said. Gloria stood to hug her and Gillian was instantly brought back to the late nineties with Gloria's scent of Love's Baby Soft perfume.

"So glad you're back," Gloria said. "Not much has changed around here, you'll notice, but I like it that way. Except all the computers, of course. I dare say I was typing memos on typewriters when I started. But that hasn't been for a long time."

"It looks like you're doing great," Gillian said.

"A few aches and pains, but I don't complain too much. How is your mother? I remember you were always worrying about her," Gloria said.

"She's fine," Gillian said. "Remarried. She lives in a Mc-Mansion with her husband, a divorce attorney. He handles all the bills now." Gillian remembered a day when she had sat on the chair next to Gloria's desk, crying because her mother had yet again forgotten to pay her bills and the phone and the electricity had been shut off. It wasn't that her mother didn't have the money to pay; she just didn't remember to do it. Gillian had spent her morning on the phone with the companies, trying to figure out a way to get the bills paid—that was before there was internet billing, and Gillian didn't have a credit card.

"That's a relief," Gloria said. "Not having to worry so much. Anyway, are you on your way to the orientation? It's in the faculty lounge, which is downstairs on the second floor now. The one that was up here has been converted to the headmaster's conference room. He's expanded."

"Okay," Gillian said. "Thanks! I'll come back to say hi again after this is all over. Are you doing okay?"

"Sure," Gloria said. "My daughter doesn't call enough and

I'm not getting around the way I used to. But I'm happy to be here. Now go to your training. Don't be late! You know Headmaster Kent doesn't like that."

Gillian did remember being humiliated in front of all the other students at a morning assembly for walking in after everyone else had sat down. "Miss Gillian Brodie," he had bellowed, "seems to have better things to do than everyone else at this school. It is just common decency to be on time for the morning assembly." Some of the other kids called her "Common Decency" for weeks after that. She shuddered at the thought.

Now she was thirty-eight years old and she was on time, but she didn't care if someone attacked her for lack of common decency. She knew she was commonly decent and she had been through much worse in her life. But despite how long had passed, going down the stairs of the clock tower building to the current faculty lounge brought her back to her high school days. There were classrooms in this building as well, so she had spent many hours lingering in these hallways, gossiping on the steps, telling secrets in the bathrooms, loitering outside a classroom while waiting for a crush to emerge. All the longing—to know, to be known, to be seen—came rushing back. She didn't envy, really, the girls who were in her care. Being in high school was intense.

There were three other people sitting in the room when she entered—another woman and two men. All looked older than her; one of the men wore a wedding ring. There was a central round table in the room with five chairs around it, and that's where they were sitting. She sat in the fourth chair and assumed Kent would sit in the fifth. "Hi," she said. "I'm Gillian Brodie, new here."

The bald man with the wedding ring held out his hand and said, "Roger Fletcher. Fifth-year dorm parent. And life-long coach. I coach intramural softball and golf."

The man to his left, who had a military-style blond flat-top, smiled at her and said, "Joe Riccola. Second-year dorm parent and intramural swimming coach."

The woman, who looked not much older than Bunny, said, "I'm Brittany Greene. Dorm mom for three years. I also teach health, wellness, and cooking."

"They didn't have health, wellness, and cooking when I went here," Gillian said.

"An alum?" Brittany asked.

"Yeah, class of 1997."

"You were the ones who put the banner on the clock tower," Brittany said.

"We have to tell every class of kids they'll get expelled if they try to copy you," Roger said.

Gillian laughed. "Sorry about that—it was definitely our best prank." As she said that, Headmaster Kent walked in, wearing a three-piece Tom Ford sharkskin suit. Not exactly what she'd expected for a staff training session, but he had always been stylish.

"Good morning," he said. "Good to see you all. Roger, Joe, and Brittany, welcome back. Gillian Brodie, so good to see you! Welcome. We do this training every year, even if every-one is returning. Just a reminder of rules and regulations and that we are caring for teenagers. We need to stand in for their parents—make sure they eat, sleep, shower, go to class. That they don't drink alcohol. That they do their homework. There's a reason we call you a dorm parent and not a resident adviser. It's to remind you that you have responsibilities."

As he talked about the rules and regulations of the dorm and the punishments that could be used to keep the kids on the straight and narrow, Gillian paid as much attention as she could, jotting down notes that seemed relevant. "Quiet time. Homework. Lights-out." She had read the handbook on the plane and the former dorm mother of Vallejo had left her a letter. She'd told Gillian about the rules and her tips for enforcing them, but also warned her about the mice that moved into the dorm when the girls got sloppy about their snacks. That was what Gillian feared more than misbehavior in the hallways—an infestation. But that wasn't one of the things Kent mentioned in his talk. Gillian started making her own notes about what she would say to the girls at their Welcome Night meeting.

During their lunch break, Gillian tagged along with Roger, Joe, and Brittany as they went down the hill in Roger's car to the Village Market to pick up sandwiches and sodas.

"So what's your other job, Gillian? Coaching or teaching?" Roger asked after they were all in the car.

"I don't have one," she said. "Do I need one?"

"Normally they don't have dorm parents just be dorm parents—you need to do other things, like teach or coach intramural sports."

"Nobody asked me to do that," Gillian said. "I'm not really qualified for much. I'm not very athletic." She was surprised that they didn't ask her more about where she came from, what she had done before. Maybe they had googled her and knew everything, or maybe they didn't care. Either way, she preferred not having to explain why she was there and who she was.

"I guess you were a last-minute replacement for Theresa, who was the dorm mother of Vallejo for eight years," Brittany suggested. "Maybe they didn't have time to also line you up for something else."

Gillian took a deep breath as they arrived at the market and got out of the car. She didn't expect to be questioned in this manner. "They didn't say anything about another job. I guess I can be a publicist if they need one, which is what I was in New York. But how often does a sleepy private school need a publicist?"

"Maybe that's what they were intending," Joe said, holding the door open for the rest of the group.

"Theresa did leave me a letter," Gillian said.

"Read it," Brittany said. "The girls didn't love her, but she was good at her job. The girls will love you because you're from New York and know celebrities. Don't worry about that."

Gillian smirked to herself: *Of course they weren't asking any questions. They thought they already knew everything.*

"It's honestly better if they don't love you," Joe said. "Because then you can get them to behave better."

"I'm not too worried about the students," Gillian said. "But Theresa did make me nervous about the mice."

"Theresa hated the mice," Brittany said. "I think they're ultimately what drove her away."

They all stood in front of the counter and looked up at the offerings on the wall. There was silence for a few moments as they made their decisions.

"You do the best you can and make an example of someone on the first days. After classes start to get harder and
sports practice is more intense, they usually calm down and
are tired at night," Roger said.

"It must be weird to be back living in the dorm you lived
in in high school," Brittany said.

"Super weird," Gillian said. "It's bringing back all the
memories."

"Just wait until the kids get here," Joe said as he ordered a
caprese sandwich.

"I'm counting the minutes." Gillian smiled. She thought
about the reunion she and Miranda had at the beginning of
junior year after they had been separated for the summer. It
had been so exciting to know that she was going to share a
room with her best friend (after the uncertainty of arriving
at school freshman year). They had hugged in front of Vallejo
and handed each other mixtapes from the summer. Miranda
had spent the summer living with her parents in Morocco, so
her tape was filled with electronic pop and European rock;
Gillian's was all folk musicians she had heard at the festivals
she had attended in Northern California—Janis Ian, Ani
DiFranco, Dar Williams. The two tapes went on to be their
soundtracks for the year.

"I really missed our music sessions," Gillian had said.

"Me too," Miranda agreed as they walked into the dorm
side by side. "I don't think my taste is as good without you."

"We complement each other," Gillian said.

They went up to their room and spent the rest of the day
listening to their tapes and telling each other about the reasons they put the songs on. And by doing so, they merged
their tastes into one cohesive soundtrack.

FOUR

....

Move-in day was like nothing Gillian had ever experienced; it certainly had changed since the move-in days of the 1990s. Starting at six A.M., overstuffed SUVs began pulling onto campus. Large orange bins were lined up at the curbs, and men in reflective vests that said GLEN ELLEN ACADEMY on them helped families unload their bursting cars. At first, Gillian looked out from above, watching as girls (Vallejo was all-girl, but the school was coed) shunned their mothers and pouted at their fathers and siblings. They gently took their most prized possessions from the cars themselves—laptops covered in stickers, makeup bags, even a few ratty-looking stuffed animals—leaving the hard work of unloading suitcases, mini-fridges, bulk-sized boxes of granola bars, and cases of LaCroix to others.

It was fun to watch from her perch, but once the early bird crowd had moved along and the actual move-in times had begun, she went downstairs to help. She was the dorm mother, after all, and she needed to welcome the girls who would be her charges and reassure their parents, so she stationed herself outside the dorm. Everyone who arrived looked at her a bit sheepishly, as if the mountains of things they were bringing were unusual—everything from those pillows that looked like chairs to framed pieces of art to ragged stuffed animals. At least when the mothers left, the rooms would look nice and orderly for an hour or so. But seeing the crates of shoes and mountains of suitcases and bags of linens was humbling for everyone involved. Regardless, Gillian tried to introduce herself to the available parents, the ones who looked the least stressed, and to give a reassuring smile to the girls. She wanted the girls to feel like she would be there for them, even though she felt like she didn't quite know how to be the leader they would need. She didn't feel very qualified to help teenagers with their problems—she felt like she had been a teenager so very long ago. Although she did admit to herself that being back on campus was bringing back all those old feelings.

A few girls arrived more modestly—in beat-up Honda Accords or newer-looking Kia sedans. Those girls generally had a large duffel, a suitcase, a laptop bag, and just one parent with them. They didn't require the help of the unloaders or even the giant orange tubs. Their belongings were portable. Maybe they'd arrived from out of state and had shipped their containers and fridges ahead of them. But more likely, these were the scholarship students, the ones who had worked hard to get here, for whom this was a life-changing opportunity. Gillian made note of those girls, as she knew the transition would probably be hard for them. Joining this cavalcade of ostentatious wealth and privilege, meeting kids who might feel entitled to be here, or even resentful of it. Her own transition to boarding school life had been filled with mistakes and missteps—it was like there was another language the rich girls spoke. She learned to say, "My mother is in real estate," rather than "My mom is a real estate agent." And "We're spending Christmas in the city," rather than "I'm going home to Sacramento for Christmas." It made the questions go away faster—which was always her ultimate goal.

Bunny came up behind her and bumped her on the hip. "Hello, stranger. What did you do since I last saw you?"

"Went to my dorm mother training," Gillian said. "How was the rest of your stay in the hotel?"

"Fun. I had filet for lunch and dinner. And it's so great to reunite with my girls. They're on their way up with all their stuff. I can't wait for you to meet them." As if summoned from a dream (or maybe Bunny had been watching the Lyft drive up the hill), a car arrived carrying their other friend, Julia. "Julia is from New York. Park Avenue, to be precise," Bunny said. "Most of her things will arrive via UPS tomorrow—she travels light, with just a suitcase."

Julia hopped out of the car, a Birkin bag on her shoulder with a MacBook peeking out of it, and let the driver pull her Gucci rolling bag from the trunk. Julia had a short jet-black bob, wore ballet flats and black leg warmers, a tailored skirt that hit high on her waist, and a cropped sweater that just met the top of the skirt. She looked like she belonged in Paris in the 1920s. Her features were delicate and pale. She struck Gillian as the kind of girl who struggled to gain weight, rather than worried about losing it. Bunny was probably twice her size. "Isn't she just the cutest little elf?" Bunny said.

Julia walked up to them and hugged Bunny. "I had the worst morning," she said to Bunny. "I'm so glad to see you."

"What happened?" Bunny asked.

"My mother called to tell me that they finally came for my

dad and reminded me not to get fat this year. Typical. I mean, my dad is literally going to jail and all she cares about is my weight."

"I'm sorry," Bunny said. "She can be such a jerk. Besides, it would literally be impossible for you to get fat."

As Gillian listened to their banter, it finally dawned on her that she was going to spend the next year dealing with teenager drama, some of it interesting and some of it banal, often in the same sentence. "I'm Gillian Brodie," Gillian said, holding out her hand.

"She's the dorm mom I told you about," Bunny said. "She's cool."

"Great," Julia said. "Because I need a drink."

Gillian shook her head. She smiled maternally at the girls and said sternly, "It is my job to tell you that underage drinking is not condoned in this dorm."

"True, true," Bunny said, shrugging. She turned to Julia. "Rainbow is almost here. Her dad came to get her a few minutes ago, with all her stuff. He brought the pickup truck."

"Is she mortified?" Julia asked, putting her hair behind her ear.

"I guess she's used to it by now."

"Right," Julia said. "Well, my father's been arrested for tax evasion as of this morning, so I'd take a cute dad with a pickup truck any day at this point."

"I'm sorry," Gillian said.

"It was just a matter of time," Julia said. "I'm glad they waited until I left for school."

"Rainbow's dad *is* cute, isn't he?" Bunny said.

"He really is, like the way that Philip is hot on *The Americans,* except that he doesn't look like a creepy eighties dude.

Should we go up?" Julia asked. "I'm exhausted. Where are our rooms?"

"We've got the fifth-floor corner," Bunny said. "We each have singles and a common room. I already installed my mini-fridge. I'm sure Rainbow will have hers too."

"Great," Julia said. "It's such a hassle getting one here, I'd have to order a new one. There is a cute mini Smeg that maybe I would get. But now that my dad . . . ugh. Who knows."

"We don't need it," Bunny said. "Really, don't worry."

"Fine, fine," Julia said. "But you know how I feel about being a mooch."

"We're like family," Bunny said. "Besides, you know how much of your Crème de la Mer I'll use this year. It's worth at least one fridge."

"True," Julia said.

"You guys don't need Crème de la Mer," Gillian said.

"Someone once told me that the thing that makes a wrinkled old woman is a careless young woman, so I'm not risking it," Bunny said.

"Who told you that?" Julia asked.

"A very nice lady named Marie Claire," Bunny said.

"You're all ridiculous," Gillian said.

Just then, a rusty pickup truck overflowing with suitcases and boxes came around the bend. "There she is," Julia said.

They ran to the curb and the truck screeched to a halt. A brunette with a pixie cut and a short tie-dyed baby doll dress on hopped out. She was wearing Allbirds sneakers. She was a mix of Instagram influencer and Grateful Dead fan. Bunny and Julia leapt on her and all three hugged for a long time. "Rainbow!" They yelled so loudly that Gillian jumped a bit. A greeting as if they hadn't seen each other for years, but even Gillian knew it had just been a matter of hours, or even minutes. She smiled, remembering the intensity of friendship at that age. Then she inhaled deeply when Rainbow's father walked around the truck to start unloading the ungodly amount of things in the back. It was Aiden Lloyd. Of course it was. She stopped and looked around; in her mind it felt like a soundtrack was playing, the kind of music that would be in a romantic comedy like *As Time Goes By*. It was as if he were walking around the truck in slow motion. It all felt surreal. Every memory flooded through her—the good and the bad. She had loved him so much and he had broken her heart. It wasn't that simple of course, but on the other hand, it totally was.

A look of shock and then, after a moment where she could tell he was processing, a huge smile came across his face. The type of smile that revealed his dimples on both sides; she couldn't forget those dimples. She could feel her cheeks get hot, her stomach buzz, her armpits grow damp. It was like a time machine, shooting her back to feeling exactly as she had at age sixteen. Except possibly he was cuter than he had been in high school? She inhaled deeply, wondering if he smelled the same, and smiled back, trying to be cool. He was wearing a blue-and-black plaid shirt and black jeans. Everything a little bit faded, like he didn't quite care enough to get new things but he had thought about how he looked when he'd opened his closet. "Gillian Brodie. Fancy meeting you here," he said.

"Greetings and salutations," she said, her smile wide. She was embarrassed at her enthusiasm, but also couldn't quite contain it.

"Looks like you two are already acquainted," Bunny said, with some surprise in her voice.

"Indeed, we are," she said to Bunny.

"Wait, you went here too—right, Mr. L?"

"I did," he said. "And not only that, but Gillian and I were in the same class."

"The famous class of 1997," Rainbow said. "Reunited." Gillian couldn't tell if Rainbow was excited or dismayed by this development; her tone was exaggerated sarcasm. Had Aiden spoken fondly of their time in high school? Might Rainbow know something that Gillian didn't?

"We're going upstairs now. We have to work on our outfits for tonight," Julia said. "Coming, Rainbow?"

"Got this, Dad?" Rainbow asked, jabbing him in the ribs.

"We're in the fifth-floor corner," Bunny said. She turned around, linked arms with each friend, one on each side, and proceeded into the building.

"I guess I'm on unloading duty," Aiden said, smiling. One of the helpers rolled over an orange bin and Aiden started pulling boxes and suitcases out of the truck bed. Gillian made a few unconvincing moves to help, but he waved her away. "I've done this a million times," he said. "Or at least it feels like it."

"The unglamorous side of parenthood," she said.

"There are more unglamorous sides," he said. "Especially as a single dad. I'll take this over her crying over a mean kid in school or a poorly placed pimple any day."

"Poorly placed pimples *are* a big deal," Gillian laughed.

"Believe me, I am well aware," he said.

The last item he pulled out was a Smeg mini-fridge in red.

Gillian hoped it matched with Julia's vision for their common room.

"That's cute," Gillian said.

"She demanded it," he said. "They cost a thousand dollars. Can you imagine? They come up to my waist and they can't even keep ice cream cold."

"Are they better than other fridges?"

"Of course not," he said. "But they do look cool. And who am I to say no. I mean, I send her here, so what's another thousand dollars?"

"Right," Gillian said. She couldn't even begin to imagine all the expenses associated with children, especially ones like these girls.

"Things haven't changed that much around here since we left," he said. "Except all the phones and social media."

"Just those small things," Gillian laughed. "Can you imagine if we had Instagram in high school? Or even could text each other?"

"It definitely would have been weird," he said. "I think I probably would have spent a lot more time hiding in my room."

"You wouldn't have been posting every moment to show off?"

"Not at all—the exact opposite. I wouldn't want anyone to know my business."

She started counting on her fingers. "You must have had her right after we graduated."

He shook his head. "Being a dad wasn't what I planned to be doing in my late teens and early twenties, but in retrospect I wouldn't trade it for the world," he said.

"I can't imagine taking care of anyone else now," she said. "Much less when I was nineteen."

"Well, you have all these girls to take care of now."

"I don't have to keep them alive like a baby," she said. "I just have to make sure they go to class and are in their rooms by ten."

"In the category of unexpected life turns, I wouldn't have expected to see you here, of all places," he said, smiling.

"Me either," she said. She looked at the distant hills, then back at him.

"You can Google it the way they all have," she added. "But what I will say is that I'm proud of the way I handled things." It had been a long-term client, one of her first, a top-tier director named Brendan Reid who had always been nothing but professional with her and her staff. Only then the #MeToo accusations started to come out, first Harvey Weinstein, then John Lasseter, and then dozens of others and Reid was one of them. Gillian's client furiously denied the claims against him, and she believed him. At first. She helped him write an op-ed about abuse in the industry and placed it in *The Washington Post*. But then ten women came together to write a rebuttal that described all the lurid things Reid had done to them. The worse the allegations got, the sicker she felt about it.

She dropped him from her client roster, but before that was public, other accused sexual harassers started contacting her, asking her to defend them and help them with their image. The *New York Post* called her "the playboy's publicist." She had to take matters into her own hands: she told a reporter for *The New York Times* that she had been duped by her client. Then she did the only other thing she could think of: she closed up shop. She got her assistants jobs in other firms and wrote a letter to all of her clients telling them that she was leaving the business. She took a screenshot of a generic version of the letter and put it on the agency Twitter account. She sublet her office to one of her senior publicists who wanted to start her own company and retreated to her West Village apartment—which she could no longer afford—and then, ultimately, luckily, to the Gem. She tried to think of it not as an admission of defeat, but as a new beginning.

"I'm sure you did everything right," Aiden reassured her. "I read some about it and from knowing you and reading between the lines, it felt like you had been betrayed by an old friend. Your main crime was trusting someone who you knew well. I can't imagine having that happen in public though—I really did feel for you." He squeezed her shoulder just for a second.

"Thanks," she said, her shoulder feeling warm where he had touched it. "It wasn't the best time of my life." But all she could think was: *He had read about me.*

"I guess trusting your old friends is a mistake you've made a few times. And it's never really worked out for you very well." He laughed ruefully. "My 'mistake,' on the other hand, was the best thing that ever happened to me. I probably would have really ruined my life if I didn't have this beautiful little person needing me all those years." He gazed across the lawn to where Rainbow was huddled with Bunny and Julia, manically whispering.

"I guess one's early twenties are pretty complicated no matter what," Gillian said, thinking about how she had thrown her entire life into work at that time—she had chosen work over friends and relationships and even family. She didn't even have time to feel lonely. "Back then, I was working fourteen-hour days and complaining about how when I came home at ten o'clock, my roommate's boyfriend would always be in our living room. And you were changing diapers."

"Not great either way," he said. "But it did help me grow up. In any case, it seems like we both made it through. I do appreciate being in my late thirties—feels like a breeze in comparison to my twenties. She's grown and I can focus on myself for the first time in a long time." He gestured to the giant orange tub filled with suitcases. "Anyway, I should bring this stuff in. But it's so good to see you. I really have been thinking about you and worrying about you. I should have reached out . . . but . . ."

"I get it," she said. "It's good to see you too."

"I'll give you my number. Text me when stuff here settles down," he said. "And good luck. These girls . . . they need a lot more than they let on. They really are still kids, even though they live here and dress and talk like grown-ups."

"It's a funny time, being a teenager. You feel like a grown-up, but you aren't quite yet. Transitions, I guess."

"Does being here make you think about when we were here?"

"I kind of can't help it. Up until now, I've tried not to think about it all too much. But it's hard, being here."

"If you want to talk about it, I'm up for it. I know what happened. . . . Well . . . it changed everything."

"That's true," she said. She tried not to let her chin tremble, which would show how she was really feeling. It was hard to untangle the crush she'd had on him with the betrayal she felt.

"Do you ever . . . talk to Miranda?" he asked.

"Never," she said. "Do you?"

"When Rainbow was first born, we talked sometimes, just because I needed some outside support. But then I was so busy and . . . it just felt weird to talk to her. We got back in touch later, and talk occasionally."

"I was so mad at her. I know I made a mistake too, but because of the aftermath I could never stop holding my grudge."

"I get it," he said. "I tend not to be a grudge holder, but I understand the impulse."

There was something comforting about a grudge, Gillian thought. Whenever you felt a-sea, your grudge was like an anchor—a rage to return to. But, oddly, she didn't hold one against the client who'd ruined her business. Although she should. Weirdly, she felt like he had freed her. After everything went down, she spent the final day in her office—a beautiful, modern all-glass space that she had spent a fortune renovating with the best office designers in New York. She had a glass desk and a white leather chair. Usually she was surrounded by outfits in garment bags sent over by fashion publicists, gift bags her clients had gotten from parties they had attended (and then left with her to send to their homes after the event was over—celebrities loved free stuff, but they didn't like to carry it home), and the multiple iPhones she used to keep track of all of her clients. Top clients paid extra to have an exclusive "private" number to call her on. At any given time, there were four or five labeled iPhones on her desk. But on the last day there was none of that.

The iPhones were dark. The gifts were gone. The garment bags were empty. The lights were off. Gillian sat at her desk looking at a printout of the letter she had sent to every client, ready to tweet it. She weighed the pros and cons. On the one hand, she had communicated to her clients and her staff; she didn't owe the world an explanation. On the other, it was always good to have a press release. Boxes containing her clients' books and press clippings were packed up behind her. The former decorations of an office, the description of her life. When she looked at the books and the framed covers of *Vogue* and *People* and *Town & Country,* of beautiful stars in perfectly fitting dresses, it reminded her of what she had done. Of the beauty she had helped bring into the world. But now, seeing everything packed up, it felt ephemeral—worthless, really. It was just a fantasy: stars and dresses and beautiful homes. The people inside the dresses were miserable and mean, they never got to eat anything, and they rarely did anything, their brains atrophying as they focused on minor obsessions. She had perpetuated the fantasy. And if she was going to be totally honest with herself, the fantasy had been what had drawn her to the business to begin with.

It had all started when she was in college, when she helped her friends who had written the "Yale Green Plan"—a proposal produced by undergraduates to help convince the university administrators to be more eco-friendly—get coverage for it in the *Yale Daily News* and, ultimately, bring it to the attention of the university. The high of getting that coverage and having it actually translate into something real had been palpable. She considered the day the piece about the Green Plan ran in the *Yale Daily News* one of the best of her life. One of her professors, an author who was familiar with what professional publicists did, had suggested that she look into a publicity internship. The professor connected Gillian to Ken

Sunshine, who gave her an internship and eventually a job. But that piece was when her love affair with PR began. And she had continued at it throughout her twenties and thirties. She had been good at her job for a long time, maybe too good; it was her entire life and that was why it was time to stop.

On that last day, her assistant, Kayley, had come in with her coat. "It's time to go," she had said. And she had sent Gillian home with a box of her most cherished belongings: the white super-soft cashmere shawl she had bought in Paris and kept on the back of her chair, the Montblanc fountain pen she had used to sign the lease on her office space, an engraved paperweight from Tiffany's that said, ALWAYS BE PITCHING — a gift from Ken when she left to start her own business — and a bottle of Dan Aykroyd's Crystal Head vodka, which she took one shot of, straight from the skull-shaped bottle, and then put a towel over, to keep it from staring at her.

"That's good advice," she said now to Aiden. "About the kids — how they want to be grown-ups, but they aren't yet. I guess we were that way too. Anyway, I'm glad we ran into each other." She said her number out loud as he typed into his phone. She felt it buzz in her back pocket. A victory.

"Me too," he said. He put his hand on her shoulder, gave her a big smile and a wink. Then he pushed a giant orange bin through the open front door of Vallejo.

FIVE

....

Gillian had slipped notes under every door in the six-floor dorm about the first night's meeting in the big downstairs lounge.

Mandatory First Night Meeting
8 P.M.—Entryway Lounge
See you then!
There will be (good) cookies.

The entryway of Vallejo was pretty magical, she had to admit. It was a double floor, so the first thing you saw when you walked in was a soaring ceiling, a giant sparkling chandelier, and huge ten-foot-tall portraits of the Glen Ellen Academy founders on either side of the chandelier. The portraits were classic late-nineteenth-century realism with somber brown backgrounds. When she was in school, they had called the founders Wally and Molly, even though their names were Winston and Millicent Royce. The story about them was that they got rich during the gold rush and bought a bunch of land that they planned to create a utopian farm on, but when they had twins, they realized it would be better to build a school for them.

First they built a manor house for themselves, which became the headmaster's house; then the clock tower, which also housed classrooms; and, eventually, administrative offices. Then they realized their little precious children were lonely and needed friends, so they opened up the school to children from the area and built a dormitory. When little Rosie and Rowan left home, they kept the school going. Accidentally, it became a Glen Ellen institution. Jack London even sent his daughters to the school for a time. Gillian loved the history of the school and looking up at Wally and Molly every time she walked through the door. Always wishing them a silent hello. She hadn't realized how much she had missed them until she returned and their pinkish smiles beamed out at her. They were like a soothing presence, reminding everyone who passed under them that they now had a new family here in Vallejo.

Before the first night's meeting, she went over the dorm rules, which Headmaster Kent had given to each of the dorm parents in a Glen Ellen Academy binder, and revisited Theresa's note. Judging by the letter she had written to Gillian, Theresa had seemed pretty fed up with the job. The letter had ended with "The thing about these girls is that they will take everything you have. They're all damaged in some way or another—just remember that when you're exhausted at night. You have to preserve yourself. I recommend getting away at least once a week. Remind yourself who you are outside of the Gem." Theresa was clearly burned out, but

Gillian assumed it was a job you could do for only a short period of time. Gillian wasn't planning to be a dorm mom forever; this was just a temporary detour, she told herself. She didn't know what she would do next: Would she start a new business? Go back to school? She shook her head and tried to ground herself back in the moment. She had spent some quality time with the Headspace app recently and it regularly reminded her to focus on her breath, stop letting her mind wander. Now, especially, was not the time for mind wandering.

Gillian headed downstairs early and arranged the plates of cookies she'd had delivered from the Basque Boulangerie Café in downtown Sonoma, positioning them around the room to create some spaces for chatting. Vallejo housed half of the girls on campus (the others lived in Castro). The boys' dorms, Solano and Altamira, were across the quad. Boys were not allowed in Vallejo or Castro after eight o'clock and rooms with boys in them had to have open doors. Although Gillian had a feeling that these kids probably felt like these hetero cisgender rules were antiquated, she also didn't really know how to update them; nor, seemingly, did the school. Regardless, she would soon find out how the kids interpreted them.

The first girls to bound into the room were Bunny, Rainbow, and Julia. They all looked younger than they had when they'd arrived on campus with their mounds of stuff. They were wearing yoga pants and asymmetrical tie-dyed sweatshirts. Each one had a little decal on the hem that said, MADE BY J. Gillian wondered if "J" was Julia. Bunny piled a plate with cookies and held it out to her friends. Rainbow took two; Julia shook her head. Bunny took a bite out of each one on her plate and then decided to eat the entire pistachio macaron. Then all three girls came over to Gillian. "So what's going on between you and Rainbow's dad?" Bunny asked, beginning the interrogation without fanfare, her mouth still full of cookie. Bunny clearly felt like they were already best friends; Gillian was going to need to be more careful.

"I don't know what you mean. We just ran into each other today," Gillian said, swiping at her cheek to keep herself from blushing (though it didn't work). "We went to high school together."

"I think he likes you," Rainbow said shyly. She took one of the partially eaten cookies from Bunny's plate and put what remained in her mouth, which Gillian could tell she regretted, as it was dense and hard to chew. "He talked about you after we were finished moving my stuff in. How you were friends in high school and stuff." She brushed crumbs off her top.

Gillian's heart skipped a beat, but she played it cool. "We always had fun together in high school, the three of us," she said.

Bunny laughed and turned to Julia. "Remember when you were dating that boring guy Joseph last year?"

"Ugh, don't remind me," Julia said. "I'm still sorry about that. What a snooze he was. I'm so glad he's off at MIT doing his 'fancy engineer' thing. It's official: I'm going to be single forever. Dating is so not worth it. Ask my mom. She's beautiful and rich and has a clothing line that they sell at the Barneys Co-op and the only way she can get men to go out with her is if she tells them she works at Barneys. The minute she tells them she's an entrepreneur, they either stop calling or they try to take over her business."

"Who needs boyfriends when you can have best friends?" Rainbow laughed and linked arms with both girls. "My dad is a good guy. But I've seen a lot of women come and go. Not that you wouldn't be a good girlfriend for him, Gillian."

"I'm not looking to date your dad," Gillian said, surprised that Rainbow would be so forward and knowledgeable about her own father's romantic life. "My focus right now is on being the best dorm mom I can for you girls."

Two other girls, more awkward, less well dressed, entered the room, whispering to each other. Gillian could tell that they both idolized the three best friends and also feared them a bit. She wondered if the other kids had a name for Bunny, Rainbow, and Julia—when she was in high school she and Miranda had called the popular girls "the Deltas" after the *SNL* sketch about the sorority "Delta Delta Delta." The three most popular girls had matching blond ponytails and all had names that started with *D*—Danielle, Dana, and Dawn.

Gillian went over to introduce herself to the shier girls. They were new to the school, in their sophomore year. Gillian remembered the terror of her first night at boarding school, her first real night away from home and what she imagined was the first night of the rest of her life—never again would she feel quite at home anywhere. By the time she graduated, Vallejo was the place she had lived for the longest in her whole life—they had moved almost every year. Her mother—always the real estate agent—loved to upgrade for a better place when one became available and then downgrade when the place became unaffordable. Gillian's mom had decorators make her apartments look trendy, but the furnishings were never comfortable or cozy. It always felt like living in a model home.

If anything, returning to school reminded her that this had become home more than anywhere else ever was. She made a mental note to tell the girls that when she gave her introductory speech. As the room filled up, the seas parted. Two very slight, dark-haired teenagers walked in, one male, one female, but they looked almost identical. They wore black from head to toe and their small faces were almost obscured with heavy black-framed eyeglasses. Each wore a thin metallic belt and combat boots. They held hands. They were glamorous yet seemed extremely shy; both were looking down at the ground as they entered. Nobody dared talk to them, but hushed whispers crackled around the room: *The twins. The Eccentrics. "Let's Hang Out."*

"You must be Farrah and Freddy," Gillian said, approaching the duo.

"We are," Farrah said meekly. Gillian had to inch closer to hear. She could see Bunny over her shoulder mimicking their shuffling walk to Rainbow.

"Welcome," Gillian said. "I assume you don't live here," she added, addressing Freddy.

"No," he said just as quietly. "I can't. And I know that I'm not allowed in after eight, but usually we get an exception for this meeting. We go everywhere together, so she'll come to my introduction later."

"Great," Gillian said. "And congrats. I hear you have a song that everyone likes."

Farrah smiled and pushed her dark, thick hair behind her ear. "It's just something we did for fun—we don't want a lot of attention about it," she almost whispered.

"I won't bring it up again," Gillian said, trying to be as sweet as possible to these bashful children. She couldn't

believe that Bunny, who was brash and outgoing and confident, was intimidated by the twins—they clearly just wanted
to blend into the background, while Bunny wanted to lead
the parade. But they were talented and maybe that was what
scared Bunny more than anything.

Gillian backed away from the twins, who were clearly
uncomfortable, only then they were mobbed by a group of
girls holding out phones and asking to take selfies together.
Gillian hadn't planned to start her remarks so early in the
evening—she wanted to encourage more mingling—but she
could tell that Farrah and Freddy wished that they could dig
a hole in the middle of the floor and disappear into it.

It was time. Gillian shouted, "Hello, everyone. Ahem!
Quiet down! Just a few words!" The hubbub did not recede.

Then Bunny put her fingers in her mouth and whistled.
"Shut up, girls!" she shouted. The room quieted instantly.

"Thanks, Bunny," Gillian said. "I want to welcome everyone to another great year at Vallejo. I'm Gillian Brodie, your
dorm mother. I'm in room 601 and I'm here for anything you
need, except I can't do your homework for you. That you
have to handle yourself. Everything else, I'm here for. We do
have a few dorm rules, which I know you're familiar with.
No visitors after eight P.M. If there's a boy in your room before eight, the door has to be open. Obviously, we have a
no-tolerance policy for alcohol and drugs. If you are caught
drinking or being drunk, you will get a dorm confinement—
which means that you can go to class and the dining hall, but
nowhere else for a month. If you are caught twice, you'll be
expelled. Curfew is nine P.M.; if you miss curfew once there
will be disciplinary action. Quiet time begins at ten P.M.; you
will get one warning and then disciplinary action. Please be

careful about food in the rooms, as I know you all have fridges. Everything must be clean and also kept sealed. I have a note here from your last dorm mother about some mice who moved in last year—"

"Hansel and Gretel!" Julia yelled.

"Well, I hope they found a new home during the summer," Gillian said. "For all of our sakes. Cleanliness is next to godliness. I want to just tell you one more thing, on more of a personal note. As you may know, I was a student here a long time ago, before you were born really, and don't make fun of me about that. But I realize now that living here in this very dorm was the most at home I ever felt in my life. High school is hard—I'm not going to tell you that it's easy. To be honest, I had a lot of ups and downs here and I didn't always think of it fondly. But I also had some of the best times of my life here. I know sometimes you won't feel like appreciating it and it's the worst to have an old person like me tell you to appreciate it. But I just wanted you to know my experience. Now, do you have any questions for me?"

Bunny raised her hand. "Regarding noise, is it one warning per day or one warning per semester."

"Per semester," Gillian said, trying to sound convincing. And a little disappointed that nobody responded to her revelation about her complex feelings about the Gem.

"Strict!" Bunny responded.

"Let's all try to respect one another," Gillian said. "Now, the serious part of the meeting is over and you can get back to getting to know one another. One last thing: the seniors will all be assigned a sophomore as a little sister. Please be kind to your mentee and your mentor. I'll post the pairings tomorrow on my door. Seniors, you should reach out to your little sisters right away and set up a meeting time for within a week. Then the rest of the meetings are up to you!"

After she was done talking, the room thinned out almost immediately. Farrah and Freddy tried to scurry out before anyone, but Gillian watched as Bunny, Julia, and Rainbow blocked their exit. Gillian tried to hear what they were saying, but they were all speaking in hushed whispers. Gillian was worried that her new Deltas were bullying the twins, so she went over to join the conversation, but when she got there, Bunny clammed up and Rainbow said, "Well, we can't wait to hear your new song."

"It would set a great example for these new girls if you could all get along," Gillian said. Bunny sighed audibly and Freddy and Farrah joined hands and started backing out of the room. "I know you can do it."

When everyone had left, she cleaned up the room a bit. She knew someone from the housekeeping staff would come and throw away the trash and vacuum the floor, but she didn't want to leave it in total disarray. Besides, she needed to process Rainbow's offhand comment about Aiden. What had she said exactly? That she had seen a lot of women come and go. She had also said that her dad was a good guy. Still, the "a lot of women" line stuck with Gillian. Aiden had always been a flirt and a people pleaser. And yes, he was attractive and had a successful business and a nice head of hair. He was the kind of guy women fell for. But what did he want? Why had he chosen Miranda all those years ago when Gillian was also an option? And who was Rainbow's mother?

Back then, Gillian had told herself not to be disappointed that Aiden hadn't come running to her after the breakup with Miranda. She had told herself a story that she was his

second choice—his backup—but it wasn't actually true. Once
he left high school, he didn't think about Gillian, even though
she thought about him. And now, if he was thirty-eight and
Rainbow was eighteen, then it was possible he had already
met her mother at the beginning of college—likely, even. So,
when he and Miranda broke up at the end of high school,
he met someone new. Gillian was never an option. And then
they had a baby She didn't know if he had ever been married. She hadn't thought to ask that question. He'd said that
he'd thought a lot about the past, about what had happened,
and that he wanted to talk about it. She, of course, thought
about it all the time; it had shaped her life in so many ways—
her inability to trust, her fear of intimacy, of betrayal.

Once the room was in respectable order, she put on her
black Tahari blazer and headed over to the headmaster's
house, where she (and all of the faculty members and dorm
parents) had been invited for a reception. The walk across
campus gave her time to mentally prepare for her first faculty
event. There were still a few teachers at the school from when
she was a student, but the majority were new since then
(it had been over twenty years, after all). And, of course, now
she knew the other dorm parents, or at least knew their
names. But regardless of how old or new the teachers were,
most of the people in that room would know one another
and would have established relationships and she would be
the new kid on the block.

On the one hand, maybe she would be more interesting
because she was new, but on the other hand, most of them
probably knew about the failure of her business, her public
humiliation at the hands of the director. What would she say

when they asked her about it? Maybe it was better that they already knew—had already googled her. She didn't really have great answers to "What happened?" and "Why'd you do it?" even though she should have a pitch for herself. To people who had asked, she had said that her brand had been tainted by the director's behavior and betrayal and she couldn't move forward in good faith representing other clients. Not exactly cocktail party conversation. But she had been to many parties in her day. She held her head high and headed to the reception.

The headmaster's house, also known as Wally and Molly's house, was nestled behind the clock tower. It was an old red brick building, like so many on campus, with white columns in front and a deep porch, complete with a porch swing and ceiling fans and a fire-engine-red front door—details that Gillian had always appreciated. The home had been a kind of mystical place when she was a student. There was only one way to be invited there—to get on what they called "Wally's List," which was basically the top five percent of grade earners in each semester. On the first week of the subsequent semester, there would be a reception for Wally's List honorees at the headmaster's house. Both she and Aiden had made it every semester. Miranda had made it only once.

The side parking lot was full of cars—Gillian reminded herself that most of the faculty didn't live on campus like she did. So she was not the first to arrive, not by a long shot. She steeled herself and walked up the steps. The door was a bit ajar behind the screen, so she took that as a sign to just walk right in.

It was a bit weird to be in Headmaster Kent's house as a

faculty guest rather than a scared student. The entryway was simple and traditional, its main feature a wide staircase up to the second floor and an open doorway on each side—one into the dining room, where there was a buffet of snacks, and the other into the living room, where most of the guests were gathered. The floors were festooned in beautiful handmade Persian rugs. The art on the walls felt vaguely familiar—like being in a modern art museum. She looked around to see if she could find her "friends" from her training session, but they were nowhere to be seen. Gillian also didn't see the head-master, though she did see her tenth-grade English teacher, Mr. Bloomfield, so she headed over to him. Mr. Bloomfield had been the fun, young teacher when she was in high school. He had coached the varsity soccer team and chose more inter-esting books than just the standard Shakespeare and Faulkner they expected to read in school. She wondered if he was still considered to be cool and progressive.

She approached as he was talking with another teacher, someone she vaguely remembered from her high school years but couldn't quite place. She had never taken his class. Maybe he taught French or Latin. With them was a much younger man who was dressed very smartly—he was wearing a button-down shirt, a suit vest, matching pants, and slip-on Gucci shoes (no socks). "Mr. Bloomfield?" she said. She couldn't remember his first name and it would have felt oddly inap-propriate to address him that way anyway. They stood in front of a fireplace with what appeared to be a Picasso draw-ing hanging above it. She squinted at it: it was signed by Pi-casso. But it could have been a reproduction. On either end of the mantelpiece were matching ornate hand-painted vases that did not have flowers in them. She assumed they were too fancy to risk letting flowers ruin them.

"Gillian Brodie!" he said. "Call me Jason, now that you're one of us." He gave her a quick one-armed hug.

"I can't believe you remember me," she said.

"Well, I was told you were going to be here. So I looked back in your yearbook. You were in one of my first classes here at the Gem."

"You were the coolest teacher back then," she said.

"Not anymore," he said. "But it's okay. I kind of prefer old-man status. You remember Anthony Rapke?"

The bald man standing next to Jason Bloomfield held out his hand.

"Hello, I'm Gillian Brodie. Nice to meet you," she said. "I'm the dorm mom for Vallejo."

"Welcome back," Rapke said. "You've got some real characters over there."

"I like them so far," she said.

"They're just needy," Bloomfield said. "You can handle it."

"They all feel abandoned by their mommies," the guy in the vest said.

"Celebrity clients are needy," Gillian said. "I'm used to big personalities. I should be able to handle some teenagers."

"Famous last words," a voice boomed over her shoulder.

She smiled and turned around. "Headmaster Kent," she said, laughing.

"Welcome, dorm mother Brodie," he said. He gave her a big hug, which she hadn't been expecting. "How's it all going?" She felt Bloomfield, Rapke, and the stylish man scattering, so she focused just on the headmaster. He was wearing another suit that seemed made for him. Bespoke, as they called them in London.

"Fine so far," she said. "Although these guys were just warning me that those girls are going to walk all over me."

"I mean, they probably will," he said. "But you'll learn."

"Any words of wisdom?" she asked.

"Remember that they look up to you. And they think you're unbearably old."

"Okay," she said, chuckling.

"And stand your ground. I know it's intimidating because they know about that director, but you have integrity—you always have. And remember: it's okay not to be cool. They already don't think you're cool. Even if they do think you're intriguing. They'll never think you're cool, so don't even try."

"They've already all researched me," she said. She was surprised that he thought she had integrity, since she was the one who had kicked off the scandal in high school by getting together with Aiden. Maybe because she had held her head high in the aftermath, even though she'd been crumbling inside.

"Of course they have," he said. "They feel like they know you. They feel like they have an advantage. But you always have the upper hand because you enforce the rules. And you can use me if you *really* need an enforcer. Like how I stepped in back when you were in high school, to quell what was going on. I know it was really hard on you."

"Is he giving you the enforcer speech?" A glamorous blonde swept in and took Kent's arm. Gillian tried to remember this woman's face, but it didn't ring a bell. She was around Kent's age. Her pale hair was definitely dyed (albeit very well). She wore a glittery tunic with slim black pants underneath, a large turquoise necklace, and her fingers were adorned with rings, the largest being a huge diamond with sparkling sapphire baguettes on her left ring finger.

"I guess so," Gillian said, with a small laugh.

"I'm Elisa Kent," she said, holding out a bejeweled hand. Gillian also noticed a diamond tennis bracelet that caught the light.

"Gillian Brodie," she said.

"Welcome to Glen Ellen," Elisa said. "If there's anything I can do, please let me know. I know everyone in town. If you need the best cheese, the best pillows, the best produce, I know where to get it all."

"So generous," Gillian said. "Thank you."

"My wife is the social one in our relationship," Kent said. "She's got a read on everyone. Usually I'm the odd man out at her parties, but I know all the folks at this particular shindig. This is the one time I get to play matchmaker. I think you'd really like Lila Keene, our history teacher. Let's find her. It'll be good for you to have a friend. Helps keep you grounded."

He took Gillian's arm and squired her away from his wife and around the first floor of the house, pointing out historic touches, like the original sconces that Wally and Molly had installed and little nicks in the door frame where they had measured their children. "I'm sure you remember this part of the house from when you were on Wally's List. But we've done some renovation since you've been here. We wanted to keep the place authentic when we upgraded it. So we held on to those little details. The icebox, however, we got rid of, and now we have a Sub-Zero," he laughed. "That's my little old-man joke. Even I'm not old enough for an icebox." Then he gestured to the groups of people standing around. "But the most authentic thing about this place is that we have the best teachers. Over there is the math department—they stick together. There's science. Some of our athletic coaching staff: we hired some professional coaches a few years ago. It took the burden off the teachers and makes the kids feel sports are more legitimate—or, at the very least, the kids listen to the coaches more and the teachers complain less. Just one of the things that our alumni donations have brought to us."

They progressed into the dining room, where a bar was set up on the sideboard. Kent was talking so much that she didn't even have time to respond. "Ah, and here is the history department." Three men and two women were standing near the bar, all holding full glasses of red wine. The men were older; Gillian recognized the one with the ponytail as her American history teacher, but the others didn't ring a bell. The women seemed to be about her age. "Xavier, Gary, Mike, Lila, and Jody, this is Gillian Brodie, our new dorm mother for Vallejo."

They all smiled warmly. Lila held out her hand. "Welcome," she said. "You get to see the other side of our kids—I always wonder about that."

"I like them so far," Gillian said.

"Well, I'd love to have a drink with you one of these days to hear more about what they're like when they're not in class," Lila said.

"I'd love that," Gillian said. They exchanged numbers, but as Gillian was sending Lila a confirmation text, she saw Gloria standing by herself near the front door. Gillian could tell that she was trying to figure out if she had been at the party long enough to leave it.

"I'm going to go check in with Gloria. I'll see you soon."

Lila smiled as Gillian walked over to greet Gloria.

"Oh, Gillian," Gloria said. "It's nice to see you here. I hate these types of parties. But Headmaster Kent always invites me."

"They can be exhausting, parties," Gillian said. "But I haven't been to one in a while, so I'm kind of enjoying it. This house looks so different from when I was in school. It's . . ."

"Fancy?" Gloria said. "I know. Headmaster Kent likes nice things. Well, really it's his wife who likes nice things."

"I met her," Gillian said. "Her jewelry . . ."

"Costs more than my house," Gloria said. "I keep my mouth shut though, about what he buys. It's none of my business."

"Is his wife rich?" Gillian asked. "Or did the school pay for all this?"

"Oh, I'm not the one to ask," Gloria said. She glanced around skittishly. "You know what, I'm about ready to go home and put my feet up and pet my cat."

"Same," Gillian said. "Except I have a dorm full of anxious teenagers to check on."

"Well, you come by and visit me at my desk," Gloria said. "I still always have candy, and sometimes I have gossip too."

"Both are very tempting," Gillian said. She smiled at Gloria as she exited the building.

Gillian waited a beat after Gloria was gone. She stood in the entryway and glanced around the party. It had thinned out a bit since she had first arrived, but there were definitely still people chatting and holding full glasses of wine. She left hers on the entryway table and went out the front door.

* * *

Gillian managed to get back to her room without seeing any of her students. She wondered what they were up to—worrying that they were getting into trouble without her eyes on them. But then she reminded herself that they weren't babies; they would survive the night. She went into her room, locked the door, and asked her Alexa to play Louis Armstrong and Ella Fitzgerald while donning the bathrobe she had stolen from the Ritz-Carlton on her last business trip to L.A. "Stolen" was probably a misnomer, as they had absolutely sent her a bill for it. But she had put it directly into her suitcase after taking a shower and hadn't thought twice about it. It was a comfortable robe, after all. And every time she looked at it, she thought about that beautiful hotel room, the pool on the roof, even the carafe of coffee she had ordered each morning that had felt so luxurious. And how she billed it all to the client—including the robe. She missed her expense account.

She unlocked her phone and scrolled through her contacts. So many of the people she would have reached out to just a few weeks earlier had evaporated. That was probably the hardest pill of her "retirement" to swallow. It was the complete disappearance of the people she considered social friends: the people she saw at parties, who she got drinks and dinner with—the producers, the writers, the editors, those who understood the world she inhabited and sympathized with her about it. None of them were reaching out to her now, and none of them would return her text if she wrote to them. She had nothing to offer. Even her last assistant, whom she had helped to get a new job and whom she had considered a friend, would think of it as a chore to talk to her old boss on the phone.

Gillian's only real non-work friends in New York, if you could call them that, were the other regulars at WXOU—Dennis, Keith, Harold, and Lady Roxanna. But she wasn't really on a phone-call basis with them. They were people she saw at the bar. They actually knew a lot about her life—they knew whom she was sleeping with and whom she was representing—and had enjoyed her stories—especially the ones about celebrities behaving badly. But the friendships only went so far. At the end of the day, they were barflies together, no more and no less.

Once Gillian had passed Keith on the street as he was exiting a building and hadn't recognized him; he'd had to run up behind her and tap her on the shoulder. It took her a moment to place him; she was so used to seeing him in his one spot in the corner of the dark bar. They laughed about it after, but neither one ever forgot it. Their friendship was one of circumstance.

She was tempted to call Aiden; seeing him had reminded her of what it was like to have a real friend. Just their short chat had felt more meaningful than most of the conversations she had had in the past few years—all of them about business, clients, a little small talk. But if she had learned anything about dating, it was that it was too soon to call—she had just seen him. She didn't want to be needy or desperate.

She hadn't spoken to Miranda since graduation. Just the thought of her all these years later would make Gillian's heart speed up and her stomach rumble. She always wondered when she was in L.A. if she would accidentally run into her. But it had never happened. Even though Miranda

was the only one who might understand what she was going through right now. It had been so long that she didn't
even know how to contact her anymore. She googled her,
only to find her wedding announcement. Then she googled
her married name. She found an out-of-date "mommy blog"
that ended in 2015, when her youngest turned five. Gillian
scrolled through a bit to see what they were up to—they
seemed to live in a nice house not far from the beach. Then
she clicked on "Contact me." And there it was, an email address. Gillian clicked on it and composed an email.

> Hi Miranda. It's Gillian Brodie. I know we haven't been in
> touch in a while. Like literally since high school. But I've
> been going through a lot—maybe you've seen it in the news.
> Anyway, it's a long story, but I'm actually in our old dorm at
> the Gem. I'm the dorm mother of Vallejo. Can you believe it?
> Anyhow, I just wanted to say hi. I know it's weird that we
> haven't talked in, what, twenty years? And at the end, well, I'm
> sorry about what happened. I really am. It's taken me a long
> time to get to that, but I've gotten there. Being here makes me
> think about you. I miss you and would love to talk. xo, Gillian

She hit Send. She held her breath with anticipation. Would
Miranda write back? What would she say? Gillian hadn't
meant to apologize; she wasn't entirely sure if she felt sorry
for what she did. She didn't regret kissing Aiden even after
all these years. But she did regret how Miranda felt and also
how Miranda had made her feel.

Writing to Miranda had sparked something in Gillian. She
texted Dennis: "Hi Dennis, it's Gillian AKA Tempranillo.
Just wanted you to know that I'm out of town for a while, so

you don't have to order wine for me." And then she texted her mom: "Hope all's well! I'm in California for a while. Would love to catch up." Finally, she texted one of her former clients, one of the few she had trusted with her personal cell phone number: "Hi Jessica! It's Gillian. I wanted to let you know that I'm living in Northern California now—Sonoma—so if you're up at your place, let me know."

Nobody responded in the next ten minutes, so Gillian took a deep breath, tried not to feel totally and utterly alone, and headed to her bathroom to put on a sheet mask.

As it set, she thought about Aiden and wondered if he was on Instagram. She looked him up, and there he was with a public account that had been started relatively recently. The most recent photo was of his overstuffed truck side by side with a baby photo of Rainbow. The caption said, "Senior year. My baby's all grown up. And has the mini-fridge to prove it." He had tagged the Smeg in the post. She laughed. She couldn't help scrolling back through his posts to see what he had been up to the past few years. It was a curated account with no reference to romantic relationships, but there were photos of Rainbow, many beautiful photos of the Sonoma area, and some travel photos from France and Italy. It seemed that he owned a vineyard, which he linked to. She researched the vineyard and found that it wasn't far from the school. He really was a local now. She stayed up way later than she should have, completely immersed. She wondered what he'd been up to for all these years. She hoped she would be able to find out.

SIX

....

Morning was not the leisurely time that she hoped it would be. It was the first day of class and girls were banging on her door. She put her robe on, now officially blessing the Ritz-Carlton gods for having provided a good one. A robe was going to come in handy in this line of work. In the hall, she found three of the new girls whose names she didn't know yet. "Miss Gillian," the shortest one said, "Angelica threw up all over the bathroom. And now she's sleeping on the floor." Gillian looked at her watch. It was six o'clock in the morning.

"Okay," she said. "Hold on." She grabbed a roll of paper towels and some Fantastik from her kitchen and followed the girls down to the second floor. The hallways were a mess—a hodgepodge of fun had gone down, she deduced. Everything from manicures to craft making to beer drinking. Had she been so immersed in Aiden's Instagram that she hadn't heard what was going on? Seemingly so. She gritted her teeth and sighed—she had messed up. She should have done a late-night check—they had told her to in the training but she had been too tired. Now that she thought about it, her dorm mother had done a hallway check every night. She would have to institute it, no matter how tired she was.

Gillian followed the girls into the bathroom, which smelled like Amstel Light, Chanel's Coco Mademoiselle, and vomit, a deeply disgusting combination. She held her breath and went into the stall where Angelica was lying; she was a tiny girl, no more than one hundred pounds. It was probably her first night of drinking. "Can you get me a glass of water?" she said to the short girl who had spoken up at her door. The girl nodded and hurried away.

Gillian sat down behind Angelica and put her head in her lap. She brushed her hair with her fingers; it had only a little bit of vomit in it. Maybe the other girls had known enough from watching movies to hold her hair back. "Angelica," she whispered. "Wake up. You're going to be okay." Angelica, who had beautiful honey hair and olive skin, blinked a little, revealing green eyes.

"I don't feel good," she said.

"I know," Gillian said. "You know you're not supposed to drink. I'm going to have to write you up. Let's get some water in you and then I'll walk you over to the infirmary."

"No doctor," Angelica said. "My mother . . ."

"Your mother isn't here," Gillian said. "And they might give you some fluids. That's it."

"First day of school," Angelica moaned.

"Yes, indeed," Gillian said. "Maybe you'll learn a lesson that it's a bad idea to get wasted the night before classes start. You know the rules here. You'll be on dorm confinement for the next month."

"Never again," Angelica said.

"Good plan," Gillian said just as the short girl arrived with a S'well bottle of water. She held it to Angelica's lips. "There you go," she said. "Remember to drink water when you're drinking alcohol. When you're *old enough* to drink alcohol. That's a lesson for all of you. One glass of water after each drink." She looked around at the three girls clustered outside the stall. She handed the bottle back and they all took long sips. It had clearly been a long night for everyone. "See, you've already learned something on the first day of school. Now, if I catch you girls drinking again, you'll all be living at home with your parents, so let's shape up." One of the girls actually looked scared, so Gillian felt like she was doing her job. She knew that there was a no-tolerance policy for alcohol, but she also understood that her own negligence was part of the reason this had happened.

The friends helped Angelica up and brought her back to her room. Gillian wiped down the bathroom floor and the toilet and tried not to throw up herself. She could have let the janitorial staff clean up, but she didn't want anyone to know what had happened in the dorm, covering up for her own mistake. She was mad at herself, at the girls, at the stench of the bathroom after only one day. What had she gotten herself into? She used to own her own business and fly on private jets and now she was cleaning up teenage vomit. What a turn of events.

As she walked back to her room, smelling of vomit and, oddly, covered in glitter, Rainbow and Julia ambushed her. "You stink," Rainbow said.

"I know," Gillian said. "What happened last night?"

"*Some* of the girls celebrated their last night of freedom,"

Julia said. "But not us: we were quietly and soberly in our rooms, covering our books with brown paper."

Gillian tried not to respond sarcastically, instead ignoring the facetious lie. "Do you even *have* books anymore?" Gillian asked.

"Some," Rainbow said. "But we do read a lot on our iPads."

"What were your last nights of summer like?" Julia asked.

"I remember going to a concert the night before senior year started, but my summers were pretty boring—I worked at a day camp in Sacramento," Gillian said. "I always looked forward to school starting, because we always did a second-day-of-school picnic. We accidentally did it our first year and then it became a tradition. That's how I met your dad, Rainbow. He showed up at our picnic and ate our sandwiches."

"My dad does love a picnic," Rainbow said. "I feel sometimes that that's why he opened a winery, so he could have more picnics."

"There are too many bees around here to have a nice picnic," Julia said.

"Bees are a sign of a healthy ecosystem," Gillian pointed out, remembering some of the talking points from a client who had a nature preserve on his estate and occasionally did interviews about it.

"We should do a second-day picnic tomorrow," Rainbow said. "I'll get you a beekeeper suit, Julia."

"Or maybe just one of those hive smokers. Those are cute," Julia said. "They calm the bees down, right?"

"I can provide the sandwiches and the picnic blanket," Gillian said.

"You're definitely more fun than Theresa was," Julia said.

"We needed someone a little more like us. But, you know, grown-up. You're like that."

"Thanks, I think?" Gillian said.

"That's a compliment," Rainbow said. "You're a little insecure. I guess it's endearing."

Gillian was surprised that Rainbow had picked up on her insecurity. She wondered what the tip-off had been. It was true that since she had closed her business, she didn't feel confident in her decisions, she had lost most of her important relationships and friends, and, most importantly, she had lost her routine. In New York, she had been at the gym by six-thirty in the morning, at the office by eight-thirty, at a party or dinner at seven, and home by ten, ready to do it again the next day. When her business closed, she had no idea what to do with all the hours in the day. She had spent her last weeks in New York wandering the streets, idly going into shops. She had lost her appetite and her energy—so she had stopped working out, but also going to restaurants. And then she had moved to California, where everything was new. Now she was relying on the schedule of school to occupy most of her time. She hoped the school and these girls could fill the void. Somehow Rainbow had noticed all of this.

When she arrived back in her room, she took a shower to wash the nastiness of the girl's bathroom off her and then looked at her email—no response from Miranda. But what could she expect? It was her own fault. Miranda had reached out a few times after graduation, but Gillian had never responded. Why would Miranda respond now?

Gillian had held a grudge for her entire adult life. She had spent the last seventeen years focusing on her career—clawing her way to the top and befriending the people who would help her make it. Plus, her clients required her attention day and night—and they considered her a friend. Sometimes she was their only friend. While it might seem cliché for a celebrity to say that their publicist was their friend, many of them felt like their publicist was the only person who really cared about them, who had their best interests at heart. And yes, it was the job of the publicist to make them think so (and also to make them forget that there were other clients as well). So it wasn't like she had spent the last decade and a half friendless; on the contrary, her friends had been on the covers of magazines and on billboards. It was her job to get them there and it was also her job to be their friend. And she liked it— lived for it, really. Some of them had even been people she would have chosen as friends if they hadn't been paying her. But that hadn't left much time for the real world. And when the real world came crashing down, her fake friends—a.k.a. her clients—were gone. And she had nothing to show for it other than a few pairs of nice jeans and some fancy beauty products.

If anything was clear to her about this move to California, it was that it meant a total fresh start for her. She had to act like her past had been erased, like she had no identity before she'd arrived at the Gem. She had to forget her past, Miranda, and her publicity career, all of the things that they represented. She had to live in the here and now.

That decision made, she remembered that she had gotten Lila's phone number at the party and she'd seemed eager to connect. Gillian sent Lila a message asking if she wanted to get a first-day-of-school glass of wine later. She was going to do things differently this time—she was going to be active in her own life, try to make friends, try not to be selfish. She got an instant "Yes! I'll pick you up." Then she headed down to the downstairs lounge to see if any of the girls needed a first-day pep talk.

SEVEN

....

That night, Gillian did her first hall check of the night after everyone returned from dinner. She made her presence known on all the floors, reminding everyone of the rules. She would be back at ten to remind them that quiet hours had begun. But that left more than an hour and a half to get off campus. One night a week, a teacher filled in for her, giving her a much-needed break. This week's teacher was Reese Howell, a young math teacher, who told Gillian that she had considered taking the dorm mother job. Gillian left her in her suite like a babysitter.

Gillian walked out to the front gates at eight-twenty, as promised, and hopped into Lila's waiting car, a Saab convertible. "Your car is so cute," Gillian said. "Thank you for picking me up."

"It's old, but I like it," Lila said. "I'm happy to get out of the house. Syllabi are all done, but no grading yet, so this is a nice time of year. Plus, it's nice to have a new person around here."

"How long have you been teaching here?" Gillian asked. She estimated that Lila was in her early thirties.

"This is my sixth year," Lila said. "I like it. I grew up in San Francisco, but I always liked coming up North with my family on little vacations. And when I was at U.C. Davis, we would come here on the weekends. *That's* when I realized how cool the wineries were. When I was a kid, we'd just go camping in Point Reyes Park—my parents were more campers than wine drinkers."

"It's really beautiful there," Gillian said. "But yeah, here in Sonoma County, it's amazing to have access to the wineries. And the cute little towns like Healdsburg and Sebastopol. And the restaurants. It's all so lovely."

"They're great. So I kind of knocked around the county, waitressing for a few years, but then I met Jody, who you met at the party. And she taught here and you don't need a teaching credential like you do to teach in public schools, although they do like you to have a specialty. I sent them my undergraduate history thesis and a sample of my pottery and they loved it. So, here I am. I like that it's steady work and I like having the summers off. I do have to do pottery workshops once a week, but that's fun too—they have a really nice studio." Lila pulled up in front of the Glen Ellen Inn. "This is my favorite place in town. Great snacks and a good wine list."

"I came here the other night with Bunny. She said her parents had an account for her here." Gillian rolled her eyes and Lila laughed.

"I wouldn't doubt it—they've kind of delegated parenting to all sorts of outside sources, including restaurants and hotels."

"I feel bad for her," Gillian said.

"She's definitely had a weird life," Lila said. "But she also likes to overdramatize it. I did meet her parents in her first year and they actually were very sweet and they were a cute trio together. A little *Gilmore Girls*–esque. Her parents are more like her friends than authority figures."

"I love that show," Gillian said. "My mom and I were a little like the Gilmore Girls too. It was just the two of us. But I was more like the parent and she was more like the child."

"Oh wow. That show, it's like comfort food," Lila said. "I always wished I had a mom like Lorelai. You're lucky. This place can be like our Luke's. There are even attractive bartenders."

Gillian smiled and followed Lila inside. This time, instead of sitting out on the patio, they sat at the bar. Lila ordered a glass of wine and a glass of sparkling water. Gillian ordered a vodka martini, since she wasn't driving and she wanted to celebrate surviving her official first day as a dorm parent.

"Do you live in Glen Ellen?" Gillian asked as they settled themselves at the bar.

"Technically I live in Kenwood—I rent a little cottage on the property of this larger house. It's nice and private and I have a little hot tub on my deck. Gorgeous views. It's perfect just for me. And I feel safe there. There's a gate and it's nice to know that the family is near. When I first lived here, I was in a freestanding house by myself and . . . I don't know, it just kind of freaked me out."

"I get it," Gillian said. "It gets . . . quiet here at night. I'm not used to hearing nothing at all."

"Totally," Lila said. The bartender put their drinks down in front of them. Lila sipped her water first. Gillian wondered if she even normally drank. "I think you'll get used to it. And maybe even start to like it."

"I hope so," Gillian said, holding up her martini glass. "Cheers. To a new beginning."

Lila lifted her wineglass. "To a new beginning and new friends." They clinked glasses and both smiled.

"So," she said. "Is there anything I should know about working at the Gem? I only know about it as a student."

"I heard that you were an alum," Lila said, winking. This made Gillian feel sheepish, like she hadn't earned the job. "Everyone is pretty chill. Most of the faculty is pretty boring. Almost everyone is married, except for me. Bill Spencer, the biology teacher, just got divorced, but it was because his wife cheated on him, so he's kind of a mess about it. The new math teacher, Jean Hargrove seems cool, but she's a lot older. I feel like basically she wanted to retire in Sonoma but wasn't quite old enough yet. I don't think she'll hang out with us."

The bartender glided past them and smiled. "Do you two need anything? A snack? Our oysters are fantastic—we serve them with a Bloody Mary mignonette. Our ginger calamari is also great for sharing."

Gillian smiled at Lila and shrugged. She hadn't eaten dinner and calamari sounded good. "Are you up for calamari?" she asked.

"Of course," Lila said.

The bartender nodded and noted the order in the computer, then topped off Lila's wine and her glass of water. Gillian realized that wine really was the best deal in Sonoma. Everyone was proud of their creations and the restaurants valued their connections to the wineries. You were much more likely to get a top-off when drinking wine at the bar; she would have to switch to wine from vodka. It was intimidating, because she didn't know the wineries or the vintages that everyone else took for granted. But she figured she would learn, and that nothing on these lists would be subpar.

When the bartender moved down the bar, Gillian returned to the previous line of questioning. "So what do you do around here? Like, for fun?"

"Mostly, I have friends in the area who don't work at the school. From college and stuff like that. School isn't my whole life. And I was dating someone, although that didn't really work out. Do you know people in the area?"

The idea of having a life outside of the school honestly hadn't occurred to Gillian, but of course the faculty members would have that. It was a kind of childish notion to think that teachers interacted only with other teachers. Aiden could be her non-faculty friend . . . "It turns out I know someone from high school who still lives around here," she said.

"You should call them—it's good to get out of the campus mind-set. I'm not saying we shouldn't be friends. Just that . . . you'll see. It's nice to have an escape."

"I'll try," Gillian said, crossing her fingers under the bar that Aiden would be her friend, or more than friend. Or whatever. Even in her own mind it was hard to have hope. Their past was just so complicated.

"Or there's always dating. There are some good, mostly divorced guys on Tinder around here. Or you can find someone here on vacation. That's always fun." She shrugged and blushed. Gillian wondered how many times that had happened.

It was strange getting to know a new person. She wasn't sure how much to tell Lila or how open to be. Ever since high school, she had lost her ability to trust her friends, always feeling that they were about to turn on her. She was dying to tell Lila about her crush on Aiden—how she couldn't stop thinking about him, how she had found his Instagram, but how their shared past was knotty. And even more than that, she wanted to talk about Headmaster Kent and his fancy house. She wanted to know if he *really* had a Picasso. But none of these topics felt safe yet. Probably as a result of her work in PR, Gillian was careful about who she shared information with. She assumed everyone was like that and wondered what Lila wasn't telling her about. Surely Lila was aware of some sort of faculty gossip or intrigue beyond a kind of boring guy getting divorced. But was Lila as withholding as Gillian? Only time would tell.

Trust was such a strange thing. Establishing it, feeling comfortable. Gillian didn't want to think that she had been damaged by the betrayal by some of her clients, although she was quickly realizing that she had. Maybe that was why thinking about Aiden felt so nice. Somehow he felt safe, a trusted person from the past when trust hadn't been so hard. Although he had also broken her heart—could anything worse happen? She decided to try the Aiden topic but without too many specifics—leave out his identity, his connection to the school. See how Lila reacted.

"I do have a little crush on someone," Gillian said.

"Tell me," Lila said, turning toward her eagerly. Her voice deepened a bit. It was her first expression of true interest. Gillian felt reinforced in her decision to reveal at least some information.

"Well, we're old friends, from high school, and he lives in the area. I actually bumped into him already. And he's nice, but nothing has happened."

"Do you have his number?"

"I do, but we haven't texted each other, other than to just confirm that we have each other's number."

"Do you have any inside jokes that you could write him about?"

"Yeah, but they all bring up . . . issues, if you know what I mean. He does own a winery, so maybe I could ask him for wine advice."

"Oh, you'll find plenty of those around here. I dated one last year who was kind of self-centered. It didn't work out. I thought it would. He was so nice at the beginning . . . but then after, like, three months . . . it just kind of faded."

"That happened to me all the time in New York," Gillian said. "I would meet someone and think they were cool and we'd go on a few dates and then they would just evaporate."

"It's harder to evaporate here," Lila sighed. "You definitely run into people. But there's something about that three-month window. I start to like guys more right around then, and it's like that's when they're starting to check out."

"I guess some men like novelty," Gillian said. "In New York, it's so hard, there's always someone better."

"My mother always used to say there's a lid for every pot," Lila said.

"In New York, there's a lot of pots and not enough lids," Gillian said. "I actually had more success meeting guys in Los Angeles, but maybe it was because I was just passing through on business. I did have one guy that I would see when I was out there. He wasn't exactly like a boyfriend, but he also wasn't exactly not. He was a professional piano player—a pianist. So he traveled a lot. But he was based in L.A. and when we were both there, I would see him at his cute little house in Venice Beach, on a canal. And sometimes he would pop in on me in New York if he was there playing. But we were never in the same place for more than twelve hours."

"You could still see him now," Lila said. "It's a quick flight to L.A."

"I don't know if I like him enough to actually see him for more than one night at a time, which is what I used to do," Gillian said. "Besides, I don't think I can leave the girls overnight unless someone is there to cover for me. I only get coverage one night a week—like tonight."

"You're just as bad as those skittish men," Lila said. "Full of excuses."

"I sometimes wonder if I chose him because I knew I would never have to actually be serious with him. Something about me is afraid of commitment," Gillian said. "Seems to me if you want it, you're bound to be disappointed. So it's better not to want it. Maybe I've always felt that way. I don't know."

"That seems sad," Lila said. "Not to be honest with yourself about what you want."

Gillian shrugged. "I don't know any other way. My dad left us. I was betrayed by my two best friends in high school. I've never really picked the right guys to date." Saying those words out loud was big for her, making her chin waver just a bit. She blinked her eyes to keep her composure. She hadn't expected to be so honest.

"Oh," Lila said. "I'm sorry, that sounds like a lot."

"Yeah, I guess it is," Gillian said. "At this point, I don't really trust myself to make good decisions about love. So I don't really have my hopes up about my old friend here, but

I do honestly love the crush part of it. It's exciting to be curious about someone. To feel those butterflies."

"The crush is kind of the best part," Lila said. "I'm sure you can think of some reason to be in touch—that's all you need to get things rolling."

"I'll think about it," Gillian said, but she knew she wasn't going to reach out. She needed one more accidental meeting to cement their destiny. "We've already run into each other once accidentally, so I kind of want to leave it up to fate."

"Whatever," Lila said. "Fate is a bunch of bullshit."

"I don't think so," Gillian said.

"You of all people shouldn't believe in destiny," Lila said.

"Why? Because my business failed? Maybe that was fate too. Maybe I was destined to be back here."

The bartender brought out a heaping plate of ginger calamari with grilled pineapple on the side. "Voilà," he said.

"Thank you," Gillian said. She watched as Lila took the first bite and smiled.

"It's really good," Lila said, licking her fingers.

Gillian took a piece and savored the ginger flavor in the fried batter. "Yum. I've never had anything like this."

She was becoming more and more convinced that fate had brought her back here for a reason. Now she just had to find out what that reason was.

Lila dropped Gillian off at the front gates. They promised that they would text the next day and figure out another time to have a drink. As Theresa had said in her letter, it *was* important to remember who one was outside of the school, and sitting at a bar with Lila talking about life and love had reminded Gillian a little. It had felt good. Normal. As normal as life could be right now.

It was a short walk to the dorm from the gates, but Gillian wandered a bit, thinking about whether she was truly destined to be back here in Sonoma. If she had been destined to be here in the first place, back in high school. If destiny was real or just a bunch of nonsense, like Lila said. She had heard spiritual people talk about destiny and how it is comforting—it makes you feel that all the things, even things that feel bad or wrong at the time, happen for a reason. Gillian had never exactly bought into that idea, but after it came out of her mouth at drinks, she wondered if she actually believed it.

The second-day-of-school picnic had been brought about by the fact that the one "luxury" item Gillian had brought with her to school was a picnic blanket. Miranda found it in the back of Gillian's closet as she loaded in her garment bags of designer jeans and bejeweled cardigans. She held up a red-and-white checkered blanket folded like an American flag at a military funeral. "What's this?" she asked.

"Oh," Gillian said. "My mother found it at Marshalls. It's a picnic blanket. She saw the photo of the quad on the front of the brochure and decided that we would be having a lot of picnics."

"I love it," Miranda said. "We should have one. Let's go to the dining hall and get snacks and then sit outside on this perfect blanket. I bet we'll meet people."

The dining hall food was fully paid for with Gillian's scholarship, so she could eat as much as she liked. And the blanket was ready to be used. "Let's do it," Gillian said.

They grabbed tote bags from Miranda's stash and headed

down to the dining hall. Surreptitiously, they made some sandwiches and filled their totes with bags of chips. They grabbed cookies and Snapples from the refrigerated section. They took a few pieces of fruit—"for the vitamins" was Miranda's explanation. Then they headed outside with their loaded totes and set up Gillian's blanket. They laid out the food on paper plates they had lifted from the to-go area. They opened a bag of chips and each sipped a Diet Coke spiked with Mr. Pibb—Miranda's concoction, though Gillian had quickly taken to it. They were only just getting to know each other, but Gillian felt a generosity of spirit in Miranda—she was already wearing a pair of her jeans and a Ralph Lauren polo shirt. The jeans were a bit long, but Gillian wore chunkier shoes to keep them from dragging on the ground. Miranda told Gillian about growing up all over the world as the daughter of a diplomat. It all sounded so glamorous to Gillian, who said only that it was just her and her mom in Sacramento. She was about to get to the part about Gillian having to serve as the mother in the relationship when who should approach but a floppy-haired boy.

"It's the second-day-of-school picnic," Miranda said to him, smiling. "I'm Miranda and this is Gillian."

"I'm Aiden," he said, his eyes sparkling in the sun.

"Sit down and have a sandwich," Gillian said. "They're fresh from the dining hall. Made by yours truly."

"Don't mind if I do," he said. "I'm from Connecticut, so all of this outdoorness here is truly amazing." He flopped down and took a sandwich from the plate they had placed on one side of the blanket.

"Did your parents come with you all the way from Connecticut to move in?" Gillian asked.

"Oh yeah," he said. "They used it as an excuse to go to Hawaii after they dropped me off."

"My parents live in Morocco right now, so they just gave me a plane ticket," Miranda said. "I'm sure they're at some diplomat gala at this very moment."

"My mom is really going to miss me," Gillian said. "We've spent a lot of time together, just her and me."

"It's nice to have a parent who loves you and wants to hang out with you," Aiden said.

Gillian blushed. She'd never thought that being a daughter would be something to be proud of, but somehow Aiden made her feel proud. "Thanks," she said.

"It sounds like you and I are a lot alike, Aiden," Miranda said.

His gaze shifted from Gillian back to Miranda. Gillian could feel him weighing both of them in his mind—which one he liked better. Gillian tried not to let Miranda's comment hurt her heart. Aiden had complimented Gillian, but Miranda was turning the conversation to her benefit. This wouldn't be the last time that happened.

Their first few months of school, the three of them spent all of their time together. Both Miranda and Gillian had crushes on Aiden. At first they tried to keep it secret from each other, but it was too hard. "He's just so cute," Miranda finally admitted. "I like him too," Gillian said. But they made a pact not to date him because it could hurt their friendship. And he kept them at arm's length in terms of romance. They were just three really good friends. Having a crush was fun. Having friends was fun. When it was just the three of them, Gillian forgot that she was a scholarship student at a rich-kid school, that she didn't quite fit in. In their little group, she did.

Gillian arrived back at Vallejo feeling buoyed that maybe things weren't so bad. She hoped the girls were behaving well. She took the elevator up to her floor and dropped off her bag and said thank you to Reese. Then she walked the halls. Most of the doors on the sixth floor were closed and the music turned low. She hoped that they were really sleeping or quieting down and not just waiting for her to check, poised to turn the volume back up. She went down the stairs to the fifth floor, where there were a few girls in the hall, but they scattered when they saw her. Maybe Angelica's experience had rattled everyone. Maybe Reese had been a good influence on them. The door to Bunny, Rainbow, and Julia's suite was open, so Gillian poked her head in. The girls were scattered to the edges of the common room. Bunny had her headphones on and her phone in front of her face. Julia was sitting at a sewing machine, feeding some silky fabric through it. Rainbow held a small mirror and seemed to be examining her pores. Nobody was doing homework.

"Hope you all had a good first day of class," Gillian said.

"We already have senioritis," Bunny said.

Rainbow giggled. "Well, Julia doesn't," Rainbow added. "She still wants to get A's."

"Shut it," Julia said. "I'm focusing on fashion this year. It's my independent study. If I don't get an A in my independent study, then something is really wrong."

"You always get A's even if you don't study," Bunny said.

"Getting A's is okay," Gillian said.

"I'm about to get a huge zit next to my nose," Rainbow said.

"I told you that I have the Mario Badescu sulfur stuff," Bunny said. "You just have to put it on before you go to bed."

"I'm afraid it'll get on my pillowcase," Rainbow said.

"Just let it dry first," Gillian said. "That stuff does work."

"You're the best dorm mom," Rainbow said.

"Don't think that you can butter me up for when you do something wrong. I'm unbutterable."

"We would never, ever try to do that," Bunny said, grinning.

"It would not even remotely cross our minds," Rainbow said.

"Can we interest you in a protein cookie or this very ambrosial flower?" Julia asked. She pointed to an unopened gift basket on the floor next to Rainbow.

"'Ambrosial.' Good SAT word," Gillian said. "I'm fine, thanks. See you tomorrow. Remember, it's the second-day-of-school picnic. Which I invented!" She closed their door and continued on her mostly uneventful hall check. Maybe she had already had a positive influence on the girls. Or maybe they were just tired after their first night of partying. Regardless, it was a quiet night in Vallejo and she was glad for it.

Over the next few days they all started to settle into a routine. Gillian made sure the girls got off to class, did their work, went to bed at a decent hour. During the day, when she wasn't on duty, Gillian read books in her suite, went for runs, and periodically stopped off at Lila's classroom to see if she had a break. They would get a coffee together in the teachers' lounge and chat about nothing and everything.

Julia suggested to Gillian that she could make some throw pillows for her suite and helped Gillian pick out a fabric for them. Gillian wanted to connect with all the girls, so she spent the evenings in the dorm lounge so that they felt comfortable—by doing this she found out about Rainbow's newfound shellfish allergy, Angelica's fear of disappointing her parents, and Farrah's commitment to learning the guitar, which was always more of Freddy's instrument.

Gillian fell into the habit, after the last hall check, of watching old episodes of *The Bachelor* via streaming. She was so outraged by them that she started texting Lila about the show and got Lila hooked as well. They developed a rating system for group dates, a kind of overall drinking game for the show: if there's a helicopter, you open a bottle of wine; if there are fireworks, you have to drink tequila; and if one contestant rats out another, you get to open a second bottle of wine. By the end of the season they watched, Gillian felt like she could trust Lila with anything.

EIGHT

Bunny, Rainbow, and Julia were in Gillian's living room, which was still shabby, but she had dressed it up a bit with the throw pillows Julia made, a kantha quilt, and scented candles from some of the fancy shops in Healdsburg, the chichi town about half an hour from Glen Ellen. Bunny was hugging the pillow Gillian thought of as "Grover" because it was furry and blue, while Julia sat on the window seat, which looked out at campus, sewing buttons onto her handmade homecoming dress and Rainbow absently moved around the pieces of a puzzle Gillian had left out on her kitchen table. Once when she had been in a greenroom, she'd heard a writer talk about always having a puzzle out in her living room because it gave people things to do when they came over. Gillian had remembered it when she set up her home here in Vallejo. It seemed that girls were always coming and going from her living room, and having the puzzle there was a good crutch. The girls of Vallejo had already done a one-thousand-piece puzzle of a Van Gogh sunflower painting and were now working on a *New Yorker* cover featuring dogs in a dog park. The worst thing about puzzles was what to do with them when they were finished. Take photos? Frame them? Breaking them down seemed so demoralizing. The puzzles took so long to do but were so quickly dismantled. She tried not to think of them as a metaphor. She had settled on keeping the assembled puzzle on display for two days after it was finished, photographing and Instagramming it, and then putting it away.

The whole effect of her living room—cozy and fun—was so different from her New York apartment, which had been decorated by a designer with the latest furnishings and fabrics. There was a homeyness to her Vallejo suite that she was proud of. She loved being in the living room by herself or with the girls, who at this moment were on a topic that had been a regular one for weeks: bemoaning their homecoming fates. "It's just not fair," Bunny said. "It's our year to be the homecoming court and we're going to be overshadowed by dumb Farrah and Freddy performing their *song*."

Despite Bunny's best efforts to hijack the homecoming committee, hers was not the only voice on it, and the rest of the students and the faculty adviser, Ms. Wilcox, had insisted on having the twins perform "Let's Hang Out." Rainbow had argued that even though everyone at the Gem had listened to the song all summer, it was fall now so it was out of style. But Ms. Wilcox had countered with the fact that they should be celebrating the accomplishments of their classmates.

"It's just a song," Gillian said. "And it's just homecoming. In my opinion, you should embrace the twins, let them play their song." She was constantly surprised by how much these girls knew about the world. How much more they knew than she had known at their age. And yet, at this moment, they still cared about homecoming and they were still being brats. She wanted to shake them and say, *You are so much better than this—be kind to your fellow humans*. Of course, at the same time, she remembered her own high school social anxiety.

"I know you think homecoming is dumb," Julia said. "But to us it's important. Besides, Ms. Wilcox is a dictator. Why is there even a committee if she's just going to make all the decisions."

"All's fair in love, war, and homecoming dances," Gillian said. Julia groaned. "I'm just trying to show you perspective in the world."

"Is that what you told your clients when they had a new album out but they got bumped from the cover of *People* magazine because Kate and William had a fight? To have some perspective?" Julia asked. They loved asking this type of question, creating parallels between Gillian's former life and now. Sometimes she wanted to snap at them that they were nothing like her clients and they should be happy about it. But drawing the comparisons seemed to bring them endless entertainment.

"I mean, as a last resort, maybe," Gillian said, thinking that Julia would be a good publicity assistant. "Celebrities are particularly lacking in perspective."

"Do you think Freddy and Farrah are going to become famous?" Rainbow asked.

"I don't know anything about their music," Gillian said.

"We'll play it for you," Julia said. She pulled out her phone and searched for "Let's Hang Out." The song blared from the phone's speakers. It had a catchy intro and then the first voice Gillian heard was Farrah's. She had a kind of raspy voice that Gillian didn't expect, in the Janis Joplin mode. And then Freddy came in, harmonizing. It made Gillian smile. And the song was sweet—it was about two kids trying to figure out how to ask two other kids on the playground to hang out with them. And the chorus was catchy: "Do you like to shout, do you like to pout, do you like to flout . . . our parents? Let's hang out." Gillian looked around as the song was playing and realized that everyone was smiling—even Bunny.

"That song is great," Gillian said. "But do I think they'll be famous? It's hard to know. Being famous is such a weird thing. I wouldn't say it's necessarily pleasant. And they don't particularly seem like they want it. You really need to want it, I think." She had seen plenty of talented people fall by the wayside in the instant-gratification culture, but she had also seen people rise to the occasion—take their moment and run with it. It had a little to do with talent, more to do with drive and savvy. She had also seen plenty of people who wanted it and got it and then regretted it. But what could she do? Once you were famous, you couldn't take it back. People still recognized Phoebe Cates.

"The twins do post a lot on Instagram," Julia said, leaning back against the window glass and holding her dress up to the light in the room so she could see if there were any imperfections. "But their photos are a little boring. A lot of pictures of them working on songs. Nothing of them having fun."

"Obviously they don't ever do anything fun," Bunny said. "We already knew that about them."

"Do you think they have fans outside of our school?" Julia asked.

"I usually don't know the people in the comments," Rainbow said. "So I bet they do. They're at cult band status already."

"I'm sure they have a new song almost done," Julia said. "They've been teasing it in their stories. We're their guinea pigs."

"It's not like they do anything else," Rainbow said. "They don't socialize or even really participate in class." She connected some puzzle pieces and looked contented.

"What if they premiere the new song at homecoming?" Bunny asked.

"We should film it!" Julia said. "Maybe then we can become influencers and get free stuff and we won't have to go to college."

"It seems to me that this is a cool opportunity," Gillian pointed out. "They're your classmates. They have a good song. Maybe they'll have another one. Maybe just try to enjoy it?"

"I'm just bored with this whole situation," Bunny said. She seemed irritated by the suggestion that they embrace the twins' popularity rather than rail against it. "Why can't our school just be normal?"

"Your school is cool. You should be proud," Gillian said. "It'll be special."

"I wish it were just a regular year," Julia said.

"That's what I want," Bunny said. "A boring, ordinary year where we get all the attention."

"Think about the stories you'll tell your college roommate.

You had future rock stars perform at your senior year homecoming dance," Gillian said.

"Oh boo," Rainbow said. "Stories schmories. Do you think they're sitting around talking about what people will think of them at the dance or even considering what *we* might think of *them*? We should stop wasting our time."

"Exactly," Julia said. "At the very least, we should be using them to make ourselves famous. Get them to tag us and stuff."

"*Ugh,*" Bunny said. "Why can't we just be in high school and not worry about our social media status. I'm quitting everything and only using my phone for group texts."

"That would be good for your college essay," Julia said.

"IT NEVER STOPS!" Bunny said. "Why can't we just be authentic and be ourselves? Why does every action have to be for a purpose? It must have been so fun to be in high school in the nineties like you, Gillian. You didn't have to worry about any of this."

"We had to worry about other things," Gillian said.

"Like what?"

"Like not knowing who was calling us or if someone had received our message or where they were or what they were doing or whom they were with. The FOMO was way more intense because it was all theoretical."

"Okay, *fine*. The nineties were also annoying. And you had to wear flannel, which was not great."

"When I was in high school in the mid-nineties, there were more crop tops and oversized blazers than flannel."

"CROP TOPS," Julia practically screamed. "What's old is new again. But we wouldn't wear an oversized blazer."

"Obviously," Gillian said. "Well, I think you should focus on the positives here. This is going to be a fun show and you are a part of it. Who gets to introduce them?"

"I guess I get to introduce them as senior class president," Bunny said. "They want to perform throughout the night and have the last song be 'Let's Hang Out.'"

"What's bad about that?" Gillian asked.

"Well, the last thing people will remember is their song, not the homecoming court."

"But then you can dance in your crowns and sashes with your adoring subjects," Gillian said.

"Okay, that sounds not bad," Bunny said.

"We're so lucky to have you," Julia said. She got up from the window seat and stood behind Rainbow at the puzzle, her dress draped over her arm. She quietly found a few matches and clicked them into place. Rainbow looked annoyed.

Gillian wasn't sure if Julia was being sincere or not, but she wanted this conversation to be over, so she gave them each a big hug and a broad smile, saying, "I'm lucky to have you living in my dorm. Now get out of here and go do your homework."

The girls smiled, blew her air kisses, and filed out. Talking to them made Gillian feel like she was always going around in circles, which was kind of exhausting, but she secretly loved their conversations. These girls were way more interesting and engaging than she had expected teenagers would be. When they were gone, she looked at her phone: still no word from Aiden. It had been over a month since she had run into him on move-in day, but she still looked at her phone with hope about seventeen times a day.

Her phone was empty of old friends but showed her new

life blooming. She did have a text from Lila: "Long day discussing why Sally Hemings was erased from history until our lifetimes."

Gillian didn't want to text back. It seemed exhausting to write what she could say in just a few moments. So she called. "So what's up with Sally Hemings?" she asked when Lila picked up.

"Oh, you know, the kids are just outraged that it took until the early 2000s for society to know and accept that Thomas Jefferson and Sally Hemings had children together."

"It *is* kind of crazy that it took that long. They're not wrong to be incensed."

"I know. Well, now that they've all memorized the *Hamilton* soundtrack, they know that Thomas Jefferson wasn't the saint he seemed to be when we were learning American history."

"Does the existence of *Hamilton* make teaching history any easier?"

"It certainly doesn't hurt," Lila said.

"Well, I just got through talking with the girls about how they need to be more generous with Farrah and Freddy and appreciate that they go to school with talented students."

"I'm excited to hear them perform. Do you think they'll sing 'Let's Hang Out'?"

"Yeah, that's what's giving Bunny a heart attack. She's afraid they'll steal her thunder. But they have to play their hit. I once represented this indie band that refused to play their hit radio song on their tour. They had finally gotten venues like the Beacon Theatre and the Troubadour, and they were sold out, but the internet was going crazy because they weren't singing their hit. So when we got to New York, which was the end of the tour, the promoter insisted that they sing it or else he was going to cancel the show. They were all pouting and acting terribly, but I told them that if they agreed to do it, I'd get it in the papers and also we'd record it and put it on YouTube and that it would rehabilitate their entire reputation. So I pitched the story to the *New York Post*, which loved it and put them on the cover, and then we paid a fan to record the song, and that fan is still making money off of the streams. And all the promoters who were so mad around the country began clamoring to have them again."

The morning after the show, when the piece ran in the paper and Gillian was sitting in the band's hotel room and sending the article out to promoters, she got instantaneous responses. Joel, the lead singer, was throwing dollar bills on the bed for each new gig she booked. By the end, there were thirty-five dollars on the bed. They used the money to buy a bottle of whiskey.

"You were good at your job," Lila said.

"I was," Gillian said. "And a lot of days I really loved it. It was glamorous and exciting and I was in the middle of big things like movie premieres and fashion shows—I even went to the Oscars once. But sometimes that isn't enough. There was always this sinking feeling in the back of my mind that it was all just silly, that no one *actually* cared, and when my client lied to me and I had to shut down my business? I don't know. It's wild to think that's what I did every day. And now my life is nothing like that at all."

"I bet you'll make a comeback," Lila said. "I'm sure there aren't many people who are as good and smart and instinctual as you are."

"I don't know if I want to. A big part of me feels like that time is over. It was so exciting while it was happening. But I don't really miss the adrenaline. At least not right now. These past few weeks of just worrying about high school problems have been pretty refreshing."

"I bet," Lila said.

After all her years of being "friends" with only her clients, it felt remarkable to have a friend who was truly in it only for the friendship. It was something Gillian honestly wasn't used to—having someone listen to her and be interested in her. Plus, having someone to watch silly television with. That said, she still held some things close to the vest. Even though she trusted Lila, for some reason, she wanted to keep that one detail vague still.

"I guess I should do my last door check," Gillian said, looking at her watch. She had realized that she needed to keep the girls on their toes with random checks of the halls and common areas at different times throughout the night. She felt like it was working because she hadn't had to pull a vomit-stained girl out of a bathroom since that first morning.

"I'll see you tomorrow," Lila said. "Don't forget that it's Parents' Day."

"How could I?" Gillian said.

She was trying not to panic. Aiden would be here visiting Rainbow in the morning. She had to get ready.

NINE

....

Homecoming also always coincided with Parents' Day, which further reinforced the "haves and have nots." She remembered watching the way the rich kids' parents arrived early, in fancy cars with huge boxes piled with gifts and snacks. She never forgot the time during her senior year when Brixton Taylor's parents showed up with a photographer, an interior decorator, and a carpenter and sent them into Brixton's room to put up wallpaper on one wall and build shelves on another. The photographer took "before and after" photos and Brixton claimed that the redesign would be in *Elle Decor*.

Legacy kids would be accompanied by parents decked out in Gem gear featuring the mascot, the White Wolf, named after Jack London's book *White Fang*. Wally and Molly had hung out with Jack London; he was their neighbor, after all, so it made sense for them to name the school mascot after one of his most famous literary canines.

Scholarship kids like Gillian often were left to their own devices—either because their parents couldn't afford to come or because the students didn't want anyone to see their parents. Gillian herself had tried to get her mother not to come for the weekend after the first year, when she'd shown up wearing her best pink suit, the one she wore to open houses. The rich parents had been wearing chic tennis outfits, or the sort of fancy casual designer clothes that only rich people knew how to wear, or White Wolf gear, indicating a sense of belonging. Gillian's mom had stuck out in her formal wear, but for Angela Brodie this was the fanciest day of the year. And if Gillian was honest, it would have been even more embarrassing if her mom had shown up in her old sweatpants and cat sweatshirt, which was her idea of leisure wear. Angela had tried extra hard to talk to the dorm mother, the teachers, and the other students, telling them how proud she was of her daughter, and Gillian had felt her humiliation grow throughout the day. In retrospect, her mom was being a proud mom and she should have loved her for it. But at the time, she was just mortified.

Remembering the feeling from those days, she checked in with Bunny, who she knew would not have parents visiting. Gillian thought Bunny might be sad about not having visitors on Parents' Day. But Bunny's text response was "Fuck them and their Monte Carlo bullshit. I'll have way more fun without them. Besides, I'll just go out to dinner with Rainbow and her dad."

Gillian felt a little pang of jealousy, as she would have preferred to go out to dinner with Rainbow's dad. But she just smiled and wrote back, "That sounds nice."

The days leading up to the big event weekend had been filled with flowering bushes being planted and trash cans being repainted. The dorms were fully scrubbed and vacuumed, and more emails than usual were sent out to the faculty

distro, reminding everyone about the weekend and the expected behavior with parents (mostly, Gillian assumed, the
donating kind of parents).

Mentally prepping to see Aiden again, but also to reassure
parents that their daughters were perfect angels who never
went afoul of the rules and regulations of the Vallejo dorm
and were supervised by an actual adult, Gillian dressed more
formally than her usual jeans and a hoodie. She unearthed a
pair of slim-fitting black pants and a very light knit three-
quarter-sleeve Eileen Fisher tunic. She blew her usually
messy hair straight, contoured her cheekbones, and tied an
Hermès handkerchief into a sleek high ponytail. She checked
herself out in the lobby mirror: she could have been a Gem
parent herself. It was a style she called "casual rich lady"—a
curated blend of effortlessly casual slightly oversized cotton
with fancy (but understated) flourishes. She would have confidence in the person in the reflection to care for her (imagined) precious child.

Before she went down to meet the parents, she took a quiet
walk through the halls of the dorm, spraying lavender, making sure the whiteboards didn't have obscenities written on
them, and checking that the trash cans didn't have anything
incriminating in them. She remembered what her mother
had thought of the dorm ("A little shabby for the tuition, but
nice") and what someone like Bunny's mother would think
("If you just knock down a few walls, replace the window
treatments, and update the fireplaces, maybe it would be liv-
able"). Then she settled herself behind a table near the dorm
entrance across from the security desk with a sign on it that
she had made herself with a piece of oak tag and some wash-
able markers. It said, DORM MOTHER—ASK ME ANYTHING.

She hoped her plan wouldn't backfire. Yes, she would have to answer the questions of nervous parents, but that was an acceptable trade-off for a virtual guarantee that she would also see Aiden when he came inside to pick up Rainbow and Bunny.

The second parent through the door was not Aiden, or even a friendly face: it was a mother who was clearly on the warpath—an elegant woman wearing a Halston jumpsuit, her face shimmering in the way rich women's faces did, her hands and clavicle lit up with sparkling highlights, her dark hair exceptionally soft and perfectly wavy. It broke over her shoulders as if she had just stepped out of a shampoo commercial. She carried one of those quilted leather Chanel purses that looked like they had a gold necklace for a strap. She was not a casual rich lady; she was a proud rich lady. "You must be the publicist," the woman said sternly. She had waited semi-patiently while Gillian had drawn a map for the disoriented mother of a member of the golf team, but the minute that woman had walked away, she'd moved in.

Gillian looked up, confused. "I was a publicist," she said. "But now I'm a dorm mom."

"My children need you," the woman said.

"And you are?" Gillian said.

"Mina Shirazi. I am the mother of Farrah and Freddy."

"Hello, it's lovely to meet you," Gillian said, holding out her hand. Mina Shirazi shook it forcefully. "You have talented kids."

"Yes, thank you—I agree, they are so accomplished. They always have been. Even when they were babies, they harmonized their cries from their cribs."

Gillian smiled; it was refreshing to see a mother who so openly exulted in her children's success. Although she also couldn't seem to picture the perfectly coiffed and dressed Ms. Shirazi caring for drooling babies. "It's good to see them working on their art," Gillian said.

"Yes," Mina said. "But I am aware that talent alone is not enough and I'm afraid we don't have the skills to propel their career forward. They need a publicist, a marketer maybe. I have hired them a manager, but he is not focused on the smaller details. I want them to get some real recognition."

"They're so young," Gillian said. "They have plenty of time."

"Maybe, but in the music world, they are not young. There is so much they could be doing now to expand their fame. I want them to go viral and release a single. What should they do on social media? Should we set up concerts?" Mina asked. "These are the things we wonder."

"They might need a few more hits before they can go on tour," Gillian said.

"Exactly," Mina said. "You know this world. Yes, they need to write a hit. The manager should be pushing them. Do they have the right team? Every day I research and make phone calls to all the top people, just trying to find out what to do. I am beside myself with worry about it."

"Don't forget that they're still kids," Gillian said. "They also have to enjoy their last year of high school."

"I'm just afraid that they are squandering their only chance," Mina said.

Gillian paused and took a deep breath. "It's not such a great tragedy to miss out on a life of being famous. I've worked with a lot of famous people and most of them are pretty miserable. If your true goal is for your children to be happy, I'd embrace what they have but not push them toward more."

"You're just jaded because of what happened to you," Mina said, her tone turning a bit vicious.

"I won't deny that I'm glad to be out of that world," Gillian said. She was no longer surprised that everyone she encountered knew her business and felt no compunction about referencing it. "But I also assure you that famous people are paranoid, isolated, and drive themselves kind of crazy. It's kind of nice to be able to live anonymously in this world. And you don't value it until you can't. You have lovely children who happen to be quite talented. But I would value their loveliness over their talent if I were you. But, of course, they're your children." Gillian couldn't quite believe she was parroting back the exact thing her famous clients had said to her in a condescending manner. Yet somehow saying it as an outsider made it less condescending—or at least she hoped that was true.

Mina nodded. "I see. Well, thank you for your perspective. My children have told me that they like you. That you defended them against these popular bullies at the beginning of the year. I am their mother, as you note, so I know what's best for them." She then opened her Chanel purse and pulled out a business card. "Please call me to arrange a retainer fee."

Gillian took the card and smiled. She was flattered but she knew that she would never call Mina Shirazi for work. It would be a conflict of interest with her current job, for one. She would, however, reach out to Farrah to see if she needed help managing her fame-hungry mother. "Thanks," Gillian said. Just then, Aiden walked through the door of Vallejo carrying a tote bag overflowing with corn and carrots—the kind with the greens still on top. She caught his eye, nodded, and shook Mina Shirazi's hand. "It was great meeting you," she said. "Please excuse me." Mina seemed a bit stunned that Gillian was leaving her presence, but Gillian tried not to think twice about it. She walked away with purpose.

Gillian approached Aiden, who was wearing his uniform of jeans and a buttoned chambray shirt that appeared slightly shabby but fit him perfectly. She wondered if he purposefully aged his clothing. There was just one little smudge of dirt on his cheek. Everything about this moment brought back to her the day she'd found out he was dating Miranda.

The three of them had been hanging out as friends for two years; the pact between Miranda and Gillian had stuck and Gillian had finally accepted that he would never date either of them. They listened as he talked about other girls, and he theoretically gave them love advice, even though neither of them really dated anyone, letting their mutual crush stand. It was a normal Friday night at the beginning of the second semester of senior year—the three of them had gone to a viewing of *Reality Bites* in the chapel, where it had been projected up on the wall. Usually after that they would have gone to the Friday night ice cream parlor that was set up in the dining hall, but Aiden claimed he needed to start reading for Monday. Gillian was surprised, because normally Friday nights were sacred for the three of them. Gillian and Miranda walked back to their room and got ready for bed as usual. Gillian put on her eye mask and earplugs, as she always did, and fell asleep.

In the morning when she woke up, Miranda wasn't in her bed. Sometimes that meant that she had gone down to breakfast early or was hitting the library. But it was Saturday. Gillian got ready for her day—put on fresh sweatpants and a Gem T-shirt. She grabbed her book and went down to the dining hall. And there they were: at the trio's regular table. But there were only two chairs and Miranda had her head on Aiden's shoulder and his arm was around her. All of a sudden, in just a few hours, everything had changed. Gillian left her tray on a table near the entrance to the dining hall and ran out into the quad. Her heart was racing. She didn't even know what to do. Her trio had become a duo, and she was the odd one out. Tears ran down her face. She had never felt more alone in her entire life, more betrayed. Her two friends were now a couple and she had lost everything.

"What's up with the veg?" she asked Aiden playfully now, trying to smile away the painful memory.

"I was just going to see if I could get those girls to have a cookout with me," he said. "They're all vegetarians, so burgers don't work. But freshly picked corn and carrots sometimes do."

"Sounds like a wild time for a bunch of vegetarians," she teased. She knew for a fact that Bunny was not actually a vegetarian, although maybe she acted like one with her friends.

"That's how we roll here in California," he said. "I'd invite you to the picnic, but I assume you have official duties."

"I guess I do," she said, gesturing toward her table. Mina was gone, but there was another parent, this one with a popped collar, leafing through the dorm rules packet she had left on the table. "But I'm free during the dance. I don't have to chaperone this one."

"Oh," he said. He looked around nervously. "I guess I am too. We do have a lot to catch up on. I could get a drink if you want. I like to go to the Fig Café."

"I'd be up for that," she said. She felt like his invite was a little reticent, but she jumped at it anyway. "I haven't been there yet."

"It's the best," he said. He looked at his phone, as if to check a calendar. "I'll meet you there at seven."

She resisted the urge to say "It's a date" and instead just smiled and said, "See you there." Inside, she was beaming.

Gillian had spent the entire day after she had realized that Miranda and Aiden were together hidden out in her secret place in the library—in the far back corner of the fourth-floor reading room. She tried to concentrate on reading, but that didn't work. So instead she wrote a letter to herself. It was the most honest she'd ever been with herself—telling herself that she needed to branch out, to not be intimidated by the other kids at school even though they were richer—that she deserved to be here, that she was worthy of love. All the things you wish were true but also know are patently not. Eventually, emotionally exhausted, she fell asleep in the comfy reading chair. When she woke up, Miranda was sitting next to her. "I didn't want to wake you," she said.

"I don't understand," Gillian said, her eyes rimmed with tears. "I saw you together."

"Let me explain . . ."

Gillian sniffled, "We had a pact."

"I know," Miranda said.

"Ugh," Gillian said. "You." It was all she could say. She was so mad.

"I'm so sorry," Miranda said. "I know this hurts you, even though that is the last thing I want."

"Then don't date Aiden. Things should go back to how they were before. I can't believe you got together with him."

"Things can't go back," Miranda said. "We're in love."

"Since last night?" Gillian said.

"Well . . ." Miranda said. "It's been going on for a while. We hung out over Christmas. My parents came back from Morocco and I was in New York City and he was in Connecticut. And he came down to meet me and . . . I don't know . . . it just changed."

"With me not being there," Gillian said. Tears welled up in her eyes. Dumb Sacramento.

"Everything can be the same in our friendship," Miranda said. "We both love being friends with you."

"But now I'm just a third wheel. And you know I wanted him too."

"I know," Miranda said, tears welling up in her eyes. "I feel terrible, I really do. But I really hope we can still be friends." She gave Gillian a hug. Gillian inhaled deeply, but she couldn't stop crying. What was she going to do? These were her only two friends at school. Her first three years were behind her—the time when she could have met more people, made different friends. Now she was a senior and she felt like she had committed her entire life to these two. And now they were in a relationship.

As Miranda hugged her, Gillian resolved to make new friends, though she knew that for the time being, she had to just accept that her two best friends were in love and she was merely an accessory. And to add insult to injury: they were roommates.

"I need to be by myself for a little while," Gillian said. She knew that she was going to have to give in to be friends with

Miranda again, since she didn't have many other friends at the Gem, but she couldn't give in so fast.

"Whatever you need," Miranda said.

Gillian waited for Miranda to leave and then left the library herself. She walked back to the room and cried her eyes out. The next day, she put on some of Miranda's concealer and walked back out onto campus with faux confidence. She was going to put on a happy face and try to forget about it. She had no other choice.

She went back to her dorm mother table and stayed there for as long as she could bear, answering parental questions about emergency procedures (detailed in the handout she happily passed along) and rule enforcement (nightly checks, one warning and then discipline) and the school social media policy (no bullying). But after a few more questions, she couldn't take it anymore. Besides, the flow of parents was slowing down. It was time for lunch and the water polo game. When she was on the verge of losing her voice, she folded up her poster and dumped her remaining handouts in the recycling bin. Everything was available on the school website anyway. Official duties complete, she went up to her room to figure out what to wear on her date. She had her own priorities, after all.

TEN

....

Gillian tried to hide her annoyance when she found Bunny sitting forlornly outside her door scribbling in a floral notebook. "What's going on?" Gillian asked as she opened her door.

"Just hiding from the shitshow that is this day," Bunny said, standing and walking into Gillian's room.

"I thought you were fine with it. Besides, Rainbow's dad is here and he wants you guys to have a cookout with him."

"Whatever," Bunny said. She made such an overblown teenagery sad face that Gillian couldn't help but smile. Bunny let out a deep sigh in return, as if she knew she was being ridiculous but simultaneously could not help herself.

"It'll be fun," Gillian said. "And you said you wanted to hang out with him. Remember?"

"I do remember thinking that it would be fun for you," Bunny said.

"You're being very ornery. I think you should perk up and enjoy the day. Let your friend's dad cook you a hot dog."

"I'm a vegetarian," Bunny said.

"I have observed you eating a steak," Gillian said. "And a rare steak at that."

"I'm a school-year vegetarian," Bunny said. "I can't eat the meat in the cafeteria here."

"I have also personally witnessed Rainbow's dad carrying a tote bag filled with corn and carrots for all the vegetarians in your crew—real and fake. Now go, put on your cutest cookout jumpsuit, and have a good time with your friends. It's your last homecoming." She gave Bunny an unsolicited hug, which Bunny slumped into. Maybe she had just needed a hug. "I know it's hard, but you'll get through today."

Bunny galumphed down the hallway, sighing loudly. Gillian waited until she'd entered the stairwell to go down a flight to her room, listening until Bunny closed the door behind her. A dorm mother's job was never done. She went over to her window and looked out at the campus, which was dotted with families sitting on checkered picnic blankets. A buffet was set up under the oldest oak tree, with the cafeteria staff, dressed up in school colors, doling out hamburgers and fries; a group of girls in sundresses were playing badminton against their dads, who were wearing golf pants. It was like an advertisement for the school. She didn't doubt that there were photographers around capturing the day for social media and future brochures.

Gillian headed over to her closet and looked through it to try to find something that was both classy and casual enough to wear out with an old friend in Sonoma—that town being much more casual than New York. She was excited to be seeing Aiden on purpose rather than in a random sidewalk encounter, but she was also nervous about it. Both the clothing decision and the feelings of enthusiasm and trepidation were all converging in her mind. She settled on a pair of black pants, a simple tank top, and a cropped cardigan. The date wouldn't be for hours, but knowing what she would wear helped make her feel better. Then she texted Lila and made a plan to meet up with her for a late lunch.

The teachers had it a bit harder on homecoming weekend than the dorm parents. They had back-to-back meetings, which could be set up by either a parent's or a teacher's request. And Lila's schedule was packed, mostly with nervous parents asking about college applications. But she had penciled in a break for lunch, so Gillian headed out to meet her in her classroom. She picked up sandwiches and bags of chips from the outdoor buffet and brought them into the clock tower building, where Lila was on the fourth floor.

On her way up, she stopped on the third floor to say hi to Gloria. "Oh, Gillian," Gloria said when she walked in. Gillian put a sandwich and a bag of chips on Gloria's desk.

"Straight from the outdoor buffet," Gillian said.

"I couldn't," Gloria said. "These are for the parents."

"And the faculty and staff!" Gillian said. "It's totally fine."

"I would never take something that didn't belong to me," she said. "Unlike certain people . . ."

"What are you talking about?" Gillian asked.

"Now's not the time," Gloria said. "But I have a lot to tell someone and I think you're the person. You have an honest heart."

"Okay," Gillian said, curious about what Gloria was talking about, but also sure that Gloria would tell her when the time was right. "Just call me when you need me. In the meantime, this sandwich is for you."

"Thank you," Gloria said. "Enjoy the rest of your day."

Gillian couldn't help smiling. "I have a date tonight . . . with Aiden."

"Oh God," Gloria said. "But he . . ."

"I know," Gillian said. "It's so weird, because I hated him so much back at the end of school—he had broken my heart and betrayed me—but all these years later, I still kind of like him. He just gets under my skin. I can't really resist him."

"And his girlfriend? Whatever happened to her?"

"Well, I didn't know for a long time," Gillian said. "I never returned her calls after high school. But I just got nostalgic for her—maybe because I'm here. I don't know. Anyway, I googled her and there she was: a mommy blogger in Los Angeles. She didn't write me back, which isn't really surprising. I mean, I didn't respond to her when she reached out to me."

"Well, you never know," Gloria said.

"I don't know why, but for some reason I stopped hating him and I never forgave her."

"Probably shows you who at the end of the day was your real friend—Miranda. She was the one who really hurt you."

"A good point." Gillian never really could figure out why she could forgive Aiden and not Miranda. Maybe Gloria was right; maybe Miranda was more of her true friend. Or maybe somehow she blamed Miranda more because Miranda should have been more of a custodian of her feelings. She could tell, however, that Gloria didn't want to discuss it any further.

"Well, thanks for lunch," Gloria said.

"Anything for you," Gillian said and continued on her journey up to Lila's classroom. Lila was in there alone, gazing out the window at the campus. Her view took in Vallejo; Gillian remembered sitting here in high school—it had always been a history classroom—and looking back at her dorm room, wishing she were curled up in her bed instead of studying pictures of the Rosetta Stone. She loved how the tiny campus created a little cocoon of views.

"How's your Parents' Day going?" Gillian asked.

Lila jumped a little, as if she had been lost in thought. "So far so good. The students who are in more academic trouble have their meetings this afternoon. This morning's meetings were easy."

Gillian put a sandwich and bag of chips on Lila's desk. "I picked this up for you on the quad."

"You're a lifesaver," Lila said. "I was just thinking about going down there, but it seemed overwhelming."

"It was fine," Gillian said. "But nobody really knows who I am, so I can slip in and out incognito. I also got a sandwich for Gloria."

"That was nice of you," Lila said. "I've never really talked to her."

"You should," Gillian said. "She was one of my only friends when I went here. I told her everything. She's a really good listener."

Lila took a bite of her sandwich. "I don't know if I'll get another meal before the dance tonight. I'm a chaperone. Are you?"

"I'm not a chaperone, no. But I'm giving myself the night off because I have a date. I got Reese to cover for me, since she also isn't chaperoning," Gillian said. "Or at least what might be a date. I'm trying not to get too excited . . . but I am."

She would have to admit it soon. If it was a real thing,

which she hoped it would be. Something about seeing Aiden
with Rainbow and seeing the care he clearly exhibited with
his winery had reminded her of the tenderness he had shown
toward his friends in high school. Plus, Aiden had been the
one she had always talked about school stuff with—the one
who read her essays and told her how to improve them, the
one who would fight with her about the importance of a
book in the canon or if their history curriculum was political. Miranda cared less about that kind of stuff.

"That *is* exciting," Lila said. "But probably good to try to
manage your expectations. It's just a first date."

Gillian could tell she was trying to be supportive but
maybe was a tiny bit jealous. There was nothing like a new
romantic relationship to ruin a new friendship.

"I know, I know," Gillian said. She took a deep breath and
tried not to get upset. It was true that Aiden had never lived
up to her expectations. Why would now be any different?
She had told Lila about their brief romance in high school
and the way her heart had been broken when Miranda returned. "It's just hard to be totally hopeless all the time."

"I know," Lila said. "But if your expectations are low,
then you're more likely to be surprised."

"That's definitely true," Gillian said. She finished her
sandwich as the reality of her situation started to dawn on
her. She was a single thirty-eight-year-old woman living in
the middle of basically nowhere in charge of a bunch of high
school students and her only romantic hope was one of their
fathers. It was not an ideal situation. There had to be someone else around who was a better match for her. "Well, if I
have to join Tinder, I will. But I'll wait until after tonight."

"Tinder, the app of last resort," Lila said. Gillian smiled. "Also, I have to say, being single isn't so bad. At least for a little while. I've been doing it for about a year and . . . I'm in a good relationship with my wine fridge."

"You're never lonely?"

"Never," Lila said. "How can I be with this job? I'm surrounded by people all the time. And the times I've let down my guard a little—like last year with that wine guy—well, I get disappointed. I'd rather just be me."

"Sometimes I'm the loneliest in the middle of a crowd," Gillian said.

"But this isn't a crowd—it's a group of needy teenagers and faculty members and guilt-ridden parents writing to you all the time."

"I guess I've just always seen myself eventually with another person. Even though I've done nothing to help make that happen," Gillian said.

"The other thing I often tell myself is that life is long. You never know what's going to happen."

"If anyone is the poster child for the 'Life is long' motto, it's me," Gillian said.

"Or maybe Toni Morrison," Lila said, laughing.

"Or maybe Toni Morrison," Gillian agreed. People always liked to use the Toni Morrison example, pointing out that her first book, *The Bluest Eye*, wasn't published until she was thirty-nine. Although it wasn't like Toni Morrison had been sitting around doing nothing before that book came out— she was an editor at Random House and a mother of two children. Regardless, it was a gentle way of being reminded not to be so self-centered or time-bound. Life was long and things didn't always happen in the sequence you wanted. She had to remind herself that the world did not revolve around Gillian Brodie after all.

Of course, that was a hard thing to tell yourself. It was something she knew professionally—as a publicist, she'd found it abundantly clear that the world revolved not around her but around her clients. And yet somehow when the news had blown up and she had become the center of the story, it was like everything got reframed. And all of a sudden, she thought about herself a lot. Pitied herself. She also started thinking more about all the things she had missed out on in her years of catering to celebrities. Love, friendship, personal autonomy. She did, however, have Diamond Medallion status on Delta. Were airline perks a sufficient replacement for intimacy? All of those years she had thought they were, but in retrospect, the deal felt slightly hollow.

There was something lovely about Lila's approach to the world. It was genuine and uncontrived. And Gillian truly believed that Lila's calling was to be a teacher, and she had only respect for her. Ever since she had gotten to Glen Ellen, she had slept more deeply at night than she ever had in New York; the days exhausted her, but she didn't have the same late-night worries. Gillian could only imagine how tired Lila was at the end of the day.

And yet, despite the sound logic of what Lila had said, Gillian wasn't quite ready to give up on love yet. Gillian had lived a version of Lila's truth for many years, and it was true that her bathroom was unsullied by a man's toothpaste misuse and her refrigerator was hers alone. But she was willing to compromise a little. Just a tiny bit. That said, it was nice to have a friend who was level-headed and emotionally objective.

"I'm lucky to have you as a friend," Gillian said. "You've really helped me through these first crazy weeks here."

"I'm glad you're here," Lila said. "I've needed an on-campus friend. And it's been a little hard to make one since not everyone here feels the same way."

Gillian could tell that Lila was a little bit uncomfortable with saying the words out loud though. She didn't want to push it. "I guess I should go—you probably have a line of parents waiting for you."

Lila looked at her iPhone. "Yeah," she said, a bit glumly. "I guess I do."

Gillian gave her a quick hug and took the detritus from lunch into the hallway to throw it away. Then she headed downstairs, but instead of walking straight across the quad, she took a detour by the headmaster's house. Parked next to the house were a Corvette and a Range Rover. She wondered how much a headmaster made in salary. Maybe his wife was rich. What did she know? At some point, had it started to seem normal to him to take private jets and buy art from any gallery he wandered into? She recalled what Gloria had hinted at in the office—about people taking things that didn't belong to them—and thought she should really follow up on that.

It was wild to reflect on how much her life had changed since her teenage conversations with Gloria. She had gone to Yale, started her own company, been on tour with bands, gone to the Oscars, flown on private jets, and visited private islands. And yet, here she was, back where she'd started. And somehow, being back on campus and living in her slightly shabby dorm mother suite felt better than all of those luxurious times. She wondered how many students had confided in

Gloria over the years, what she had seen, what she knew. Gloria had the most comprehensive knowledge of every student and faculty member who had gone through Glen Ellen Academy.

Gloria was the true Gem insider. All the roads ran through her. And if there was anyone who could inform Gillian about the ins and outs of the school, it was Gloria. It always had been.

ELEVEN

....

Gillian returned to Vallejo, taking the long route around the back side of the campus buildings so that she wouldn't run into any students or parents. She was on a mission and she couldn't be distracted. Besides, the parents weren't here to talk to her. Back when she was a student, she had been jealous of the hauls the rich kids had brought back after Parents' Day. But she hadn't thought that her fellow students had appreciated what their parents had done to send them away to school—the expense, the logistics. In retrospect, Gillian's mother had also done so much to support her daughter in school, even though they didn't see each other every day like when they had lived together. Angela had called weekly on Monday nights, had sent monthly care packages filled with Oreos and Goldfish crackers, and had called Headmaster Kent when the students all turned against Gillian to tell him to step in and fix it. There wasn't much he could do, but Gillian, despite being embarrassed, had appreciated the effort from her mother.

When she returned to the dorm, she had a few hours before she had to leave to meet Aiden at the Fig Café. She only had two ways to decompress; one was running, and that was out of the question on a day when the campus and its immediate surrounding area were filled with students and parents. So the only other option was to read.

When she'd shuttered her business, she had decided that she needed to start reading again, to take up the pastime she had enjoyed as a child and again in college. (But not in high school, when reading for pleasure had been deemed "uncool.") She had great memories of escaping from her college studies by devouring *The Giant's House* by Elizabeth McCracken, *Housekeeping* by Marilynne Robinson, and *The Virgin Suicides* by Jeffrey Eugenides. Back then, she had loved going to the contemporary fiction section of the college library and checking out something that nobody else was reading. Sure, she loved Jane Austen and Virginia Woolf and even James Joyce as much as the next English major. But more recent literature felt fun and escapist.

On the first Saturday after she closed up shop, she'd headed to Three Lives, a tiny little bookshop near Bleecker Street that made you feel like you were going back in time, and she'd bought all four of the Elena Ferrante Neapolitan novels. She had started the first one that day, with a picnic lunch on the Christopher Street pier featuring a can of rosé and an Italian sandwich from Faicco's. She had finished the first book within days, and then when she'd gotten caught up in her move to California, she hadn't started the second. Well, now was the time. She pulled the book off her nightstand and snuggled herself onto her bed. She could see out the window that the lawn picnics had mostly wrapped up, and the complimentary buffet was being deconstructed. Gillian was glad to escape to the gritty streets of Naples.

After reading a few chapters, napping a little, and staring into space, she realized it was time to get ready. She went into the living room and played an old favorite on her portable stereo—*Birth of the Cool* by Miles Davis. It was an album she had purchased at a used CD store in high school when she had wanted to feel sophisticated. It was one of the few jazz albums that felt familiar to her; she had never really become a "jazz person." Even so, this one album made her feel fancy and cultured. And that was what she wanted in advance of seeing Aiden. The outfit she had picked out earlier—black pedal pushers that showed off her slim ankles, a black crepe tank top, and a cropped light pink cardigan—would hopefully come off as sophisticated yet casual. She still wasn't entirely sure about the California dress code. This outfit was definitely more New York than California—it was seventy-five percent black, after all. But it wasn't one hundred percent black, so she felt she should get some sort of medal.

She spent an hour moisturizing and contouring her face. She pulled her hair up into the most casual messy bun she could make—he'd never know it took twenty minutes to get it perfect. When Reese arrived, she thanked her and then took the stairs down to the lobby so she wouldn't run into anyone in the elevator. She called a Lyft from her phone and met the driver outside the gates, even though the inner roads were open for Parents' Day. There was absolutely no reason for her to be sneaking around, and yet it kind of made the whole endeavor feel more fun. More dangerous.

She arrived at the Fig Café before Aiden and took a seat at the bar. She preferred a first date at a bar; it made some casual touching more possible but also felt less confrontational. It was oddly easier to talk to someone side by side than across

a table. She ordered a glass of rosé and sipped it slowly, calm-
ing her nerves in advance of his arrival. Even if nothing came
of this, it would be nice to reconnect with an old friend.
That's what she told herself. She thought back on Lila's comments from the afternoon, about how nice it was to be single.
She tried to remind herself of all the years she had enjoyed
quiet nights alone on the couch in between work travel
and parties. But now that she didn't have that crazy external
stimulus all the time, it was harder to justify time alone. Still,
she was capable of appreciating it. That was something she
had to remember.

As she'd said to Lila, she had always thought of herself as
a person who would one day be in a relationship. But somehow it had never quite happened. Aiden was a kind of bittersweet reminder of the one thing that she'd never gotten to
have. In so many ways she had achieved everything a person
could want in life—an Ivy League education, a successful
business, a beautiful New York City apartment, a glamorous
life. Yet she had never managed to find real and lasting love.
And weirdly enough, Aiden was the one who'd stuck in her
brain as the person who represented real love for her. Maybe
it was because of how she had observed him with Miranda in
those early months—how they truly did adore each other.
Their genuine affection for each other was one of the things
that had helped her get over being so angry at them. It was
clear that they were both so happy. And there was a part of
her that never gave up on wanting that—but another part of
her that never seemed to be able to believe that another person could provide it. Her jealousy and her love of her friends
had all gotten wrapped up together in one big complicated

braid. But when she thought about love, somehow Aiden seemed to be the only one she could imagine.

She had just reopened *The Story of a New Name* and finished her glass of wine when she felt a tap on the shoulder. She jumped just a bit and pushed the glass away from her, as if to hide the fact that she'd already had one drink, and turned around to find Aiden standing there, hands on hips, grinning. His hair freshly washed, his clothes changed from earlier in the day. He smelled like citrus. He had gone home to get ready. That was a good sign.

"Hi, stranger," he said. "Sorry I'm late—I had to shower because we ended up going horseback riding and I smelled like barn."

"Oh, the girls must have loved that," she said. "Sounds so fun." So the shower had been more of a necessity than date prep. She tried not to feel too disappointed.

He settled himself on the bar stool next to her. "It's nice when they act like little girls for a minute instead of the teenagers I know they are. I miss that little-girl stage. They all liked riding horses, even Bunny, who started out grumpy."

"I bet Rainbow was a great kid," she said. "She's a great teenager, but I know what you mean. And yeah, Bunny, she's having a hard time."

"Rachel—that's Rainbow's real name—and I were inseparable when she was little," he said. "She doesn't need me as much now and it kind of breaks my heart."

"Rachel is a pretty name. Why did she change it?"

"Why do teenagers do anything? She always wished she had been named Rainbow. Maybe it was because all the kids in her elementary school were named July and Brooklyn and

Cloud and she was named Rachel. So she decided one day that she wouldn't answer to Rachel anymore. Now everyone calls her Rainbow, except me in our quiet moments."

The bartender leaned in to take their orders. Gillian scanned quickly; it was a stressful moment, what to order. She didn't want to seem uninformed, but she also didn't want to waste too much time deciding. She took a deep breath and picked the first syrah she saw. Aiden pointed to a glass toward the bottom of the menu with a nonchalance that made Gillian think he knew every wine and winemaker on the menu.

"If there's anything being a dorm mother has made me realize, it's that these kids need adults more than ever," she said. "They act grown-up, but they're kids. Being away from home must be hard on them, at least a little."

"Do you think going to boarding school messed us up?" he asked.

"I don't know," she said. "It was the best option for me and for my mom. Do you think you would have been happier or more successful if you had gone to your local high school?"

He sighed. "I'm not sure. Probably not. My parents moved right before my sophomore year—the sixth or seventh time they had moved in my life—so I would have been new to any school I went to. And they were busy, so they liked me being away. Besides, I was happy at the Gem. I figure that in some ways Rainbow has the best of both worlds because I'm nearby. If she's feeling sad or needs something, I can pick her up and take her for a drive. But look at Bunny—her parents so far away."

"I think she's tougher than you give her credit for," Gillian said.

"But you shouldn't have to be tough at age seventeen," he said.

"True," Gillian said. "But her life would be weird no matter what, because of her parents. So at least here there's some stability. What if she was with them in Cannes or Monaco or wherever they are right now? That would be way worse."

"I guess you're right," he said. He laughed, saying, "I just imagined her parents, who I've only met once, trying to homeschool her. They're not bad people. I actually think her mom is really fun to talk to. And they get along better than she says they do. Bunny can be a bit of a teller of tales."

"I have caught her in a few lies," Gillian said.

"She's a complicated girl," he said.

The glasses appeared silently before them. They clinked and each took a sip. Gillian's was robust; it tasted like a lot of things, but she wasn't sure exactly what. She took a second sip: maybe cherries, maybe pepper. She couldn't decide. She looked over at Aiden as he closed his eyes and swirled his glass. He sniffed, sipped, and nodded.

"You approve of the wine?" she asked.

"It's good," he said. "It's a Russian River pinot, made by this couple I've met a few times. They claim they get the best fog in the area, so their grapes are the best. It's definitely one of the better ones I've had. So maybe they're on to something."

"The best fog?" she laughed.

"All winemakers are bullshitters of some sort," he joked. "Yours looks good too—what was it, the Two Shepherds?

They're also from the Russian River Valley. It's where the best pinot is being made right now—other than mine, of course. Which is being made right up the road."

There were so many things she wanted to ask him about—his wine, his winery, Rainbow's mom. What had been happening in his life since she last saw him, twenty-one years ago. But there would be time for all of that (she hoped). She paused and tried to remember what they were talking about before they were distracted by wine. "So, back to Bunny: Remember Alyssa Houston?" she asked. "That super-rich girl that we all supposed was related to Whitney Houston?"

"Oh yeah," he said. "Didn't she have a decorator come and set up and wallpaper her room every year?"

"Yes, she had all the school-issued furniture moved to the basement and replaced with brand-new furniture from Ethan Allen that was delivered on the first day of school each year, and her parents paid double so she wouldn't have a roommate."

"She was probably better off being away from home," he said. "Because she was actually pretty normal, other than all that weird rich-kid stuff. I remember her saying that she was kind of embarrassed by the furniture delivery and she didn't even really like what she had. She kind of preferred the basic stuff that the school provided."

"She was really good at math I remember," Gillian said.

"And I think she was on the chess team."

"Oh right," Gillian said. "I wonder what happened to her . . ."

"I'm sure whatever it is, she likes her furniture now."

"I think about her when I talk to Bunny—about how she came from such a crazy family but was so level-headed and smart. Bunny could be like that if she wasn't so obsessed with social status."

"I'm sure you're a good influence on her," he said.

"I'm trying," she said. "But I don't know how much of what I say goes into her head."

They both fell silent for a moment and sipped their wine.

"So," he said slowly, "I guess there's a lot to catch up on. It's been . . . a long time."

"Or should we just pretend that we just met?" she asked.

"I guess we could do a little of both."

"I feel like I'm a pretty different person than I was in high school," she said.

He nodded. "I am and I'm not. I guess life changes you. Being a young parent definitely changed me. But also, at the end of the day, you are who you are."

"You'd still climb up to the top of the clock tower and hang the senior banner?" she asked.

"For sure," he said.

"Anything you'd change?" she asked, hoping that he'd say that he'd have been better off dating her instead of Miranda, but she knew it was wishful thinking.

He shrugged. "I'd probably be nicer to my parents. Appreciate them more."

"That seems possible only in retrospect," she said.

"I didn't realize how much they gave me until I became a parent and I didn't necessarily have the resources to do what they had done. I had to create a life that made those resources."

"It seems like you've done a pretty good job."

He shrugged. "It took a few tries. At first we were still in school, but after graduation, I came to Silicon Valley at the right time. But then I wasn't around at all. The winery means that I'm home more, but now she isn't home. I don't know. It's never quite right, but until she got to high school, we had a great time together here. I was starting the business, but I wasn't away at the office every day—our home was also my business. She loved living here—she learned how to horse-back ride, we had goats and ducks as pets. Unlimited space."

"So you never married her mom?"

"We lived together in college and then after, in Mountain View. But it just really never came up. We were only together because of Rainbow."

"Did you ever tell Miranda?"

"Of course. I mean, we were still in touch. Not dating or anything. But, you know, at that age you think you can still be friends."

"I never spoke to her again," Gillian said. "Until last month, when I emailed her after I got here. But she never wrote back to me."

"I guess you're allowed to be mad at both of us. I'm actually kind of surprised you're here at all." He recoiled a bit, as if he was preparing for her to yell at him.

She sighed; she had thought about this so much. "Well, after you turned on me and sided with everyone else at school who called me a slut and a homewrecker for hooking up with you, I was mad." She crossed her arms. "But for some reason, she was the one that I put all of my hate on."

He looked relieved; his shoulders relaxed a bit. "I guess I'm glad about that. That you didn't hate me."

"Oh, I hated you then. But somehow over the years, I stopped hating you as much, but I kept hating her." She was surprised at her own frankness.

"Then let me correct myself: I guess I'm glad that you don't hate me now."

She felt like he was flirting with her, which felt wrong but also turned her on a little. "I don't," she said. She put her hand on the bar and he took it.

"I think about that a lot, what happened in high school—especially as Rainbow has grown up. I empathize with what you girls went through so much more as she describes her friendships and crushes to me. They're just so much more intense and developed than my feelings were at her age. It seems like a cliché to say this, but I was just a dumb guy."

"These girls do have that effect on you. To make you look back and think about your own teenage-hood. I guess I've missed out on a lot of experiences by not having kids," Gillian said. "At this point, I probably never will, other than caring for other people's."

It felt like something heavy to admit to someone on a first date, like a true confession. But also it was the kind of thing that she would have said to Aiden back then, so why not now. Having children had never really been a priority for her and she had always seen her clients and her employees as a kind of family she cared for. She had never, in her years as the head of a boutique publicity firm, longed for children or regretted that she didn't have them. On the other hand, she also didn't view the age of thirty-eight as too old. She knew plenty of women in their forties who had successful careers and then turned to baby making as elder stateswomen of a sort. Those women had learned from the mistakes of their predecessors, and their babies were well dressed.

Gillian sometimes thought that her mother's lack of maternal instincts was one of the reasons she felt so lukewarm about having children. But in retrospect, Gillian's mother had been the same age as Gillian was now when Gillian had left for the Gem. Of course she would want some freedom. Gillian couldn't fault her for it. There were two reactions, Gillian figured: she could either be dying to be a mother so she could right the wrongs she felt as a child or she could avoid motherhood at all costs so as not to repeat the mistakes of her own upbringing. Was it possible to escape your own past? She wasn't sure.

"I wouldn't recommend having a kid at nineteen," Aiden said. "It's not ideal. And you still have plenty of time."

"I know, I know. You just seem wiser than other people our age."

"I told you all winemakers were bullshitters," he said, laughing. He playfully punched her in the arm. It was sweet and flirtatious. She smiled and leaned toward him a tiny bit. Then she remembered how she had always misinterpreted his signals. And maybe this was his way of reminding her. "But I do want to say," he added, "no bullshit, that I'm glad you told me how mad you were at me."

"It was really hard for me to say," she said. "I mean, I can't believe I said that after we've just met again for the first time in, like, twenty years."

"I respect that," he said. "I'm honestly in awe of you for being so honest. Most people aren't straightforward like you're being."

All of his "no bullshit" and "honestly" made her a little bit suspicious of him, but she tried to go with the flow.

"Thanks," she said, hoping she didn't sound too incredulous.

"I mean it," he said, leaning toward her. "I am impressed with you and I am sorry for how I acted back then. I was a dumb kid. I didn't know what I was doing. I didn't know anything about feelings—especially other people's. But I figured out fast that I had hurt you and that I had hurt Miranda and then I guess I just tried to protect myself. But I hope we can put all of that behind us."

She closed her eyes and took all of it in. She was just not sure what to say in response. As if sensing an awkward moment, the bartender refilled their wineglasses and put down a plate of pâté and grilled bread, which they dove into as if they hadn't eaten for days.

"This is too good," she said, closing her eyes and savoring the fat-to-crunch ratio, which was truly perfect. She suspected that the bread had also been brushed with butter, making it even more delicious.

"It is," he said.

She was still kind of in shock from the conversation they had had before their snack arrived and wasn't sure exactly what to say, so instead of saying anything, she just focused on the food: spread the mustard and pâté on the crispy triangle of fat-laden carb that had been laid in front of her.

"It's weird," he said after finishing a bite.

"What?" she asked.

"Being here with you."

"Weird how?" she asked.

"I just feel super comfortable with you, and we can just talk."

She thought about how in high school they had had heated discussions about whether it was more important to read

Hermann Hesse or Herman Melville. (She had fought for Hesse; he'd argued for Melville.) And why there were so few female authors taught in English classes—they agreed there should be more.

"It's a nice thing about old friends," she said. "It's like you can just pick up where you left off even if it was, like, twenty years ago."

"I don't have that many old friends," he said.

"Me either."

Gillian took another bite and then said, "So you aren't in touch with Miranda now?"

"Not really," he said.

"No one is a great correspondent these days," she said.

"So true," he agreed.

They were silent again. She was dying to know what he was thinking. But then she steeled herself by deciding that maybe he wasn't thinking anything. Maybe the wine was just settling in. The food was tasty. The restaurant smelled good and had the ideal level of noisy business without anything overwhelming. The setting was perfect. She put her hand on top of his, which was forward, but it was how she felt. "It's really good to see you," she said.

"Yeah," he said. He didn't move his hand away. Though she wasn't sure if he was comfortable either. But then he confirmed that everything was okay. "Should we order some more food? This was super good."

She nodded. "Should we order more food" was even better than "This is fun"; it was the universal sign for "I would like this night to continue." They were in agreement on that point. She reached for a menu, which disconnected their hands. Maybe that was his goal. But it also achieved her goal, which was to make the night longer. She never wanted this night to end.

Aiden scanned his own menu, got the attention of the bartender, and ordered all three of the pizzas and the "simple side salad." He looked at Gillian for her approval as the bartender keyed it into the computer. She nodded. The bartender then refilled their glasses again.

Gillian liked it that Aiden had taken charge of the ordering—she felt confident that as a local and a wine-industry person that he would get only the best. It was also nice to have their glasses refilled so seamlessly; this had happened to her most often when she was out with clients who had relationships in the restaurant industry. There was a kind of unspoken camaraderie between those people, and they all gave one another special perks—extra pours, extra tastes, off-the-menu items. She assumed that Aiden's role as a local winemaker earned him that special treatment. There was also the thing about being a local in a tourist town. Even though she lived here officially, Gillian still felt like a tourist. She wondered how long it took to really feel like you lived here. To be accepted. Probably a long time.

She paged through possible conversation topics in her mind and wondered if she should bring up Miranda again or ask him about other relationships. But then she thought about her own past: Did she want to detail it for him? What would she even tell him? About one-night stands after awkward internet dates? About setups that made her wonder what the person who had set her up really thought of her? About the hope she would have when she was a few dates in with someone and then he disappeared? None of those things was worth reporting.

With all the things in her head swirling around, all she could say was "I really like this place." And give him a smile. She wondered what was swirling around his head. Maybe nothing. Maybe everything. It was so hard to know someone.

"Me too," he said. "It's kind of my go-to place. I don't like to drive all the way into Sonoma at night. Too many drunk tourists cruising around."

"I guess that's an occupational hazard," she laughed.

"They just don't know how to handle their wine," he said. "But they keep the lights on. I wouldn't have a business without them. None of us would."

She was glad he had started another line of conversation. God, dating was exhausting. "It must be weird being in a place where you do something that requires such a skill, like growing grapes and making wine. But then you also have to run a business and deal with tourists. It's like having three heads—a wine-making head, a business head, and a hospitality head."

"I am proud of our little tasting room and cheese cave," he said. "I'd always wanted to be in the restaurant business and this lets me do it in the most low-key way. Still have evenings to myself. Everything is exactly on my terms, which is what I've been working toward for a long time."

"That's all you can ask for. Your setup sounds really great," she said.

He smiled as if thinking about it. "I'd love to show you one day."

"I'd love to see it," she said. She couldn't repress the smile: this was exactly what she'd wanted to happen. It meant a second date, an intimate setting. Not to mention some really good wine and cheese. She tried not to overthink it—if he had ulterior motives. If he would hurt her again.

"It's been a long journey to get it to this place," he said. Then he described the process of buying the vineyard, the first years of making wine, the expansion into retail and opening the tasting room and outdoor garden. It had taken more than ten years. About the same amount of time it had taken her to build her business. She asked him a few questions about making wine and bottling and distributing it. About how he got publicity for his tasting room and his wines. Talking about business, about publicity particularly, felt so comfortable for her.

"I wish I had had your expertise when we were opening our tasting room," he said.

She blushed. "I was good at my job, it's true." It was nice, for a few moments at least, to feel like an expert.

"I don't doubt it for a second," he said.

At the end of the night, they walked out to the parking lot together. She had called for a Lyft in the restaurant so as not to create the awkwardness of him offering her a ride back to campus. The car was waiting for her in the lot. He gestured toward his truck. "I guess this is good night," he said.

"I guess so," she said, already regretting her decision to call her own car, even though she knew in her heart it was the right thing to do. She wondered if she should buy a car of her own—but that felt like the final straw in admitting she wasn't a New Yorker anymore. She wanted the car but she also wanted to be a New Yorker.

"I meant that about wanting to give you a tour of my vineyard," he said. "Maybe next weekend? Saturday afternoon?"

"That works for me," she said. "I can be away from campus

in the afternoon, but I have to be back after dinner." She wondered if she should step closer so a good-bye hug would be possible, or if she should just smile and scurry away to the car. He stepped toward her and took away the awkwardness. He gave her a big enveloping hug, forceful and meaningful. She turned her face up at him, daring him to kiss her. He lingered, blinked his eyes a few times, as if going over the scenario in his mind, and then pulled back.

"I can accommodate this schedule," he said.

"Thanks," she said. "I know my job makes things a little hard, but it's worth it."

"As a parent of a girl in your dorm, I appreciate your thoroughness."

She smiled and tilted her head at him.

"This was fun," he said.

"It was," she said. "Thanks." She didn't know what to make of the almost kiss. It had felt like it was going to happen. The vibe was there. And then . . . it didn't. And yet, the date had been fun. He had admitted it. And he had asked her out again. To his home—or, at the very least, his property. When she got into the car, she took a deep breath. Maybe happiness was possible after all and the past could finally be put behind them. Was that too much to ask?

TWELVE

....

When she returned to the dorm, nobody was observing the rules—Gillian wondered where Reese was and why she wasn't controlling the situation. As she walked up the front path, she saw that the lights were blazing and could hear that music was playing via the open windows. It was well into quiet time, but when she went inside, she found Reese sitting in the downstairs lobby looking at her phone, and when she went upstairs, she found girls in the halls, dancing, doors open. Gillian took a deep breath. She walked through the first-floor halls and said, as sternly as she could, "Quiet time warning." It felt a little overzealous to be imposing order on homecoming night, but rules were rules and certainly there were girls in the dorm who wanted to sleep. She kept a list on her phone of everyone who she issued the warning to. By the time she got to the third floor, word seemed to have gotten out that she was walking the halls, as the doors were all closed, the music was mostly lowered, and the dancing had moved behind closed doors. At least her charges feared her enough to tell their upstairs neighbors that she was coming.

She was concerned about how the night had played out for Bunny, Rainbow, and Julia, so despite the fact that they had closed their door, she knocked on it before heading up to her room on the sixth floor. Rainbow cracked the door open and peeked out. "Hi, Gillian," she said. She held the door back so Gillian could pass in front of her. Bunny was sitting on the common room couch wearing pajamas, a silky sash, and a homecoming queen crown. Rainbow was mounting Bunny's plastic scepter above the "fireplace," which was literally a large poster of a fireplace they had taped to the wall. Julia, still in her handmade gown, was staring at her phone, her mouth wide open.

"So?" Gillian asked. "How was it? Congratulations, Homecoming Queen."

Bunny smiled and gave a royal wave.

"The twins played a new song," Julia mumbled. She held up her phone so that Gillian could see her screen.

"Was it good?" Gillian asked.

"Well, three hundred thousand people have already watched my video of it on Instagram," Julia said.

"It's, like, tripled in an hour!" Rainbow exclaimed.

"I wonder how it happened," Bunny said.

"It looks like it got picked up by the feed," Julia said. "Instagram is recommending it."

"I bet they'll be mad," Bunny said. "That you scooped them."

"I doubt it," Julia said. "They're not very self-promotional."

"Did they post about it?" Gillian asked.

"I'll check," Julia said. They were all quiet as she typed into her phone. "Not yet."

"You're the exclusive source of the twins' content," Bunny said. "Do you have oodles of new followers? You're going to be an influencer soon."

"Do you think they know you posted it?" Rainbow asked tentatively.

"I don't know," Julia said. "But a producer from *Good Morning America* just messaged me to ask permission to use the video on the air. Um, Gillian, we might need your help?"

"You went viral," Bunny said. "Maybe more people liked that other song than we knew."

Gillian sat on the couch. "Can I see the video?" Julia handed over her phone. Gillian watched it. The new song was even catchier than the first. And now that this many people had seen it, it was only going to get bigger.

"I think you should message Farrah and Freddy and tell them what happened. They might start getting calls, so you should tell them why. And tell them they can call me if they need help."

"Okay," Julia said slowly. "I was just trying to have some fun. But . . . I feel like I might have made a mistake. I mean, now people can figure out where they go to school."

"You're right. If you're already hearing from the media, well, brace for some action here tomorrow."

"UGH," Bunny said.

"Bunny, you're in the foreground of the video, wearing your crown," Rainbow said. "I bet people are going to want to know who you are."

"No comment," Bunny said, hiding her face behind her sash. "But Julia can promote her dresses, even though she's behind the camera."

"I hate this," Julia said, smoothing her dress on her lap. "All of a sudden I feel really anxious and nervous."

"It's all going to be okay," Gillian said. "Just don't say yes to anything or talk to anyone without consulting me first."

Gillian went up to her room and pulled Mina Shirazi's card out of her pocket from earlier in the day. She deserved to know that things were about to blow up. Mina didn't answer the phone, but Gillian left a message explaining what had happened and advised her, Farrah, and Freddy not to respond to any media inquiries without running them by her first. She also called Headmaster Kent to warn him, but she only had his office number, so she left a message and wrote him an email. She said she was available if anyone needed her help. Then she washed her face, put her hair in a ponytail, and got into bed. She hadn't even had time to reflect on the fact that she had another date with Aiden. She tried to force herself to sleep because it was clear that the next day would be a busy one.

The next morning before six o'clock, when Gillian looked out her window, she saw two news vans set up on the campus. The gates, which were always locked, had been opened for Parents' Day and the vans must have snuck in. Her phone was already lit up with voice mails and texts. Mina Shirazi, Headmaster Kent, Farrah, and Julia had all called and texted. The vans were invading the campus. The media was calling. She called Farrah back first and told her to sit tight. Same with Julia. She texted Kent and told him to shut the gates. She texted Mina and told her not to talk to the press. It was funny that Julia was more rattled by the entire thing than Farrah was.

Farrah took it well, saying, "Oh, yeah, well, I guess we were risking it by performing the song and not telling people not to Instagram it. That was a mistake. But we'd prefer not to do any press. I'll talk to my mother—she'll probably tell you to book a million interviews. She really wants us to be famous."

Julia was almost hyperventilating when Gillian spoke to her. "A million views. Requests from *People* magazine, the *Today* show, *Entertainment Tonight*, *Entertainment Weekly*, *Entertainment* something else. Also now I have, like, a hundred thousand new followers. What do I do?"

As Gillian was telling her just to ignore everything, she saw Headmaster Kent out on the quad wearing the same bespoke suit he had worn at the welcome party; it must have been his favorite. Or he didn't have a lot of suits. But nothing else in his home or behavior pointed to him being the type of man to be frugal about suiting. Maybe he had two of them; that was actually more likely. Cameras were being set up by small teams, and pretty women holding microphones were fluffing or smoothing their hair in mirrors. Gillian decided that she was needed outside—she could see his desire to talk to the media, to make a comment, from all the way up in her window. And she needed him not to do that. She put on a pencil skirt, a pair of gold sling-back wedges, and a black linen sweater. She tied an Hermès scarf around her neck and grabbed her phone. She called this her publicist uniform.

She headed downstairs and out onto the quad to see if there was anything she could do to control the situation.

"Gillian Brodie!"

She heard Headmaster Kent yelling her name before she could get to him. She headed across the quad while trying to assess the situation: Did she know any of the correspondents who were setting up on campus? She assumed these were the San Francisco or Sacramento crews, not the typical Los Angeles celebrity news reporters. As she tried to figure it out, another van rolled onto campus. If only these were people she knew; that would be easier for her to manage. But as of right now, it seemed to be a local story. Other than all the requests Julia was getting. When she reached Kent, she saw that he had bags under his eyes. "I got your email last night and your text this morning," he said. "Thank you for alerting me, but is there anything we can do about this?"

"Not really," Gillian said. "I mean, it would have been easier if you had closed the gate last night."

"I'm sorry," he said. "I had other matters to attend to. Like trying to explain this to the board."

"Well, other than closing the campus to outsiders, which you should do, I think we're kind of stuck. Hopefully it's just a one-day story, though. 'Dynamic Duo Performs Viral Song at Homecoming Dance.' It's not like the story goes anything beyond that. There's no scandal, just a song by two cute teenagers that went viral on the internet. If Farrah and Freddy won't give interviews to any of these people, they'll go away."

"Mina Shirazi is going to try to milk this for as much as possible," Kent said.

"I already advised her not to grant any impromptu interviews. And I spoke to Farrah and Freddy and told them to sit tight."

"Farrah has a good head on her shoulders, but Mina is a stage mom through and through. She wants them to be famous. This is just the moment she was waiting for," Kent said.

"Okay," Gillian said. "Now's not the time for blame. What we should do is pick one outlet to do an interview and to do it soon. Farrah and Freddy should also probably post a more official version of the song on their Instagram and YouTube. I'll talk to them."

"Okay, I'll go make sure the campus gates are closed. And I'll call Mina and reinforce what you said to her."

"You should also put some security at the gate to stop new trucks and on campus to keep the people already here in line."

"You're right," he said.

"Also, say 'No comment' to anyone who thrusts a microphone in your face."

"Gotcha," he said.

"Oh, and we may need to use your living room for the interview."

"Whatever you want," Kent said, looking flustered.

"This is good for the school," she said, trying to be reassuring. "The campus looks great. You have talented students that have gone viral. I bet applications will go up this year."

"We may need to implement a social media policy," he said.

"That wouldn't be a terrible idea," she said. "But in the meantime, the press for Glen Ellen Academy is great. I'll go see Farrah and Freddy and help them get ahead of this."

As she walked across campus, her phone to her ear, she caught sight of Bunny out of the corner of her eye, doing an interview with one of the fluffed ladies. She had told the girls not to talk to the press, and there Bunny was. Gillian hoped she wasn't saying anything inflammatory, but clearly she couldn't control Bunny. She had a wild feeling of adrenaline flooding through her body, of rising to the occasion. She hadn't expected to be a publicist here at the Gem, but it was like the muscle memory just snapped her right back into place. She could see already that Farrah and Freddy didn't want to be famous. Still, she knew that she could help them not make mistakes. And maybe even protect them. If nothing else, she was the only one on campus who could help them.

Farrah and Freddy were hiding out in the third piano practice room in the basement of Solano, one of the boys' dorms. Solano was a more modern building, built after the Wally and Molly era, after the clock tower and Vallejo. The entryway was brighter than Vallejo's but was also grand; it was filled with archival photos of the Gem through the years and featured full-sized statues of Wally and Molly that had been donated by an alumnus who worked for the company that owned Madame Tussauds. One of the senior responsibilities was to dress up Wally and Molly for holidays and relevant events. They were currently wearing Gem sweatshirts and sweatpants. Wally held a stuffed White Fang, and Molly was holding little blue-and-white pom-poms. Gillian saluted the figures as she had been taught to do in high school and headed down the stairs.

The practice rooms were a new addition to the school since she'd graduated, but they made sense because she remembered friends being tortured by their roommates' musical practice. Playing an instrument wasn't required the way sports were, but judging from the brochures the alumni office sent her, the school remained committed to the arts. And they were proud of these practice spaces. She peeked into the windows. All the rooms had pianos; the first also had a cello, the second had an upright bass, and the third, where she found Farrah and Freddy, had a drum kit.

The door was locked from the inside. Gillian knocked and Farrah got up from the piano bench to let her in. "Thanks for coming over here," Farrah said. "We're afraid to go out there."

Farrah returned to the piano bench. She was wearing what appeared to be pajamas—a Gem T-shirt and flannel Christmas-themed pants that were too long for her, so they pooled around her feet. Her hair was pulled back in a ponytail for a change. It was nice to see her face, which was normally covered by her hair. Freddy was parked behind the drum kit and was dressed almost exactly as he had been on that first night she'd met him—in a black T-shirt, black jeans, heavy black glasses, a metallic belt, and combat boots. Gillian wondered if he ever took the outfit off.

"They'll leave pretty soon," Gillian said. "They got what they came for: a pretty backdrop. A feel-good story about some kids going viral."

"Ugh," Farrah said. "Are they going to show Julia's video?"

"I told her not to respond to anyone. So, anyone who shows it doesn't have permission and could be sued."

"Our father is a lawyer," Farrah said. "He can write mean legal letters if we need him to."

"I guess that means you have him on retainer," Gillian said, trying to make a joke. Neither Farrah nor Freddy smiled.

"Our mother wants us to talk to a record label. There was one that had contacted us over the summer," Freddy said.

"That's probably also not a bad idea," Gillian said.

"She's probably doing it now," Farrah said.

"Have you guys thought about doing an Instagram post, just so your fans have somewhere to share their love and excitement with you? Maybe just something short of you guys at the dance last night? It doesn't have to be the song."

"We weren't sure what to do," Farrah said. "We aren't used to all of this attention. We just like writing songs. We really didn't want to perform last night at all, but Ms. Wilcox said it would be a good showcase for us."

"In retrospect," Freddy said, "it was a mistake. We shouldn't have played the song."

"I don't think it was a mistake. You have a new song, so you wanted to share it," Gillian said. "And now it's happened and your song is really good. So people are excited about it. I heard it on Julia's Instagram. Now you just need to capitalize on it."

Farrah's phone buzzed. "That's our mom. I'll put her on speaker." She put her phone on the top of the piano. "Hi, Mom."

"Farrah dear, I just got off the phone with Dane at Epic. He's thrilled about the response to the video. He thinks now's the time to start recording. He loved the song in the summer, remember, but he wasn't ready yet. Now he is. He wants you in the studio in L.A. the day after tomorrow. They can release the song on iTunes and Spotify next month. And then an album by the end of the year."

"Um," Farrah said. "That sounds like a lot. I don't know if we can do that and also go to school?"

"We only have a few songs," Freddy said. "And we have to go to school."

"We'll figure it all out," Mina said. "Dane said he could get you some songs that are already written."

"We're singer-songwriters," Farrah said. "We have to write our own songs."

"Maybe you can just do an EP," Gillian said.

"Hi, Gillian," Mina said.

"I should have told you she was here," Farrah said. "But I was a little distracted by all the work you just agreed for us to do."

"Gillian's part of the team. I'm glad she's there," Mina said. "Gillian, the phone is ringing off the hook with requests. I'm pushing back, but it's hard."

"I'm sure Dane would want you to wait until the song is released," Gillian said. "But I think they should do one interview now. Has the *Today* show gotten in touch?"

"They have," Mina said. "You like them best?"

"They're good because eventually, like when the record comes out, the twins could do a concert on the plaza. Whoever we go with, we should let them air a clip of the footage from the dance, showing how much everyone loved the song. But not enough to take away from its release. People have been resharing it like crazy since Instagram started promoting it from Julia's feed."

"So, tomorrow morning for the interview?" Mina said.

Gillian nodded at Farrah and Freddy. "Yes, that's right."

"Are you kids okay with that?" Mina asked.

"I'm amazed you're consulting us," Farrah said, trying not to be too serious but also trying to remind her mother that she wasn't always in charge.

Farrah and Freddy made eye contact with each other and seemed to have a silent conversation. Gillian tried to observe both of their faces simultaneously to see if she could intuit what they were saying, but all she could pick up on were uncertain smiles.

"Okay," Farrah said. "We'll do the interview if Gillian can arrange it. And we'll go to L.A. to record the song."

"Great," Mina and Gillian said simultaneously.

"You guys should probably stay out of sight today anyway," Gillian said after they hung up with Mina.

"We will," Freddy said.

"We don't want to talk to those weirdos out there," Farrah said.

"Good," Gillian said.

"And Gillian, tell Julia that we're not mad at her," Farrah said. "She sent me the weepiest message. We get why she did it. And we hope she gets more followers."

"Okay," Gillian said. "I know she feels really bad. It's generous of you to be understanding. I will say, I did see Bunny out there talking to the press, so I'm not sure what the result of that will be."

"Why does she hate us so much?" Freddy asked.

"She's just jealous," Gillian said.

"She has everything," Farrah said. "I wonder why she doesn't realize it."

"Being a teenager is hard on everyone," Gillian said.

"I just wish she would leave us alone," Freddy said.

"I know," Gillian said. "But one thing that will happen if you start to become successful is that you'll see people's true colors. So you've seen that Julia wants attention and Bunny is jealous. But I am learning about you that you are able to be generous and forgive people, plus you're hardworking and you like your privacy."

"And we're seeing that you really want to help us," Farrah said. "We really appreciate it."

"I'm doing my best," Gillian said.

Gillian pulled out her phone, glad she hadn't deleted all of her contacts in a fit of rage. She called her favorite producer at the *Today* show, Alexis, to set up the interview. Freddy got up from his drum stool and walked over to Farrah. He sat next to her on the piano bench and held her hand as Gillian talked and they listened to her side of the call.

"Hi, Alexis, it's me, Gillian."

A pause, then: "Yeah, Gillian Brodie."

"I know, it's been a while," Gillian said.

"Yeah, I'm okay, I mean, I'm definitely on a break. But it happens to be that I'm out here in California and I'm working with Farrah and Freddy Shirazi."

There was another pause, presumably as Alexis said that she either had or hadn't heard of them. Then: "I know, they're great aren't they?"

It felt pretty amazing to be talking to a producer again, to be making things happen. Gillian went through the details with Alexis.

"Okay," she said when she got off the phone. "You'll do the interview here tomorrow morning. They'll come and set up an uplink in the headmaster's house. It's more private than doing it in the Vallejo or Solano lounges. I already warned him that it might happen."

"Got it," Farrah said.

"And call me if you hear from anyone else," Gillian said. "But basically don't answer your phones and don't respond to any social media messages."

"Done," Freddy said.

"Great—I'll see you tomorrow at five A.M. at the head-master's house," Gillian said. "I'll let him know that we're invading."

"Thank you, Gillian," Farrah said. "I don't know what we would do without you. We'd be making all kinds of mistakes."

"It's kind of fun for me," Gillian said. "I missed this part."

"I'm glad you like it, because we hate it," Farrah said.

"I can prep you for the interview later today if you want," Gillian said.

"We're so nervous, and we have no idea what to say," Farrah said.

"And we don't really know what anyone would want to ask us," Freddy said. "We're just some teens who wrote a song."

"I used to do stuff like this all the time. I'll meet you back here at three," Gillian said.

"Thank you, Gillian," Freddy said and put his arm around his sister. Gillian was glad they had each other; it was more than most kids at boarding school had. She hoped they would overcome their shyness for the interview. Anything could happen once the cameras rolled—she had seen so many easy interviews go so wrong. She just hoped these kids could hold it together under pressure.

THIRTEEN

....

Gillian emailed Headmaster Kent about the five o'clock A.M. call time and then headed to the dining hall to meet Lila for lunch. As she walked across campus, she thought about the rollout of Stella Dean's first few songs. Stella had been one of her favorite clients—her first song had gone viral after she played it for Pharrell Williams at a performance class he visited. His reaction was so genuinely enthusiastic (and of course recorded and broadcast) that the internet had gone crazy for Stella Dean. Stella was overwhelmed and had hired Gillian to help her deal with the response and, subsequently, to help roll out her first EP. It was fun to work with her—Stella was so genuine and eager, she was likable in interviews, and her music was approachable. She had been mobbed after the initial Pharrell story, but Gillian had helped her prioritize the interviews and had coached her in how to answer questions. The onslaught was managed and Stella was able to produce quality music and live a life mostly out of the spotlight, unless she sought it. Gillian hoped the same would be true for Farrah and Freddy.

Lila was waiting at the entry to the dining hall, which looked like it was straight out of a Harry Potter movie. They grabbed salads from the salad bar and took them into the little faculty dining area off the main room. "Thank goodness for this place," Lila always said when they passed through its swinging doors. This time she added, "I need a break from those children. They are so worked up today."

Lila was dying to know about the fallout from the video and about Gillian's date. Gillian was ready to update her on the details, though first she asked, "But you were at the dance when they performed the song. What was it like?"

Lila dug at her salad for a minute. "It was exciting—I mean, it would have been regardless. They had just announced the homecoming queen and king. And you know Bunny: she milked it for all it was worth."

"I bet she was relieved. She was so worried that the twins would 'ruin' homecoming for her."

"I mean, they still stole the show, but she had her moment. She and Noah Dowd got crowned and then they descended to the dance floor for a spotlight dance and Farrah and Freddy got on the stage and sang their new song. Everyone started dancing after the first verse. I think Bunny was okay with it though. Anyway, the song is great. You heard it? It starts out slow and then builds. I don't really know what the lyrics are, but by the end it's just a total dance party. It'll be the song of the fall for sure. Do you know what it's called?"

"It's called 'Trust Me.'"

"Good name," Lila said.

"Yeah," Gillian said. "They have an interview tomorrow

morning. Hopefully all of these news vans will be gone by then."

"Something like this has never happened here before," Lila said.

"It looks to me like it's local media out there. But I guess anything is possible."

"That makes more sense," Lila said.

Jason Bloomfield and Anthony Rapke walked into the room with sandwiches on their trays and sodas sparkling in plastic cups. They sat down with Gillian and Lila. They started talking about the vans on campus, asking Gillian questions—about the satellite uplink equipment, the viral video, Farrah and Freddy's future. They loved the story and asked way more follow-up questions than she could have ever expected. Surprisingly, she enjoyed having them ask her all about it.

"Who's interviewing them tomorrow?" Lila asked Gillian.

"Natalie Morales," Gillian said.

"Is she coming to campus?" Jason asked.

"Yes, she's flying up from L.A. I think they're going to shoot some B-roll on campus tonight. Hopefully it'll be a good package, and then when their album comes out, they can go to New York and play in the plaza."

"Are they going to be internationally famous?" Anthony asked.

"They already are," Gillian said. "This was all triggered by a non-famous person's Instagram. The real question is if Julia will also become famous because of it."

"Did they ask to interview Julia?"

"Not yet," Gillian said. "But I guess I should find out if

she wants to be interviewed if they ask. She'd have to get up really early in the morning, which she might not like."

"Would you recommend that she do it?" Lila asked.

"Absolutely not," Gillian said. "But I'm biased because I think it's terrible to be famous. Julia may not agree with that assessment. But she doesn't really know any better. Anyway, Farrah and Freddy don't really have a choice at this point. People know who they are. And they're the real story anyway."

"True. I think Julia will probably listen to your advice," Lila said.

"I don't know about that," Gillian said. "These girls definitely have minds of their own. I told them not to talk to the press and there was Bunny out there, making a comment. So what can I do. I will say that Bunny was the one who didn't want any of this to happen. I think her exact words were 'Why can't we just have a boring, ordinary year?' Of course, it was so that all of the spotlight would be on her. But I think if anyone knows that the lifestyles of the rich and famous are kind of a crock, it's Bunny. So hopefully she'll influence Julia. I also think Julia was a little freaked out by all of the attention on her Instagram."

"She already dresses like an influencer," Lila said. "Maybe she'll get some free yoga pants out of it."

"I think that would be more to her liking," Gillian said. "Who doesn't want free pants? Basically my entire wardrobe is free clothes that my clients didn't want."

"From my perspective, you just look like someone who has nice clothes," Lila said.

"Thank you. I'm sure the fashion publicists who sent them

to my clients are disappointed that I'm wearing them and not people who actually have their photos taken. But yes, I've found a few good pieces this way."

"It's weird being in the middle of all this," Anthony said. "Our campus has always been so quiet, felt like it was removed from the real world."

"Sometimes the real world intrudes even on the innocent," Gillian said. "But it should go away pretty quickly." She winced, remembering the way the #MeToo stories snowballed. Only this was different. This was some kids getting popular on the internet. A heartwarming story. Those tended not to snowball.

"Are you okay?" Lila asked.

"Oh, fine," Gillian said. "I should probably just go make some phone calls to make sure tomorrow goes okay, and then I need to media-train Farrah and Freddy. And find out what Bunny said to that reporter."

"The school is really lucky you're here," Jason said.

Gillian shrugged. "I'm happy to do it. Gives me something I actually know how to do." She pushed her chair back from the table and picked up her tray. She remembered the feeling of walking into the dining hall with her tray as a teenager, the moment of terror as she scanned the room for a friendly face to sit with. The horror of potentially dining alone. Or the worse horror of seeing her best friends romantically entangled for the first time. So much had happened in this dining hall. At least that was behind her. Being single and a traveler for all of these past years had made dining alone a joy. She brought her tray into the main room, dumped her bit of remaining salad in the composting bin, and put the tray and empty dishes on the conveyor belt that brought it back to the dishwashers in the kitchen.

Then she looked at her phone and she saw that she had seventeen missed calls and thirty-five texts. From Mina, Freddy, Farrah, Kent, Alexis, and Aiden. She clicked on the message from Aiden first. Everything else could wait.

FOURTEEN

....

ast night was fun," Aiden had texted. "Rainbow told me
about Julia's video. Sounds like you have a lot on your
plate. Hope you're ok. Looking forward to showing
you the winery."

"Thanks," she wrote back. "Yeah, lots going on. Can't
wait for Saturday."

Having something to look forward to—an afternoon of
drinking wine and eating cheese with someone she had long
dreamed of spending time with—was invigorating. She joy-
fully returned the calls to Alexis, the *Today* show producer,
to iron out the details for the B-roll and the setup for the sit-
down interview. Headmaster Kent connected her with the
campus concierge (who knew that job existed?) to have the
living room in his house set up for the film crew, as well as
the access for the B-roll. She assured Mina Shirazi that there
was no need for her to fly back from Los Angeles for the interview. She even talked to someone from Epic Records to
confirm the details of the recording and release the schedule
so that it would be correctly stated during the interview; the
executives there were pleased with the publicity plan and

seemed grateful that Gillian was handling it. She had never had an Epic client before, but maybe at this point that was a blessing.

Finally, she headed back to Solano to work with the twins on preparing for the interview. She didn't think Natalie Morales would ask the twins any "gotcha" questions, but Gillian wasn't even sure if they were prepared for the basics: How does it feel to have the song of the summer? What are the origins of this new song? Why did you play it at homecoming? What's next for the Shirazis?

Before she headed back over to Solano, she checked in with Julia. She found her on the common room couch, wearing an oversized hoodie, the hood pulled tight over her face. "I can't handle this," she said. "I have, like, a million messages and comments."

"Just ignore everything," Gillian said.

"What about the company offering me a free purse?"

"Just wait to write back to them until this all blows over."

"Okay," Julia said, tugging on the hoodie strings. "This is kind of making me realize that I don't want to be an influencer though."

"Good," Gillian said. "You can buy that purse if you really want it. Be in control of your own brand. Accepting freebies makes you beholden to other people. And besides, you're a maker. Show them what you make. Your dresses are beautiful."

"An excellent point," Julia said.

Gillian couldn't tell if she was being facetious or not, but she liked that the words had come out of Julia's mouth. It was true that her parents could afford to buy her any purse on the internet; she had shown up to school on the first day with a Birkin, after all.

"Stay strong," Gillian said. "Turn off your notifications and maybe read a book for a while as the traffic dies down."

"Right," Julia said.

Gillian hesitated for a moment, because she was about to channel her old hard-charging publicist self with Julia, but she couldn't help it. She needed the video. "But can you do me a huge favor and send me the video? The *Today* show might want to run a snippet of it."

"Is that okay?" Julia asked.

"You can trust me," Gillian said.

"I do," Julia said.

The video showed up on Gillian's phone instantaneously. She headed back across campus to meet with Farrah and Freddy. She smiled at the last of the vans as they rumbled off the campus grounds—they were retreating, the producers having realized that they weren't going to get meaningful interviews from anyone at Glen Ellen Academy. Headmaster Kent had sent out a text to every student, advising them to decline interview requests, even if microphones were shoved in their faces. The students had complied. The campus care-taker, Gus, was standing by the gates, poised to close them to all incoming traffic once the vans were all gone.

She entered Solano, saluted Wally and Molly, and smiled at Farrah and Freddy, who were waiting for her near the security desk. They sat down in one of the clusters of chairs that made up the lobby. Gillian gave each of them a sandwich she had gotten from the dining hall. They ate them greedily. This was one of the first things she had taught all the young publicists when they started working with her: always feed the talent. Have granola or chocolate bars in your bag, bottles of water in every car, and it never hurts to show up with a sandwich. It reminded her of the time a band gave her a bonus after their tour was over and in the note that accompanied it, it said, "Thanks for always having a Snickers when we needed it. And sometimes before we knew we needed it."

As they ate, Gillian talked the twins through the questions she thought they would be asked and how they should answer them. Questions like: What are the origins of your songs? What did it feel like to have "Let's Hang Out" become super popular at your school? Are you working on an album? How do you balance school and songwriting and performing? The twins ate in silence, but they were concentrating deeply. Gillian knew they were taking this seriously.

"I guess our main question," Farrah said, as she crumpled up the sandwich paper nervously in her hand, "is what to do if we get a question that we don't have an answer to or that we don't want to answer."

"Redirect," Gillian said.

"But how do we do that?" Farrah asked.

"Basically, you answer the question you want to answer, kind of riffing off what they ask you. Say they ask you, 'Are you angry at your classmate who posted a video of your song without your permission?' You could say something like, 'We write songs and perform to entertain people and we're glad that our classmates are our fans. It's even been more rewarding to see how many fans we have online that we didn't even know about. We're excited to record the song officially so everyone has a chance to listen to it.'"

"That's good," Farrah said.

"It's called a pivot," Gillian said. "Politicians do it all the time. They never answer the question they're asked." She loved helping clients get ready for interviews.

"That's why it's so annoying to watch interviews with them," Freddy said.

"Exactly," Gillian said. "And now you guys get to be the annoying interview subjects. The real question is: Do you know what you're going to wear."

"What we always wear," Farrah said. She was back in her black uniform; the Christmas pajamas had been put away.

"Life is way easier if you wear the same thing all the time," Freddy said. "We did learn that from our mother. She's very glamorous, but she always wears the same thing during the day. At home she always wears cropped leggings and a crisp buttoned shirt with vertical stripes. Occasionally she'll wear a solid color—white or pale pink. And then when she needs to look fancier—like when she came here—she wears a Halston jumpsuit. She has them custom-fitted. She hates our black, but she gave us these belts. We wear them for her."

"That's a good story to tell if they ask you about your clothes," Gillian said.

"Do you think they will?" Freddy asked.

"Probably not," Gillian said. "But it's good to be ready."

"She gave us the belts when we left for boarding school. So we would have matching things," Farrah said.

"I love that," Gillian said. "They're your signature look. That and the glasses."

"She picked those out too," Freddy said.

Gillian smiled. Mina Shirazi was a force of nature, quietly shaping everything while pretending to be irritated, which was probably the best way to get her teenagers to do exactly what she wanted. Also, they knew in their hearts that she was stylish and glamorous and they wanted to be that too, just in their own way.

"There's one other thing, Gillian," Freddy said; he seemed almost sheepish. It was interesting to Gillian that Farrah was the more outgoing of the two (on a sliding scale of shyness), but that Freddy seemed the more perceptive and sensitive. His voice sounded tentative.

"Anything," she said.

"We don't really want to be famous," Freddy said. "What do we do about that?"

"Well," Gillian said. "Unfortunately, at this point you don't get much of a choice. But you can do what you love and make a living from it, which is a luxury that a lot of people don't have. And this is just one interview and you're going to record a few songs. Appreciate that people like your work. That doesn't always happen."

"We are grateful," Farrah said. "But we're also scared."

"I know," Gillian said. "I hope that after this interview tomorrow, things will mostly go back to normal except you'll have a few more followers on Instagram."

"I guess that'll be okay," Freddy said.

"One thing you might find is that you have really lovely fans and it's nice to hear from them. But you can also keep quiet when you need to. I'm here to help you stay private and out of the spotlight. You're in control of your own image—nobody else is."

"That's comforting," Freddy said.

"We're in control," Farrah said. "We have to remember that. And you're here to help us if we have questions, right?"

"Maybe we should get one of those custom needlepoints from Etsy to put in our rooms," Freddy said. "'You're in control of your own image.'"

Farrah nodded and looked off dreamily. Gillian wondered if she might be just a little bit more willing to be famous than Freddy was. But that would be for them to navigate.

Gillian paused for a moment to let the idea of being in control of their fame sink in. "I think you guys are on the right path, for sure," she finally said. "You know how to answer the questions, you know what you're wearing. Now the only question is, Have you set your alarms? Take a shower before, but you can show up with wet hair. They'll do it for you and do your makeup. I confirmed that they're sending a crew. Arrive at five o'clock and they'll start filming at six, for the nine o'clock hour on the East Coast."

"Time zones are so annoying," Farrah said.

"If you were living in New York, you'd still have to get up early," Gillian said.

"I thought rock stars got to sleep late," Freddy said.

"Not when they're doing press," Gillian said.

"We can do it," Farrah said. "We just have to walk one hundred feet to the headmaster's house."

"You're going to be great," Gillian said.

After she left Farrah and Freddy, Gillian met a local crew from the NBC affiliate to shoot some B-roll around campus. It was just a producer named Rayanne, a cameraman, and

Gillian. She wondered why Headmaster Kent hadn't sent someone else to walk with them, someone who knew the school better, but then she realized that she was probably more familiar with the nooks and crannies than any faculty member. Certainly she knew how to get to the top of the clock tower.

Rayanne asked Gillian about the history of the school, about the students. Gillian told her about Wally and Molly and their friendship with Jack London, about the homecoming traditions, and about the makeup of the student body. They talked about the headmaster's house, as they stepped inside, and how it had been the first building on the campus and about the logistics of the morning shoot. Rayanne commented on the art, but Gillian said she didn't know anything about it.

Gillian felt almost giddy as they exited the building; it felt so good to be doing something she knew how to do, doing work, having conversations she felt confident in. After being adrift for many months, and feeling like a fish out of water here at the Gem, a few moments of being transported back to her life as a publicist was truly glorious. It reminded her that she had liked her work so much, that she had been good at it, and that it had brought her satisfaction on a semi-regular basis. The end of her publicity career had been traumatic, but she realized that the worst thing about it was that it had stripped her of her confidence and, even worse, erased her memory of what she *had* liked about her work—the fun she had working with people: her clients but also the producers and the editors who covered them. She loved the rush of solving a problem, of getting a booking, of making things work. It was nice to be reminded of that; it gave her hope that there was a future for her out there somewhere.

Rayanne and the cameraman were getting in the van when Rayanne's phone dinged. "Oh," she said, looking at the screen. "What are we going to do about this?"

"What?" Gillian asked.

Rayanne showed Gillian the video of Bunny saying, "Nobody even knew they went here until their song got popular on our private message boards last spring. And it was my friend Julia who posted the video and made them famous." As Gillian watched the video, the cameraman loaded his gear into the back of the van.

Gillian was enraged inside, but couldn't show that to Rayanne. "She's just a jealous student," she said as calmly as she could. "I wouldn't pay attention to her."

"We want to interview her tomorrow," Rayanne said. "And Julia too."

"They're not available," Gillian said.

A text popped up on Rayanne's phone. "Bunny is confirmed, so I guess they are," Rayanne said.

"Listen," Gillian said. "Bunny is young—she doesn't really know what she's doing. Could you do me a favor and not interview her? I can get you footage of the twins singing their first song."

"Sorry, she already agreed—and thanks. See you in the morning." Rayanne opened the passenger door and hopped in.

Gillian gritted her teeth and went back to Vallejo. She wasn't surprised about what Bunny had said to the reporter; it was basically what Bunny said to everyone. The problem was that now she was on video saying it. She went straight to Bunny's suite. Bunny was sitting on the couch, her arms around a pillow, face puffy.

Gillian sat next to her and put her arm around her, "Bunny, what's going on?"

"I made a mistake," she said. "I talked to that reporter and now everybody hates me. The video is circulating. My mentions are horrible and I just feel so awful."

"I'm sorry," Gillian said. "But in this day and age, you have to think about what you say, because it can live online forever. And everyone can comment."

"I know, I know. I feel really bad, but it's too late now. I agreed to be interviewed by the *Today* show." Bunny hung her head.

"Yeah, it's definitely bad. But I do think it will blow over if you keep a low profile. You can back out of the interview," Gillian said. "I'll call them."

Bunny sniffled and snuffed for a few minutes. Gillian kept her arm around her. She wondered where the other girls were, but then decided that they were smart to stay out of the fray while Bunny was having a breakdown.

"I should have listened to you," Bunny said, her nose gurgling.

"You should have," Gillian said. "But I won't say 'I told you so' until later."

"The twins are going to be so famous," Bunny lamented.

"Only if they want to be," Gillian said. "And I'm not sure that's what they want."

"Can I listen while you call the producer?" Bunny asked. "So I know what you do to get out of a sticky situation."

"Sure," Gillian said. She took out her phone and called Rayanne. "It's Gillian. . . . Yeah . . . I'm here with Bunny. . . . I know. . . . Yeah, well, sadly she's not going to be able to do the interview tomorrow. . . . I know. . . . But you know how it is with kids. Her parents freaked out. . . . Yeah. . . . And Julia too. She just can't do it. She'll give you permission to play the video she took on her phone, but that's it. I'm sorry. You definitely still have all the time you need with the twins. . . . The location is great. . . . Yeah. . . . See you tomorrow. . . . Bright and early for sure. . . . Bye!" Gillian put her phone back on the table and shrugged. "There you go. You're free."

"What did she say?" Bunny asked. "Was she disappointed?"

"Sure," Gillian said. "But the main part of the piece is still happening. It's fine."

"I hate this," Bunny said.

"I know," Gillian said. She stood up and so did Bunny. Gillian gave her a hug and patted her on the back. "It's going to be okay. I promise this isn't the worst thing that will ever happen to you and the only person who will remember it is you."

"Whatever," Bunny said.

"Good night," Gillian said. "See you tomorrow."

"Next time I'll listen to you," Bunny said.

"Learning from your mistakes is the best way," Gillian said. And she headed upstairs to her room to crash for a few hours.

Bunny's outburst with the press reminded Gillian of a moment during her senior year at the Gem. She had been trying to make new friends in the wake of Miranda and Aiden getting together and she'd gone to a yearbook committee meeting for the first time. It was the second semester, so the group was already formed and everyone had their assignments. Gillian was hoping they would include her as a kind of add-on. She just wanted something to do and focus on that wasn't her lovebird friends or her schoolwork. At the first meeting she went to, the editor mostly talked and the photography lead showed some photos that were candidates for the sports pages. Sports photographs were apparently the hardest to get—you needed a special camera to really capture the athletes in action. Gillian listened and wrote a few things down in her notebook. When she came back for the second meeting, the editor asked her, "What are you doing here?"

"I want to join," Gillian responded. "I was here last week."

"What are your talents?" the editor, whose name was Ophelia, asked.

"I can write," Gillian said.

"We can all write," Ophelia said. "Do you know how to use PageMaker or take underwater photos of the polo team? Because that's what we need."

"No," Gillian said. "But I can help the people who are doing those things. I can learn."

"We don't have time to teach you," Ophelia said. "You don't know anybody or anything yet."

"It's true that I'm new here, but I'm learning about everything. I'm a quick study."

"Whatever, Common Decency," Ophelia said, referencing Gillian's most embarrassing moment and enduring nickname. She tossed her long blond hair behind her shoulder and turned back to a pile of photographs she was sorting through. "Go back to your threesome."

That conversation had stuck in Gillian's mind for years. Why was Ophelia so cruel? Why wouldn't she accept Gillian's help? And why hadn't Gillian been quick enough on her feet to make a Shakespearean reference to cut her down? Maybe she was just a bad manager—promoted to a role she wasn't ready for. What did high school seniors know about publishing a book anyway? Gillian wished that after all these years, it wasn't still the ultimate put-down to say that someone was nobody at this school. From Ophelia to Bunny, they never stopped. Gillian felt for Farrah and Freddy. Their time up until this moment had been difficult; they had been outsiders—"eccentrics," as Bunny called them. But now they were no longer nobody and that might be even harder for them. They were so quiet, so innocent, although also so talented. It went that way so often. They needed Gillian's help and she was glad she was there to give it to them. And hopefully Bunny had learned her lesson.

FIFTEEN

....

Gillian had set her alarm for four o'clock, but she woke up almost every hour to make sure she hadn't missed it. It reminded her of all of those days of having an early morning flight out of JFK. It always made the most sense to take the first flight out—you were sure the plane would be there, the crew was fresh, you got basically a whole day in Los Angeles if you got on the six-thirty flight out. But the sleep the night before was always the worst. She'd wake up every hour.

By three-thirty, she couldn't even pretend to sleep anymore. So she got up and took a long shower, then put her old publicist uniform back on. She stocked breakfast bars in her handbag and headed over to the headmaster's house.

She had told the headmaster that the crew would be arriving at four-thirty for final set-up details and that Natalie Morales, Farrah, and Freddy would be arriving at five for hair and makeup, lighting, and a preinterview. They'd be going live on the air at six-fifteen. She approached the house at around four-twenty. The NBC van was outside with a huge satellite dish on the top—the uplink—which seemed old-fashioned, but what did she know about live television technology. She was glad to see that the rest of the campus was quiet and the street outside the gates was not filled with vans. The news had spread about Natalie Morales's interview and everyone else had given up. Already Gillian was effecting positive change. She felt proud of what she had done to help the school and the twins.

She walked quietly into the house, which was still dark. The living room was already set up for the interview; the lights and camera setups had been placed the night before. The dining room had been turned into a makeup studio—there was a lighted mirror and a salon chair. And the kitchen was a greenroom, ready with a coffee carafe and some breakfast pastries. Gillian had a text from Farrah: "We're up and showered. We're just interviewing each other a little for practice. We'll be there for sure at five." She looked out the window as the guys in the van stepped outside and started stretching. She went into the kitchen and flipped the switch on the industrial-sized coffeemaker. She turned the lights on in the dining room and the living room so the crew would know it was okay to come inside.

Gillian thought back to the many Wally's List ceremonies she had attended here, those rare moments when she'd had Aiden to herself. During their senior year, they had felt bold (as seniors do) and had snuck upstairs, armed with, in case anyone asked, the flimsy excuse of looking for a bathroom. All the doors in the upstairs hallway had been closed, so they had opened each one methodically. There were three bedrooms: a master dominated by a large bed with a wooden headboard; what looked like a guest room, featuring a small desk and a single bed; and, finally, one that had essentially been turned into a closet, filled with garment racks of dresses and suits in zipped-up bags and shopping bags from Hermès, Tiffany, Bloomingdale's, Nordstrom, Saks, and some places that they didn't even recognize. A crated piece of art leaned against the wall. "What is this place?" Gillian whispered.

"The Ghost of Christmas Past," Aiden responded. He held out his arms (more like a zombie than a ghost, in Gillian's opinion) and walked toward her saying, "Woo, woo." She laughed a little too loudly and then looked around as if they could be caught.

"Do you think Mrs. Kent bought all this stuff?" Gillian asked.

"She must have," Aiden said.

"We better go back downstairs," Gillian said, becoming increasingly paranoid.

They rejoined the party without anyone having noticed that they were gone. But the image had haunted Gillian. All that fancy stuff just sitting there. What was it for?

The morning rolled forward. The crew and the production team came in; they thanked her for the coffee and then got to work. The hair and makeup team showed up in a separate car right at five, just as Farrah and Freddy were walking in. The twins' hair was wet, as promised, and they were quickly herded into the dining room by Greta and Solange.

The last person to arrive was Natalie Morales. But when she did, everyone became much more focused. Rayanne, the producer, shook Natalie's hand and they had a quick sidebar. She then brought Natalie into the hair and makeup room, a.k.a. the dining room, to introduce everyone. Freddy was asking Solange to put black eyeliner on him and Farrah was requesting that the hair woman not make her hair look *too* nice.

"Let them be themselves," Natalie instructed.

"I'll make it artfully messy," Greta said to Farrah.

"Great," Farrah said.

"It's nice to meet you," Natalie said. "Are you two ready?"

"Nice to meet you too," Farrah said. "We're ready but also nervous."

"Just think of it like a conversation with a new friend."

"Thank you," Freddy said. "Just the idea of being on national television is terrifying. So many people are watching."

"In their pajamas," Farrah said.

"Some of them might even be naked," Freddy said.

"You'll do great," Natalie said. "Don't think about all the people. Dressed or undressed. Just think about talking to me."

Greta started arranging Natalie's hair while she stood and talked to the kids. She knew that every minute was valuable. Gillian liked a time-conscious stylist. Natalie settled in the chair when Farrah and Freddy were done, but she kept talking to them.

"It must be weird to know so many people have heard your song," she said.

"It's wild," Farrah said. "It's like we're here in our little cocoon—where we know everyone and where we feel comfortable. And we sing a few songs. And mostly only people here have heard and liked them. And then all of a sudden, in like two hours, so many people know about us. The past couple of years, we've just lived here quietly, knowing our place, going to class, working on new songs in the evenings. We even have a practice space in the basement of Freddy's dorm. But we never thought anyone would hear them, other than our friends."

"That sounds really nice," Natalie said. "It is a lovely school. I think I would like living here too."

"You're welcome to come back anytime," Freddy said. Gillian wondered if he might have a little crush on Natalie.

"I'll let you know if I need an escape," she said, winking at Freddy.

"Okay," Rayanne said; she was wearing a headset and carrying a clipboard. She looked very official. "We're going on the air soon, so let's get miked up and settled in the living room."

Solange put one last swipe of bronzer on Natalie's cheeks and they all filed into the living room.

The twins were seated on a tiny love seat, which put them impossibly close to each other. And Natalie was seated across from them. The shot had been set up so that the Picasso print was clearly visible behind her.

"How does it feel to go viral?" she asked.

Freddy smiled and Farrah answered, "It feels great. I mean, it was a total accident. We've been writing songs since we were little. And singing them to each other. This was just another one that was really just for us but it happened to get put on Instagram by someone else and it just started getting shared."

"We just played songs for our friends, and one of them got a little popular last summer, so someone from a record company called our mom. But we didn't think anything would come of it," Freddy said.

"And now we're going to go and record it. We've never done anything like that before," Farrah added.

"Is it making you feel different?"

"It's weird," Farrah said. "Because once people heard our other song and liked it, it kind of made songwriting not fun anymore. We're kind of shy and we don't love talking, but singing, it's like a different language for us. Like, we had only written songs for ourselves and we loved them so much, but when we saw other people enjoying them, it wasn't ours anymore. So we stopped. But this was one that we'd always kind of sung to each other. So when we had to perform at homecoming, we figured it would be a good one."

"It sounds like songwriting is so personal for you," Natalie said.

"It's the way we communicate with each other," Freddy said. "So I think we do it even when we aren't thinking about it. The idea of sitting down and writing a song is weird, but singing a tune to one another while we're walking to class is totally normal. So we just have to capture that, I guess."

"And you're going to record the song you sang the other night?"

"Yes, this week," Farrah said.

"We're going to cut right now to a video made by your classmate that we're running with her permission and yours."

"Now we wait forty-seven seconds," Rayanne said. "I'll cue you back in."

Gillian walked over and stood behind Natalie to give the twins a thumbs-up. They were doing great and she wanted them to know. Farrah looked relieved. Rayanne gave the cue and Natalie started talking again.

"What was it like performing for your classmates?"

"I mean, we're super shy. Most of them probably don't even know who we are—I mean, maybe they do now because of our song, but we always kept to ourselves. Anyway, it's nice to give people some fun."

"We can't wait to hear the rest of your album," Natalie said. "And we wish you the best of luck."

"Thanks so much," Freddy said.

"Thank you. Back to you Hoda. And thanks to Farrah and Freddy Shirazi, for spending time with us this morning."

"And we're out," Rayanne said. "Good job, guys."

"Thank you," Farrah said. "I almost forgot about all the naked people."

Natalie Morales laughed, shook their hands, winked at Gillian, and vanished.

When Gillian got back to Vallejo, the floors were abuzz. All the girls were planning to skip their nine o'clock classes to watch the segment in their common rooms—it was on a delay on the West Coast even though it had aired live on the East Coast. Gillian couldn't remember such excitement about a television show other than the Oscars or the Super Bowl. The only person who wasn't excited was Julia. She was sitting on the floor, moping outside Gillian's door when she walked back up. "I still feel bad," she said. "I created a big drama."

"They're not mad at you," Gillian said. "If that makes you feel any better."

"It all feels strange." Her voice was a little bit wobbly.

"I know," Gillian said. "But this is all going to be over soon."

"If you say so," Julia said. "But I still don't want to watch the interview."

"You don't have to," Gillian said. "Go to class, be a regular kid."

"Okay," Julia said. She stood up and picked up her Prada zip tote, which had notebooks and a copy of *Siddhartha* by Hermann Hesse spilling out of the top. She gave Gillian a hug. "I'm really glad you're here this year. We really need you."

"I'm happy to be here," Gillian said. "Now go get a coffee and go to class."

"Okay," Julia said.

Gillian left the girls' suite and took a deep breath. It had been an exhausting day. She needed a nap.

When she got up, she headed over to the clock tower to visit Gloria. The last time she had seen her, Gloria had intimated that there was something she wanted to tell Gillian. When she got to the office, though, Gloria was cagey. She gestured, indicating that Headmaster Kent was in his office. So Gillian made small talk about the twins and Bunny and the *Today* show. At the end of their chat, Gloria said, "I have an errand to run at lunch today. Do you want to walk out to my car with me?"

"Of course," Gillian said. She watched as Gloria took her handbag out of her drawer, clicked off her monitor, and waved to Headmaster Kent.

"I'll be back in about an hour, Stuart," she said.

"See ya later," he said.

Gillian followed Gloria out of the office, down the stairs, and out to the campus. Gloria's car was parked behind the clock tower building, so Gillian followed her there. When they got to Gloria's car, Gloria said, "I have something to tell you that's going to take a bit of time. Would you mind getting in the car and going for a drive with me?"

Gillian looked at her watch, but she didn't have anything else to do today until the girls got back from dinner. "Sure," she said, hopping into Gloria's Chevy Malibu. Gloria expertly navigated around the remaining news vans on the campus and out to the main road.

"Okay," she said. "I think you know that I started here in 1988. I've been the assistant to the headmaster for thirty years now."

"So you had had the job for just under ten years when I graduated," Gillian said.

"Yes, that's right," Gloria said. "I was hired for my bookkeeping skills. I have an associate's degree in accounting from Napa Valley College. The headmaster when I started was a guy named Bruce Stone. He was an old-school guy—he'd been headmaster for many years. We got along fine and as I worked for him, he gave me more and more to do. By the time he left in 1996, I was doing all the accounting for the school. There was a finance department that handled everything else, but because I had been there for so long and knew everything that was going on, they liked having me do the books. Stuart—Headmaster Kent—started in 1995, and when I told him I handled the books he wanted me to keep going."

Gillian sat quietly as Gloria spoke, watching the wineries go by as they drove on Arnold Drive.

"Headmaster Stone was a nice, honest man. And Kent was too at the beginning. The first twenty years that I did the books—factoring in the donations and the spending, plus the school budget—they always balanced. But recently, the numbers haven't been adding up. There's been a shortfall. It's easy for me to see what was being spent by the school—salaries, supplies, upkeep. And how the donations were being used. But the past few years, a little bit from the donations has been missing. At first, it was a few thousand dollars. But then it started being more, like ten thousand, fifteen. I've been keeping track of the shortfalls—he always tells me that it's not a big deal, that the books don't always balance. And I'm worried that there are other places that I don't know about that he can siphon from too. Gillian, I'm scared." Her hands were shaking. "I'm afraid that people will think that it's my fault. But I know I'm doing it right."

Gillian was aghast. She couldn't believe what she was hearing. And yet, it kind of made sense. The shopping bags. The art. His wife's jewelry. These weren't the sorts of things a regular headmaster would have. This was a big deal. An embezzlement scandal that had been going on for years, perpetrated by the headmaster himself. "This is so crazy," Gillian said.

"I know," Gloria said; she was almost breathless. "But I feel relieved to have told you. I've been . . . holding it inside for so long."

Gillian felt lucky that Gloria trusted her, although also overwhelmed. What was she supposed to do? She didn't want Gloria to get in trouble, and she didn't really understand how the administration of the school worked beyond the headmaster. She knew there was a board; the president of the board was, after all, the woman who had sought her out. Was this something she should bring to the board? She assumed they had something to do with the finances of the school, since Helene had hired her. The weight of the revelation felt heavy on her brain.

"I'm going to help you," Gillian said. "I don't know how yet, but I'm going to figure it out."

"Thank you, Gillian," Gloria said. "I'm just in the middle of it and I want to get out. I don't want to cover it up anymore and I want to be honest."

"I totally get that," Gillian said. "Let me just figure out how everything works here and I'll get right back to you." By then they had reached downtown Sonoma. Gloria pulled into a parking spot and they both got out of the car.

"Here's my number—my cell and my home—in case you need to ask me anything else," Gloria said.

Gillian took the paper and could tell that Gloria didn't want to drive her back to campus.

"I have a few things I can do down here," Gillian said. "So I'll just take a cab back." Gloria stood next to her car, her key in her hand, shivering. Gillian held out her arms and Gloria walked into them. She put her head on Gillian's shoulder and wept. Gillian assumed they were tears of relief. If anyone understood what that felt like, it was Gillian. She let Gloria cry until she was ready to get back into her car and drive away.

Before she headed back to campus, Gillian walked around the square slowly, trying to figure out what to do. She hadn't expected something like this to happen while she was here, and she wasn't quite prepared to deal with it. But as she walked, she started to formulate a plan.

Later that evening, Gillian got a call from Aiden. When she saw his name on the phone, her stomach fluttered. Why did he make her so nervous? "How was your day?" he asked, like they were old friends or people at the start of a relationship. Either way, she liked it; it wasn't something that someone had asked her in a very long time.

"Busy," she said. "It also started at, like, three-thirty A.M., so I'm a bit out of it. But so much is going on, I'm running on adrenaline, I think."

"The kids did a good job in the interview," he said. "I watched it this afternoon."

"I'm proud of them," Gillian said.

"It's good that you were there to walk them through it."

"I'm glad too," she said. As they chatted about the twins, her mind drifted to her conversation with Gloria. Aiden would know what to do, but should she tell him? Did she trust him enough? This was Gloria's big secret, one she had been holding on to for years. Gillian needed to give it respect.

"It's good for the school," he said. "The Parents' Association is all abuzz with the link. They're thrilled. Hoping it will increase the caliber of the applicants next year."

"Oh," she said, as the gears in her brain started turning. She hadn't realized that there was a Parents' Association. Her mother had never been part of it. "Tell me about the Parents' Association."

"It's like any school PTA," he said. "Except it's mostly virtual because the parents live all over the country. They do like having me lead it, because I'm here and can give them in-person updates about what's going on. I can see the school when they're not gussying it up for special occasions. Not that the school ever looks bad. It just looks extra fancy when the parents are coming to town."

"So wait, you're the head of the PTA?" Gillian asked, amazed and a bit terrified. What would happen if she told him Gloria's story? Did she need to keep it secret? Her brain filled up with questions.

"I am," he said. "But I don't let all the power go to my head. I really am basically just a hall monitor. Checking to make sure the school is keeping up their end of the bargain. And we do a little fundraising, that kind of thing."

"It's a nice thing to do," she said. "For the school. I bet they'll be sad when Rainbow graduates and you can't be their eyes on the ground anymore."

"I'm sure they can find another sucker," he said.

She laughed. "I guess we're both kind of hall monitors for the Gem."

He laughed too. "Not what we aspired to in high school. But whatever."

"Whatever," she agreed.

As they talked, she could feel herself drifting and trying to figure out how long she had been awake. It had been one of the longest days of her life. She didn't want to get off the phone, but she could feel herself not quite answering everything as sharply as she normally would have. And she still needed to walk the floors and make sure all was quiet on the Vallejo front.

"I guess I have to go," she said. "But I'm excited for the tour of your winery."

"Me too," he said. "Meet me at the tasting room at five P.M. on Saturday. It'll be winding down for the day by then, so we can have the place to ourselves."

"Sounds great," she said.

"And don't wear heels or anything—we'll be walking around in the vineyard. It's very casual here."

"Gotcha," she said. "I haven't worn heels in months."

"This isn't really a heel kind of town."

"I've noticed that. It's one of my favorite things about it," she said. "I'll see you Saturday."

"Saturday," he said.

It had been such a weird day of so many ups and downs. She collapsed onto her bed, so many thoughts running through her head: worry about Gloria, excitement about her date, curiosity about what was next for Farrah and Freddy. She fell asleep in a familiar posture—with her phone next to her head like she had in her publicist days. Some old habits are hard to break.

SIXTEEN

....

She expected the week to pass slowly because she was so eagerly looking forward to Saturday, but so much was going on that she barely noticed the days flying by. Farrah and Freddy got dispensation to take a few days off from school and headed to Los Angeles to record their song. They sent her regular updates about how fun it was to travel without their mother, the stretch limo that picked them up at the airport, and the bouquet of candy that was in their suite at the hotel when they arrived. "It looks like flowers, but it's candy," Freddy wrote, adding a wide-eyed emoji.

When she wasn't thinking about which follow-up articles Farrah and Freddy should give quotes to (she favored placements in *People* and *The New York Times*), she was thinking about what to wear on Saturday. It was an even tougher outfit to come up with than their Fig Café night date/not date. At least that had been at a restaurant in the evening, so she could wear mostly black. This was outdoors at a winery. She would have to wear color. None of the dresses in her closet seemed to fit the bill, but she also didn't know the area well enough to shop. She couldn't ask Bunny, Julia, and Rainbow, because that would admit to them that she was going on a date with Rainbow's dad, which was already a bit of a problem, considering her current occupation. Lila offered her closet, so Gillian headed over to her house with a bottle of wine and some Comté and her favorite rosemary crackers from the Village Market.

The Lyft wound around the mountain roads of Kenwood and then stopped at a little side road with a mailbox at the end of it. It was starting to get ridiculous that she didn't have her own car, but she just wasn't ready to commit yet. Gillian got out of the car with her tote bag and looked around. The number on the mailbox matched what Lila had told her. She looked beyond the gate and there was Lila, walking up the gravel lane.

They got to a fork in the road; it was lined by a chicken-wire fence on each side. "The main house is up there," Lila said, pointing to the left, where Gillian could see a large house and a pool. "And I'm over here." They followed the fork to a small white clapboard house with a wrap-around porch. Lila walked up the steps in front of Gillian. There were two padded lounge chairs on the deck, a table and chairs, and a grill. The deck looked out at treetops and rolling hills.

"This is stunning," Gillian said.

"Yeah, I'm really lucky to have this place," Lila said. "It's like an oasis. Plus, they don't mind if I use their pool on hot days if they aren't in it, and they never are."

"I'm jealous," Gillian said.

"You're welcome anytime."

"There are definitely perks to living in California."

"There are very few downsides, as far as I can see them," Lila said.

"Wildfires," Gillian said.

"Right," she said. "And earthquakes and mudslides. But other than that, it's pretty good." She opened the front door and gestured for Gillian to walk in. The house was small but lively. It had an open floor plan: a living room with a big fireplace that rolled into a dining area that opened into a kitchen with a big stainless steel range hood. The living room furnishings were white with pops of blue. The dining table had been made from a veiny reclaimed wood, and the kitchen cabinets were painted a bluish gray.

"I'm definitely happy to be out of New York," Gillian said. She handed the bottle of wine and the paper bag of cheese and crackers to Lila.

"Oh you didn't have to do this," Lila said. She pointed to the floor-to-ceiling wine rack on the far wall of the kitchen. "I have a bit of a collection. And that's just what isn't in the wine fridge."

"Wow," Gillian said. "Really no downsides at all."

"I've actually already opened a bottle—come into the kitchen."

And true to her word, there was an open bottle of a dark rosé with a turquoise label sitting on the marble kitchen island. Two white wine glasses sat next to the bottle, each poured and ready to drink. "This is from a winery called Forlorn Hope that's not in Sonoma—it's up in the Sierra foothills. I found it last summer when I was driving around near Yosemite. It's really good."

Gillian took a glass and they clinked. "Cheers," they said

in unison. Gillian took a sip of the crisp, mineral-forward wine—it was perfect.

"I'm so excited for your date," Lila said. "I have a few things that I think would work. Let's go look and then we can sit on the deck with our glasses."

Gillian followed her through a door off the kitchen into a beautiful room with floor-to-ceiling windows that looked out on more greenery. "This must be an amazing place to wake up," Gillian said.

"It's great, but really the closet is the thing that sold me." She opened the door and Gillian walked into a closet that reminded her of some of the celebrity closets she'd seen. A wall of shoes; floor-to-ceiling shelves of perfectly folded shirts and sweaters. Dresses hung in multiple layers. The middle of the closet had an island with drawers in it where, Gillian assumed, Lila kept underwear and T-shirts and jewelry, and it also had a display rack where a few dresses could be hung. A kind of staging area. She had hung five dresses on the rack—two floral, one striped, a solid light blue, and a solid light pink. The floral weren't really Gillian's style, but she liked the other ones, simple California chic.

"Your closet should be in a magazine," Gillian said.

"Honestly, it's from one. I saw photos of a closet like this in *Town & Country* and gave it to someone from California Closets and they set this up. I know it's a waste of money in a rental, but I love it so much. It brings me joy every time I walk in. I also obviously love shopping. There's no way I could ever wear everything in here. But I picked out a few dresses I think would look good on you and would work for an afternoon winery date."

"I'm curious," Gillian said as she held the dresses up to her body. She was leaning toward the light blue dress, which buttoned all the way down the front. She could leave the top buttons undone to show some cleavage, but not be too sexy. She was dying to tell Lila about Aiden, yet something, maybe her past trauma, was holding her back. So instead she stayed on the topic of school. "Why did Theresa, the woman before me, leave? From her letter I could sense she was burned out. But it's not a bad job . . ."

"I think she got sick of the kids being entitled and she missed having her own home. She was spending summers with her elderly parents. Not ideal. She moved to Scottsdale and bought a condo there."

"I guess I can see that," Gillian said as she held the two floral dresses up. They weren't her style at all. One had floaty cap sleeves and the other an empire waist. "I can't imagine what I'll do this summer."

"You'll cross that bridge when you come to it," Lila said. "I was afraid of the summers when I first started, but now I love them so much. Teaching seems easy—especially with smart and dedicated kids like these—but it wears you down."

"I don't know why anyone would think it was easy! It looks super hard to me. I think I want to try on this blue one."

"I like that one. Go for it," Lila said. Gillian wasn't sure what the protocol was, but she stepped out of the closet, into Lila's bedroom, and changed. Then she went back into the closet, where the full-length mirror was. She looked and it did fit her perfectly. It hit right above the knee, the buttons down the front were flattering, and the fabric was cool and airy.

"Love it," Lila said. "Pair it with a jeweled flip-flop and you'll be all set."

"Thank you so much," Gillian said. "I really appreciate this. I might need your shopping expertise to California-ize my wardrobe."

"Anytime," Lila said. "Now let's go drink on the porch."

"An excellent plan," Gillian agreed.

Before the night was over, Gillian had told Lila about her conversation with Gloria. She trusted Lila and she felt like Lila might know what to do. It was a relief to get it off of her chest, even though she was almost shaking (though not as much as Gloria had been) as she related the story. "It made me so mad," she said. "That he has been taking from the school for his own purposes and basically forcing Gloria into being his accomplice."

"That's outrageous," Lila said. "I can't believe it. Although, I guess I can. He does seem fancier than he should be. Those suits. . . . But what do you do? Who do you tell?"

"I'm not sure," Gillian said. "It's weird for me because Kent has always supported me and helped me when I was a student, and he approved me to get this job. I do know Helene Waxman, who is the head of the board of directors. But I don't know. I think it needs to be dealt with. I just hope I don't lose my job over it. And I really want to protect Gloria."

"It's scary though."

"It is scary," Gillian said.

"But it's important. I mean, he's committing a huge crime. Against the school and the students. And the teachers, frankly. It's an outrage."

"I know. It's a really bad thing. Like he could go to jail. It just feels intense to be the one who knows, who has to reveal it. And Gloria has to explain it. She's the only one who really knows what's going on."

"I know," Lila said. "But now that you know, you have to tell. It's your responsibility. I don't think they'll retaliate against either of you," she added. "They'll be glad you told them. I would be if I were them."

"You're right, I have to do it. It just feels really hard. I've been in the position of being the outsider, and it's not great."

"But after everyone realizes that you and Gloria are heroes, you won't be an outsider."

"I guess," Gillian said.

"As Winston Churchill once said, with great power comes great responsibility. You have the power and the responsibility. You'll do great." Lila smiled and leaned over to give Gillian a hug. "You are a star."

"Thanks," Gillian said, although she didn't feel like a star. She felt like a rat.

They finished their wine and Lila put the dress in a hanging bag for Gillian. Gillian called a Lyft and they walked outside.

"I understand why Gloria might be nervous to tell," Gillian said. "But I just have to figure out the right way. And I have one more confession to make: the guy I'm going on a date with is also the head of the Parents' Association. I was thinking of telling him."

"Aiden Lloyd?" Lila asked, a bit incredulous.

"Yeah," Gillian said. She hadn't exactly meant to tell her . . . and there it was. Out there.

"Oh . . ." Lila said.

"What?" Gillian asked.

"Well," Lila said as she was walking Gillian up the road to meet her ride. "He was the wine guy I told you about."

"Oh God," Gillian said, stopping in her tracks.

"It didn't work out," Lila said. "Obviously."

"Shit," Gillian said. "I'm really sorry. Does this make you uncomfortable?"

"No," Lila said. "But you probably shouldn't wear that dress. I wore it on one of our dates."

Gillian took a deep breath and handed the garment bag back to Lila. "I'm sorry," Gillian said. "I had no idea."

"Me neither," she said. "But he'd be a good person to tell about the Gloria thing. He would know what to do."

Gillian gave Lila a hug as the car drove up. "I'm so lucky to have you," Gillian said.

She got into the car and waved to Lila, standing there holding the garment bag. As they drove, she thought about Aiden with Lila and how Lila had described him as somewhat self-absorbed. But Gillian would have to find out for herself. Part of her worried that even though Lila had been understanding, she would go back and think about it and turn on Gillian. Would she lose her only friend in California over this? Or was she being paranoid? She had resolved to make things different than they were when she lived in New York—to have real friends and real conversations. And she had found that with Lila.

She knew exactly how Lila felt—it was sort of like when she found out that Miranda and Aiden were together. But now she was the Miranda. She hated everything about it.

Or was Lila a more evolved person, and did she really not care? Gillian just didn't know what to think about anything anymore.

* * *

The next morning, she tried to erase everything from her brain. The sun was out, and the weather was warm but not too hot. The air smelled sweet, reminding her of jasmine on the Gem campus. Saturdays were open days on campus: there were school sports to watch—water polo and tennis and field hockey and soccer—and homework to do. Kids did laundry and sat around in small groups on the lawns, drinking lattes and staring at their phones. Gillian mostly left the kids alone on Saturdays. She had started what she called a "study break" on Sunday nights—an evening snack of cookies or chips and an organized activity like a Boggle tournament or card games. But she kept to herself on Saturdays. Let the kids feel free, unobserved.

This Saturday, following Lila's recommendation, Gillian headed to the spa at Gaige House, a little Japanese-style hotel. Gillian got her nails done and a massage and spent some time just sitting quietly on the hotel's Moon deck, listening to a creek bubble in the distance. She felt completely centered when she arrived back at her room on campus to get ready for her date. And tried not to think about how she could have lost her friend.

The gates of Aiden's vineyard, Grange Hill, were open and the Lyft drove up a winding road, edged by alternating tall palm trees and low succulents. The neat rows of grapes stretched in either direction from the main road, all with rosebushes planted at the ends. The building at the top of the hill looked like an old barn, the doors made of wood and two stories high. They were wide open to a tasting room and what Gillian assumed was a patio behind. Standing in front of the barn door was Aiden; she felt a fluttery combination of excited and nervous, attraction and fear. His role in her life, and in her memory, was so complicated, she just couldn't reconcile it all together quite yet. She decided to lean in on the excitement and attraction though, because why not? It was a date, after all. So she walked up to him and gave him a hug. He gave her a light kiss on the cheek and ushered her into the tasting room. "You look nice," he said, the compliment sending a blush through her. "Meet my baby, Grange Hill Winery." As he said that, she wondered if it was even possible to date Aiden; maybe it was hard being the mistress to a winery.

That said, it was a beautiful place. The tasting room was dark and cool, with big ceiling fans turning above, hanging from the exposed beams. There was a long bar on one side that seemed to be made from stall doors, with multiple bartenders pouring tastings for groups of tourists. On the other side of the room, there were small tables where people were finishing up bottles over mostly empty cheese and charcuterie plates.

"This is our tasting room," he said. "This place was once a working farm, and this structure was more or less the barn. There were horses kept down here and feed kept up there in what's now the gallery." She looked up to see a kind of balcony running around the edges of the room, with a staircase at the end next to the bar.

He put his arm around her waist and led her out through the tasting room to the back patio. They were assaulted by the sun, but also by the smells of ripening grapes and maybe juniper. "We're harvesting right now," he said. "It's the end of the season, but we still have the syrah and the cabernet coming in. They're the last of our grapes to get picked."

"It smells divine."

"I'll take you into the vineyard if you want."

"That would be amazing," she said. "Do you grow all the grapes for your wines here?"

"About eighty percent of them," he said. "We have another property over closer to the water where we grow some of the white grapes. And we sometimes do blend in grapes from other vineyards, mostly if our crop doesn't work out for some reason—we had to do that in 2014 and 2015. But things have been good the past few years and we weren't affected by the fires last year, thank goodness."

He led her off the formal patio, straight into the lines of grapevines.

"I love that your vines come right up to where people visit you," she said.

"We encourage them to walk among the grapes also," he said. "Although I will admit that these guys we have right here are not the ones we use for wine. They get a little bit manhandled by the visitors, so we leave them for show."

They kept walking a bit farther into the row and all of a sudden, the noise of the tasting room vanished and all she could hear was the chirping of birds and the buzzing of bees. She smelled dirt and lavender. The grapevines were at their fullest and they grew taller than she was, so it felt like being in a cool outdoor cocoon. She felt like she should whisper because it was so beautiful and overwhelming. "Thank you for bringing me here. I've never been anywhere like it."

He also modulated his voice: "Yeah, whenever I'm stressed

or confused or just need a moment, I come out here and walk. It's very . . . cathartic."

"You've done an amazing job," she said.

They walked through the vines in silence for a few minutes. The sun was getting lower in the sky and the light was a bit more muted than it had been even when she had arrived. She remembered that photographers called this golden hour. Finally, the vines parted and there was a small picnic table; it was set for two, with a red-and-white checkered tablecloth and a bottle of red wine, some of which had been poured into two stemless glasses. A wooden board filled with cheese and meat was covered with a plastic top. "This is one of our secret picnic spots," he said. "Used mostly by the workers during harvest season. But also sometimes used by special winery employees."

"You're certainly a special employee," she laughed.

"I will admit that I take advantage of the perks of this place, that's for sure," he said. "I also set them up so I would like them best. So that might be gaming the system, but what can I do."

"It's nice to like your place of work," she said.

"I certainly do."

"I vaguely remember what that's like," she said. "But I will say that I'm growing to love it here, which I didn't expect."

They settled on opposite sides of the table and he lifted the cover off the cheese plate. They clinked glasses and took a sip. "This is the 2016 pinot noir, one of the few good things to come out of that year. I think it's the best wine we've ever made," he said. "This part of Sonoma is particularly suited to the pinot noir. One of the few places in the world."

"One of my favorite grapes, I'm learning," she said. "What a lucky coincidence."

"And it pairs well with meat, which is why we're having this spicy soppressata."

"The wine tastes spicy to me," she said.

"Yes!" he said. "You have a good palate."

"I'm okay," she said. "I do prefer it when someone else picks out the wine though."

"I remember the stress of the wine list before I knew a lot. At this point, though, I'm more interested in wine production. Natural processes, no interventions or additives. That's going to get you a better result."

"But sometimes they taste funky, like dirt, and I don't love that," she said.

"That's definitely an acquired taste," he said.

"But this pinot noir doesn't have any of that."

"Nope," he said. "It drinks really clean."

"It does," she said. "How did you learn how to make good wine?"

"Well, I have good help—that's the most important thing. I have a professional winemaker and a vineyard manager and a tasting room manager. Plus, I have a part-time chef who helps with the tasting room food menu and the kitchen staff. I've learned a lot myself. I know what I like and what I don't. But I trust all those people to make this place great."

"It's a complicated business," she said.

"There are lots of moving parts. But I love all of them," he said. "And I built them up slowly. First we planted the grapes, then we started making just whites. Then reds. Then we opened the tasting room. Then we added food. It's taken years. So now it's a lot, but I learned about each part separately. It's like having a kid. They kind of expand into your life slowly—at first they sleep all the time and then they are up a little bit and then they crawl and then they walk. All the while, you get used to it."

"That's a nice way to think of it," she said. "Do you think you would do it again?"

"Open another vineyard?"

She nodded.

"Maybe," he said. "I hadn't really thought about it. I'm so entrenched here. But I also have learned never to say no to anything. I never expected this to happen, so why couldn't other things?"

He refilled their glasses, splitting the rest of the bottle between them. Gillian quickly ate a few of the crackers so she wouldn't get drunk too quickly. She was enjoying the moment too much. The sun was lowering in the sky and the evening birds were starting to fill the air with their song.

"So what else is going on?" he asked. "You've had a triumphant week."

"It's been fun," she said. "It's nice to feel like you know what you're doing for a little while. My life has been so unusual the past few months that I always felt insecure, like I never knew what I was doing. But returning to being a publicist for two days really reminded me that I do have work skills."

"I felt that way when I first got up here, like I was just a dumbass among people who knew everything. And I had been good at my job in Silicon Valley. It took a long time for me to feel comfortable in what I was doing."

"Based on what you were telling me before, you're like a scientist and a farmer and a restaurateur all at once."

"That's one way of thinking of it. I'm also, if you recall, a campus babysitter."

"All of that is way harder than being a dorm mother," she said.

"All jobs have their challenges," he said. "It seems that you've actually taken to yours."

"I mean, I didn't plan to be here, and when I said yes, I thought of it as just temporary. When my business imploded, I didn't know what to do—it was my entire life. Literally, my entire world: all my friends, my social life, every hour of my day. But then Helene Waxman called to offer this job . . . it was like she was a guardian angel. I actually may need to call her again. Something has come up."

"Are you quitting?" he asked.

"No, no," she said. "Nothing like that. But I got information . . . bad information, truly scandalous. And I don't exactly know what to do about it. And I feel awful because it's about Headmaster Kent. It's such a weird feeling—like I am betraying him, but also that I am protecting the school."

"Wow," he said. "This sounds big."

"I know," she said. "Maybe 'betray' isn't exactly the right word. What I mean is that I've known him for so long—we all have, right? He supported me in high school and also backed giving me this job. But I feel more loyalty to the Gem than to him, if that makes any sense."

"Sure," he said. "You're an independent person."

"Right, and this job isn't my career. So basically, what I'm saying is . . . that I don't care if there are consequences for what I'm going to tell you."

"Okay . . ." he said. "What is it? So many things are running through my mind."

"Well, you remember Gloria. The school secretary. I guess assistant now."

"Of course, who could forget Gloria."

"Well, she told me that she has proof that Kent has been embezzling from the school. She doesn't know how much he's taken, but it could be a lot."

"Wow," he said, his eyes growing wide. "That's insane. Truly horrific."

"I agree with you," she said. "It *is* terrible. A crime against everyone at the Gem—the students, the parents, the faculty. Everyone."

"I'm in shock," he said.

"I was too."

"But wait," he said, leaning in toward her. "Remember that room we saw when we were there all those years ago?"

"I know," Gillian said. "I was thinking about it!"

"And he does have all of that art. It's like MoMA in there. And all of those fancy suits and the cars. I always assumed his wife was rich . . . but . . . maybe not?"

"I know—when you look at everything with this information, it all kind of makes sense."

"So, wait, back to Gloria. How does she know?"

"She's a trained accountant and has been doing the books for years. She said they always balanced until the past few years, when at first a few thousand disappeared and then over time it grew and grew. She didn't know who to tell. But she told me and now I have to do something about it. It was hard for her, I'm sure. I mean, she's loyal to him and she also doesn't want to get in trouble."

"I'm sure she won't be in trouble," he said. "Although I guess people might wonder why it took her this long to tell."

"I think people will be more interested in where all that money has been going for all these years," she said. "Would you embezzle from the school you loved just for . . . stuff?"

"Regardless, he's stealing from this school. From the students. It's an outrage." He raised his voice louder than she'd heard in a long time.

"He is," Gillian agreed. "What do you think I should do?"

"You're welcome to bring it to the Parents' Association," he said. "But the final decision would be the board of directors. And they love Kent."

She sighed. She'd known it would be hard, but she thought it was worth pursuing. "Even if they love Kent, they can't want him stealing from the school. What's the protocol?" she asked.

"You'd present your evidence at the next meeting. And then the board of directors would be notified. And then I think there would be some sort of hearing process. They'll probably want to talk to Gloria. She's the one who really knows."

"That sounds like a good plan, but I should probably discuss this with Gloria first. Just to make sure she's up for it?"

"Okay, let me know," he said, sounding more definitive, like a responsible Parents' Association president rather than a person on a date.

They were both quiet for a few minutes; she was worrying that she shouldn't have told him about Gloria's revelation, that it was going to derail their budding relationship. She wondered what he was thinking. If he was going to back out of the rest of the date. If he was going to back out of them being friends. He had turned on her before; it could happen again.

"Should I not have told you?" she asked.

"No," he said. "I just think maybe we shouldn't talk about it anymore. After it gets past my level, we can talk about it again."

"Okay," she said, relieved. This whole thing was just a minefield of stress.

"Let's walk up to the top of the hill—we can see the sunset from there."

"If I talk about it a little, will that ruin everything?" she asked, still feeling anxious about the whole situation.

"You have to trust me a little bit," he said. They stood up and he put his arm around her. It was their first little bump in the road and she felt like they had weathered it well. Had communicated about it effectively. She smiled and leaned against him. She decided to let it feel good to come clean, to have someone else who knew, even if he didn't really want to talk about it. He smelled like wood and dirt, but clean. Like he bathed in a wood-and-dirt smell. Maybe Aesop made a cologne like that. Maybe a past girlfriend had bought it for him. Regardless, she appreciated the scent. Took it in. And then enjoyed the walk up the hill.

When they reached the top, he wrapped his arms around her, and they looked out over the Sonoma hills. The sky was streaked with pink and purple and the sun was just disappearing behind the rolling hills.

"This is nice," she said.

"It is," he said. Then he turned her around and kissed her. It was a slow, savory kiss. Deliberate, sexy, and, dare she even say, kind. He pulled away and she smiled and put her head on his shoulder.

"Do you remember that night in high school?" he asked. "Not what happened after, but that night?"

"How could I forget?" she asked.

"I hadn't thought about it in a long time," he said. "But now I can't help it."

It had been a cold February night during their senior year. Miranda had left town for the weekend for her grandmother's funeral. But Aiden and Gillian had followed the regular weekend protocol and had attended the Friday night movie. The movie had been *When Harry Met Sally*, which they had both seen a bunch of times. During the movie, their hands had accidentally touched, but they'd both reacted skittishly, moving away as quickly as possible. And then it had happened again and again. Gillian could still remember the electricity of those moments. Then they headed to the dining hall for the ice cream parlor, as they often did; only when they were almost there, Aiden said, "Remember the view from the clock tower the night we hung the banner?"

"Kind of," Gillian said. She had been so focused on hanging the banner and getting out of there, she hadn't really stopped to appreciate the view.

"Well, I have a confession to make: while you guys were hanging the banner, I was just looking out through the arch, and it was amazing. You can see almost to the ocean."

"Wow," Gillian said. "That's amazing."

"Let's go up there," he said. "I want you to see it."

"We could get in trouble," Gillian said.

"Nobody will know," he replied mischievously.

They went in through the unlocked door at the back, the door the cleaning staff used to take the trash out, and they tiptoed up the back stairs. When they got to the top, the door to the outdoors was inexplicably open. They had been told that it would be permanently locked after the banner situation, but either that had been an empty threat or someone hadn't done their job. Regardless, together, they stepped out onto the terrace that surrounded the giant clock, which loomed above their heads. Aiden put his arm around Gillian and pointed her toward the ocean. "Can you see it?" It was dark and she decidedly could not see it.

"I'm not sure," she said. She turned back toward him and put her head on his chest. He leaned his head on top of hers and they hugged. She felt calm, relaxed, at peace. She never wanted to leave this moment. She looked up at him to see if he was feeling the same way and he kissed her. A soft and plaintive kiss. A romantic kiss. They hugged each other tighter and kind of swayed in the wind. It was the moment she had long been waiting for and she savored it. But she couldn't ignore that one pang of regret—he was her best friend's boyfriend, after all. She knew it was a mistake. And yet she stayed there, because it was also what she wanted most in the entire world.

They stayed up there like that, probably for longer than they should have, because when they came back down, the dorms were closed for the night, a practice that had been abolished sometime in the interim. And that was how everyone found out. Each had to be walked back to their rooms by their dorm parent, in view of everyone in the dorm, and both were punished for breaking curfew. With Miranda being out of town, everyone just assumed the worst. And that was that. An almost innocent hug and kiss turned into a major scandal.

When Miranda came back, she was immediately enveloped by the Deltas—three girls who loved gossip more than anything else in the entire world. Somehow they'd found out when she would be back on campus and they met her when her taxi dropped her off. Gillian sat at her window and saw them swarming the cab as Miranda got out. Saw them talking excitedly, and caught Miranda's look of shock. *I am totally screwed,* Gillian thought.

Danielle, Dana, and Dawn escorted Miranda back to Vallejo, where Aiden was waiting for her out front. All Gillian could do was watch from above as Aiden apologized and the Deltas demonized Gillian. Aiden briefly glanced up at her window before putting his arm around Miranda and walking her toward his dorm. The Deltas did their secret handshake and came back into Vallejo, laughing so loud that Gillian could hear them three stories up. Gillian climbed into bed and put her pillow over her head. She was in for it for the rest of the year, she could already tell.

"I was so freaked out," Aiden told her. "I liked you, but I knew it was just totally impossible with our little friendship triangle. I had made my decision to be with her. I couldn't break up with Miranda for you. And with all the rumors that started going around, I had to hold firm. It would have just exploded everything."

"I knew," she said. "I was heartbroken, but I learned an important lesson from that."

"What was it?"

"Protect your heart at all costs."

"And has that lesson served you well?"

"Well, I've managed not to have my heart broken again. But I also haven't been in love again."

"You were in love with me?" he asked.

"The way one is as a high school student," she said. "I didn't really know anything. But, yes. I certainly was heartbroken when I didn't get to be with you. And then you broke my heart again when you turned on me like everyone else at school."

"I'm so sorry," he said, holding her tighter. "I really do feel awful about all of it. I think about how I would feel if Rainbow were in your position. I would be so mad."

"It was a long time ago," she said. What else could she say? She needed to put it behind them so they could move forward now.

"I guess I have to make up for that," he said and he kissed her again.

"I guess you do," she murmured.

SEVENTEEN

....

Gillian snuck into her room, feeling like a kid who had missed curfew, and went straight to the bathroom to wash off her makeup. She smiled at herself in the mirror. It had been a good night. A vulnerable night. Perhaps it was a mistake to have told him that she'd been in love with him in high school. But it had come out naturally in the conversation, and there was no way to take it back now. He had received the information well and had even said, "I guess I have to make up for that." Which was not the reaction she would have predicted if she had written the script for that moment.

Gillian couldn't even be sure if she had known herself that she had loved him then. Yes, she had been in pain when he hadn't chosen her—originally and after their kiss—but did the pain mean love? She now knew it did, and the admission was out there and there was no way to take it back.

The rest of the night had been relaxed. They had walked back to his house, which was on the other side of the property from the tasting room and parking lot—a small A-frame log cabin that seemed like a man's paradise, with a pool table, a dart board, a pinball machine, and a giant stone fireplace. There was a bedroom behind the kitchen that Gillian assumed was Rainbow's, and loft upstairs, which she figured was where Aiden's bedroom was, although she didn't get a look at it. On a lovely porch on the front, he had installed a swing with cup holders in each arm. He had given her a beer from the Russian River Brewing Company that fit perfectly in the cup holder. He also brought out a blanket and wrapped them up together in it, and they had sat together on the swing listening to the birds. He told her about his garden in the back and his quest to become self-sustaining, inspired by Rainbow. "This generation knows the world is ending and is trying to do something about it. I called her 'my little environmentalist' when she was a kid," he said.

After a second beer, he kissed her good night and called a Lyft to bring her back to campus. A chaste but romantic evening. "Let's do this again soon," he said as she got into the car.

"I'd love that," she said. Then he closed the door behind her, and she headed home.

Now she was in her bathroom, going over everything they had said. Hoping she hadn't made mistakes. Should she have told him about Kent, should she have revisited high school? All of it had seemed fine at the time, but in the stillness of her room she worried she had gone too far.

Before climbing into bed, she looked up when the next Parents' Association meeting was and the process for getting on the agenda. It was a virtual meeting, as Aiden had said, because the parents lived all over the country, so she would have to present from her home computer. She had never done anything like that before, so she would need to practice—if only she was sure Lila was still her friend, she'd have no reservations in asking for her help. This was the kind of thing she prepped other people for, not the kind of thing she did herself. But it was important. She had to take a stand for the Gem. The school deserved better than what it was getting. Tomorrow, she would submit the request to present and then she would get to work.

In the morning, she started making notes based on what Gloria had told her, but she realized that she needed more information from her before she could really get going. She looked at the paper that Gloria had given her after their car ride together and picked up the phone to call her, but as she did, there was a knock at her door. And in came Rainbow, Bunny, and Julia. "It's good to see you girls," she said.

"We feel like you've abandoned us," Bunny said. "You're too busy for your own dorm children."

"Nothing could be further from the truth," she said. "You guys are my first priority."

"You didn't even do a hall check last night. And don't call us 'guys.'"

"Sorry, ladies." They all giggled. "How do you know I didn't do my check?" she asked.

"We were waiting for you. But don't worry—nobody else knows, or nobody else was doing anything bad."

"Now that homecoming is over and our worst fears have come true, we're bored," Bunny said. "We need something new to focus on."

"Shouldn't you be doing your college applications?" Gillian asked.

"Oh, those," Bunny said. "Julia is going to get in early to

Yale and Rainbow and I are going to go to U.C. schools, so we just need to get good SAT scores."

"Are you working on your SAT prep?" Gillian asked. "I know you can really score high this time if you take the practice tests."

"So boring," Bunny said.

"It's important!" Gillian emphasized. "I'm required by Dorm Mother Law to say this to you."

"It's a biased test," Julia said.

"Maybe, but you're the beneficiary of the bias. You have every advantage in this world," Gillian said. "How did you decide you wanted to go to Yale, Julia?"

"I mean, it's great. And you went there. I want to be like you. Plus, I think my fashion sense is more East Coast."

"That's sweet," Gillian said. "But what would you say if I told you that I wished I hadn't gone to Yale?"

"I would say you're lying," Julia said. "Who wouldn't want to have gone to Yale?"

"It just wasn't for me," Gillian said. "I don't have one remaining friend from there. We were just so different from one another."

"But I'm like the people who go to Yale," Julia said. "Plus, it would make my parents happy."

"Okay," Gillian said, and then, trying to steer the conversation: "That's a rational reason. Where did your parents go?"

"Davidson College, where they met."

"A lovely place," Gillian said. "Why do you think they would want you to go to Yale, then? Wouldn't they want you to go where they went?"

"They're not like that," Julia said. "I don't know if I'm like the people at Davidson. I'm definitely not like my parents, or at least not like my father, who got arrested right before school started."

"Point taken. All I am saying is that you have all the options in this world. And you have so many talents."

"That's good advice," Julia said.

"How did you two decide you want to go to U.C. schools? Also, which one? They're all so different."

"We want to go to UCLA together and live in an apartment in Westwood. We're done with this small-town vibe. We're ready for the big city," Bunny said.

"My mom lives in L.A. In Eagle Rock," Rainbow said. "I always like it when I go down there. I like the vibe of the streets. It's fun. It's stuffy here."

Gillian was dying to ask more questions about Rainbow's mother, but she restrained herself.

"Okay," Gillian said. "Those seem like fine reasons. Although I would have preferred if you'd said that you wanted to learn something specific that UCLA was good at. Regardless, you still have to study."

"We don't even really know where to start in terms of what we'll do in college or learn. But we know UCLA is cool, so we want to go there," Rainbow said.

"Why don't we have a weekly SAT study group here?" Gillian suggested. "You guys can take sample tests and I'll score them for you. Then you'll know what you have to work on. This is important."

"We know, we know," Rainbow said.

"It's your future," Gillian said. "Be proactive now. You are lucky to have all the tools at your disposal. You just need to activate them."

"Yes, Miss Brodie," Julia said, curtsying.

"Please don't call me Miss Brodie. That makes me feel like my mother," she said. "I'm just trying to help you."

"Didn't you once tell me that grades don't matter?" Bunny said.

"Yes, your grades at college don't really matter very much in the real world, depending on the field you want to go into. But your high school grades get you into college. You just have to work hard for a few more months."

"Fine, fine," Bunny said. "We'll do it for you."

"I want to be even more proud of you than I already am," Gillian said. "Now go and do something productive." She ushered them toward the door. She had realized that they would never leave if she didn't kick them out. So it was a new skill she was working on. It was a hard one because actually she loved hanging out with them. Loved seeing the progress they had made so far. She really was proud of those girls. Of all the girls in Vallejo. She had surprised herself with how attached she had gotten to them.

When they were gone, she called Gloria at home to follow up on their conversation.

"Gloria," she said. "It's Gillian."

"Oh, how are you? I can't stop thinking about our conversation. I'm just so worried."

"Please stop worrying, Gloria, I want to help you."

"Okay," Gloria said. "I trust you, Gillian. But . . . I'm afraid."

"I know," Gillian said. "I get it. I'm afraid too. I also feel some loyalty to Headmaster Kent. But think about what he did to the school. What he did to *you*. Putting you in this position."

Gloria took an audibly deep breath. "It's true. I'm so nervous all the time. I wake up in the middle of the night worrying. I go through all the different ways out of this situation in my mind. All the ways I could be implicated. I hate it."

"I'm going to get you out of it," Gillian said. "I spoke to Aiden Lloyd about it, in confidence, and he said that we have to tell the Parents' Association. I'll help."

"You did what?" Gloria said, her voice rising. "You told the head of the Parents' Association?"

"He's a friend. Our friend," Gillian said.

"He's not my friend," Gloria said. "After what he did to you. You cried in my office for an entire month after. How do you know he won't betray you again. Betray *us*."

"He won't," Gillian said. "I trust him now. It's been a long time and he's committed to saving the school—for the sake of Rainbow and his role on the Parents' Association."

"Okay, but I need assurance that they won't turn on me."

"I'll get that for you," Gillian said.

"Thank you," Gloria said. "So assuming we have those assurances, what's the next step?"

"Assuming you want to go along with it, I will work on a visual presentation that includes scans of the budgets that made you realize the numbers didn't add up. It would also be great if you could find receipts, but I don't know if you'll have access to that. And then when you speak, I think just be open about the fact that this upset you for years but you didn't know what to do. And now it's gotten to a level where you can't be silent anymore."

"Okay," Gloria said. "I'll scan the budgets and give you my notes tomorrow. Come meet me in the office before nine. He's never in that early."

"Will do," Gillian said. "See you tomorrow. And, Gloria: you're doing the right thing."

"Thank you, Gillian."

The minute she hung up with Gloria, Gillian called Aiden.

"I know you don't want to talk about this, but I need to have one more conversation about it," she said.

He sounded sleepy, but said, "Okay."

"I've spoken to Gloria, and before she can give any of the evidence she has, she needs your assurance that she won't get in trouble."

"Like immunity in a mob trial," he said.

"Like that," she said.

He was quiet for a moment, as if he was considering all the pros and cons of agreeing to this and possibly wondering if he even had the power to do it. "Yes, she's right—she should have immunity. I'll tell the board."

"Thank you," Gillian said.

Gillian really wanted to talk to someone about what was going on, and since Aiden clearly didn't want to talk about it any more than she had to, Lila was her only option.

"Hi," Lila said tentatively.

"Hi," Gillian said, as kindly as possible. "How are you?"

"Fine," Lila said. She sounded distant.

"Are you mad at me?" Gillian asked.

"Not mad," Lila said. "Just a little sad. I did really like him, so I was disappointed when it didn't work out. But really, it's just a bit weird that I dated him and now you are."

"He's broken my heart a million times," Gillian said. "I'm sure he'll do it again, especially based on what you've told me."

"I hope he doesn't," Lila said.

"Thank you," Gillian said, relieved. "I would understand if you didn't want to talk to me. Or at least until Aiden breaks up with me. Which I'm sure he will, judging by his previous behavior."

"Who knows," Lila said, a little hurt audible in her voice. "You might be the one for him."

"I think that's unlikely. It seems to me that the only 'one' for him is his winery," Gillian said.

"That could be true," Lila granted. "So I won't ask about your date. But I am curious about your scandal."

"Yeah," Gillian said. "I'm going to present about it—well, we are, Gloria and me—to the Parents' Association. She's nervous because she thinks she'll be blamed. But I said she wouldn't."

"I'm sure it's scary for her," Lila said.

"But it's not a court of law. Nobody is going to jail right now. It's just passing along information at this point. I can't imagine they'll fire her. She's worked here for thirty years," Gillian said. "Anyway, I think that my job is to help her present the information, and then they'll pass it along to the board of directors, and then from there there's an inquiry. Based on what I can tell from the website."

"You're brave to take this on," Lila said.

"Well, I'm new here, so I don't have as much to lose," Gillian said. "And it's not fair for him to be profiting off the school. I got a scholarship here, and think about how many kids they could help with the money he's skimming off the top. Going here changed my life. It could change someone else's. Besides, I love this place—the time I've spent back here has reminded me of that. And this isn't my career. I have the freedom to speak freely."

"Freedom's just another word for nothing left to lose," Lila said.

"Exactly," Gillian said. They both tried to hum the song. "I loved Janis Joplin when I was in high school. I once had a Janis Joplin–themed party for her birthday in January. Basically we made our hair messy, wore long necklaces, and listened to her greatest hits while pretending we were at Woodstock. Not very original. But I still remember it."

There was a long pause and Lila seemed to take a deep breath. "Okay. I've thought about it and I do want to know how your date was."

"Oh," Gillian said. "Are you sure?"

"Yeah, I mean, go easy on me, but yeah."

"I don't know. I feel a little weird . . ."

"I can take it," Lila said.

"I just want to say that I know this is awkward. I've been there."

"Gillian, just spill it already."

"Okay, if you say so. It was nice, but also weird. I mean, we have such an awkward past together—he really did betray me when we were younger and we've talked about it on both dates and it's just a kind of an uncomfortable thing to have between us. But then he apologized. And then I drank too much wine and accidentally revealed to him that I was in love with him in high school."

"Oof," Lila said.

"Such a dumb move, but anyway, now it's out there."

"Did you see his cabin?"

"Just for a second. I did laugh at his leather sofa. I guess he's a man who lives alone, so he can't help but buy a leather sofa."

"Why do men always have a leather sofa?"

"They're just the worst. Sticky and also ugly."

"Terrible."

"If there was ever a gender divide in this world, leather sofas are smack in the middle of it."

"And Porsches."

"Another useless thing." They were both laughing now.

"I once dated someone who had a Porsche, and the trunk was so small, we could barely go for a picnic," Lila said.

"No forethought," Gillian said. "At least Aiden has a truck that can manage all of Rainbow's things. So he seems to at least have that practicality down. The truck can probably also fit a leather couch, though, so maybe that was what he was thinking about. Anyway, it was a sweet night."

"Do you think you'll see him again?"

"I hope so," Gillian said. "But I'm worried that this embezzlement situation is going to come between us. Like his official responsibilities will interfere with our relationship, or he'll feel that they do. The romantic in me should choose love over principle. But as of right now, principle is winning out." She glanced over at the notes she had taken on the pad on her desk.

"Principles matter," Lila said. "I'm glad you have them."

"I'm surprised that I'm choosing them," Gillian said. "But it feels important."

Somehow, it had all started to feel to her like she was meant to be here, that her experiences in New York—but also as a student here—all mattered, they all made sense. She felt like she brought something different to the campus. Her experience of getting a scholarship, the way it had changed her life—it had been her path to Yale, to Ken Sunshine, to having her own business, and even to back here, even though that wasn't what she had meant to do. She had expected life at the Gem to be quiet—an escape—but it was so much more than that. Her experiences had helped make it so that she could help people—and that felt really good. She didn't know many people who had lives as adults that were as vastly different from their childhoods as hers. Going from not knowing if the electricity would be turned off on a day-to-day basis to being on private planes with actors and musicians. Going from having two pairs of jeans to attending trunk shows where designer clothing was being given away—it was a big deal. She was proud of what she had achieved. And she wanted other kids to have access to it too. This school was for rich kids, yes, but it gave opportunities to people like her. If the funds were available to do so.

"You seem distracted," Lila said.

"I was just thinking about all the things that had to happen for me to be here for this. What a wild last year it's been."

"It really has been," Lila said. "Well, I'm glad it's you!"

"Me too. I guess I need to work on my presentation," Gillian said. "I really feel like Kent is doing this school such a disservice. I want to help change it."

"You go, girl," Lila said.

As they hung up their phones, Gillian felt like maybe their friendship could be salvaged. She hoped so, at least: Lila was smart and fun and Gillian was so lucky to have a friend who would listen to her and support her, even when she was jealous of her dating situation. She would do everything in her power to keep Lila as a friend, even if it meant she couldn't have Aiden as a boyfriend. But meeting Lila had reminded her that having a friend was even better than being in love. Since she had connected with Lila, and then almost lost her, she had realized how important friendship was in this life. Lila coming back and forgiving her felt so monumental. It felt better than anything else.

EIGHTEEN

....

The evening of the Parents' Association meeting, Gillian walked the halls early wearing her most professional blazer. A few girls commented on her "grown-up" attire—they were used to seeing her in T-shirts and leggings. "I have a business meeting" was all she would tell them.

"Are you interviewing for a new job?" Bunny asked. "Because you have to stay here until the end of the year. It's in your contract."

"Don't worry, I'm not going anywhere," she said. "I plan to stay here as long as they'll have me. It's you guys who are going to leave me behind, not the opposite."

Although if she was honest with herself, she wasn't sure if the board would want to keep her after tonight. They had put her on the agenda as the final item and all it said was "Presentation of a Sensitive Nature: Not to Be Recorded." She guessed that was for the best. Only the members of the Parents' Association would know Gloria's information for now. She didn't know when it would be made public—if it ever would be. That wasn't really her responsibility. Her job was to bring the information forward, and it was their job to act on it. If this was the end of her own tenure at the school, it would make her very sad, but it would be worth it. As she thought about it being her last night in Vallejo, though, she felt a pang of loneliness. This place had started to feel like home and she wasn't quite ready to leave it.

She logged in to listen to the entire meeting—it was, she assumed, regular Parents' Association stuff. Fundraising for new sports uniforms via a virtual silent auction, evaluation of scholarship applications, a diversity committee, a library committee. Aiden reported that the Shirazi twins had a song on the Billboard Hot 100 and Mina Shirazi thanked everyone for their support during this complicated time. That broke down into a bit of cross talk about how exciting it was for Mina that her kids were being recognized for their talent. "I've always known they were special," Mina bragged.

Gillian wondered if her mother had even known about the Parents' Association. If they even told the scholarship parents about all the things they did with the money they raised from the rich parents. A scholarship parent could have brought another perspective to the board, she thought. Every person on this call seemed to be rich and out of touch with reality. Gillian had seen the sports uniforms—they were all fine. There were better things to spend money on. She did like the library committee though. The library felt pretty crusty to her. Not that high school students were using the library for anything other than Wi-Fi and flirting. But still, if contemporary fiction and history were available in the library for the few students who might seek it out, that would be nice. A bullet point for a brochure, at the very least.

When it was Gillian's turn, she took a deep breath. She introduced herself as a dorm mother and a proud alumna of the school. She told them about how much she had enjoyed the past few months, how she loved getting to know their children. And how she had been the recipient of a scholarship to attend the school. She then introduced Gloria Rhodes, who was in her home living room, surrounded by photos of her family, and reminded the association about Gloria's long history with the school, her tenure of thirty years, her deep knowledge of how the school was run, of the students, of the policies. She tried to establish Gloria's credibility and also her blamelessness. Then she put her PowerPoint presentation up on the screen—it had just a few pages.

While the PowerPoint filled the screen, Gloria started talking. She was clearly nervous; her voice was shaking and she was obviously reading from a statement she had written down, per Gillian's advice. Gloria also described her many years at the school, her accounting history, and her job of bookkeeper, which was in addition to all the other things she did to keep the school running. Then she walked through what she had found: the early years of everything being fine and then, more recently, the money. "The numbers just didn't add up," she said, before pivoting to talk about her fear. How this had been her job for so long, how her pension and her health insurance depended on it, how Kent was her boss. Gillian tried to read the room as Gloria talked. She hoped that the parents had sympathy for her. She was a whistle-blower; she deserved protection.

When Gloria was done with her presentation, Gillian flipped the screen back so they could see her face and waited for questions. Aiden was the one who called on people—it was fun seeing him lead this meeting. He was good at it. He knew how to encourage productive discourse, as well as how to get people to stop talking when they were blathering on. There was one man that Gillian was nervous about. He had been making huffy faces throughout her intro, before she turned the microphone over to Gloria. Aiden called on Mina Shirazi first, who said, "This is an outrage. To our school. Our community. He should be fired immediately."

"First we have to go through a formal process," Aiden said.

"Kick him out, I say," Mina said. "What do you think should happen, Gillian?"

"It's not up to me," Gillian said. "But it seems to me that Headmaster Kent is stealing from this school, which puts the entire population at a disadvantage. And we should be grateful to Ms. Rhodes for revealing this crime. You should investigate in a more formal way. And you should assure Ms. Rhodes that she isn't in trouble."

The huffy man had already raised his hand before she stopped talking. Aiden recognized him, although Gillian could see that he did so reluctantly. "What if," the man asked, "this is just a big mistake on Ms. Rhodes's part?"

"A formal investigation would show that," Gillian said. "Bring in an outside accountant to check her work. There's also the possibility that an outside person will find more than Ms. Rhodes has. It's certainly worth it."

"Thank you for bringing this to our attention, Ms. Brodie and Ms. Rhodes," Aiden said. She smiled at his formality. "We'll now proceed with the next level of escalation, which is to share this issue with the board of directors. They may have questions for you and we will certainly pass along your PowerPoint, which has a lot of important information, if that's okay."

"That's fine," Gillian said. "I'll send it to you after the meeting."

"Ms. Rhodes, we will also likely need your files."

"That's fine," Gloria said. "Just give me a call. Gillian has my cell phone."

"This was a brave thing to do," Aiden said.

"Thank you," Gloria said. "It wasn't easy. I hope you all understand that."

"We do," Mina Shirazi said.

Gillian smiled at Gloria. She exited the meeting and poured herself a strong gin and tonic.

After she was done with her drink, she texted Aiden: "That was intense."

He wrote back, "The Parents' Association hasn't had to deal with anything like this since I've been on it."

"I'm sorry," she wrote.

"It was responsible for you to bring up."

"It just feels like it might make things complicated . . ." she wrote.

There was a long pause. She saw the three dots start. And then stop. And then start again. She held her breath. She was losing everything. Again. She was almost in tears.

"I think we just need to think about everything carefully," he finally wrote.

It was so vague. Distant. The tears welled up. She let them flow. It had been a long time since she'd had a good cry. Since she had felt sorry for herself properly. And now was as good a time as any. Crying reminded her of the days after the news of her downfall went public. After she'd tweeted the screenshot of her resignation letter, she had sat back and watched the responses pour in. The support and the vitriol. It took approximately seventeen minutes for the *Huffington Post* to post a take. (She assumed the writers had been working on it before she went public, but the timing was pretty impeccable.) She packed up a few more boxes in her office as the notifications on her computer and phone dinged and dinged.

When she walked out of her office building that day, with her most precious possessions in a Bergdorf's bag and her largest sunglasses on her face, the two photographers waiting outside the building immediately started snapping photos of her. Ironic for someone who'd spent her career behind the scenes. She went home that night and curled up in a ball and cried harder than she had ever cried in her entire life. It was the kind of crying that took the breath out of you, the kind of crying that made you lose your appetite, made you forget that time existed. The kind of crying that made you sleep hard afterward. The kind that made your eyes puffy the next morning.

Luckily, there weren't any photographers outside her apartment when she came out the next day to buy a copy of the paper. When she got to the deli on her corner, she saw the front-page headline of the *New York Post:* PLAYBOY PUBLICIST PENS RESIGNATION. Her phone continued to buzz, but she just didn't pick up. It was the first time in more than fifteen years that she didn't have to answer an incoming call, and while she had expected to feel sad, it actually made her feel kind of free. She tossed the *Post* in the trash and walked out to the path by the Hudson River. She walked all the way down to Battery Park and leaned against the railing, looking out at the Statue of Liberty.

Now, three thousand miles away from that tragedy, tissue box in hand, she crawled into bed, put *The Trinity Session* by the Cowboy Junkies on her stereo—it had been her go-to weeping music since high school—and laid her head on her pillow.

Then her phone buzzed. A text. She had to look at it. "Maybe we just need to keep this topic off-limits," he said. "Until it all blows over."

"That seems wise," she texted back, knowing it was the mature thing to say.

"Maybe you should come over and not discuss it in person," he said.

She was shocked. A booty call. This wasn't what she'd been expecting at all. A strange turn of events. She had been planning to have a good cry and wake up to being fired from her job and having lost her potential boyfriend. But if that was what he was asking for . . . she had to go. . . . She knew she should say she'd see him tomorrow. Instead, she wrote back, "I'll be right there."

When she arrived at his front door, he was holding it open. The house was dark inside except for a lit fireplace. He handed her a glass of wine and they settled on the couch. They chatted for a few minutes about nothing, really—how nice it was to have a fireplace, how good the wine was, how she was starting to really appreciate Mina Shirazi. And then he reached over and pulled her close. First he kissed her forehead, and then her nose, and then her mouth. She snuggled into him and wrapped her arms around him. He felt warm and smelled like citrus, like on their first date. His hand worked its way under her tunic and down her back. The fire crackled in the background and she slid her hand under his T-shirt. He slowly lowered her back onto the couch and kissed her neck. She wrapped her legs around him, wanted him as close as she could possibly get him. It was so much better now than it would have been in high school. Soon they were skin to skin, their shirts discarded on the floor. She noticed that very quietly in the background, *Appalachian Spring* was playing. Classical music, what a touch. She closed her eyes and concentrated on kissing Aiden, on being completely present. On the electricity between their skin, between their hands. It was everything she had hoped it would be and more.

As their clothes piled up on the floor next to the couch, all she could think was "After all this time, it's finally really happening."

NINETEEN

....

November 2018

The next three weeks were the best of her life. She got to do all the things she had always wanted to do with Aiden. Whenever she had dorm coverage, they drove out to the beach and drank wine on the rocks, wrapped in cashmere blankets. They hiked and watched birds at the Point Reyes National Seashore. They met for lunch at cute little restaurants in downtown Sonoma and Healdsburg.

The best part of her days were after the girls all headed off to class and her responsibilities waned for a few hours. She would head over to Grange Hill and "help" Aiden with whatever he was doing. It was November, which was an exciting time in the winery. The grapes had all been harvested, so she got to observe the destemming and crushing process, and then both Aiden and Gillian watched while the vintner introduced the yeast into the crushed grapes. The white was fermented in stainless steel casks in the cooler part of the cellar, and the reds were fermented in oak in the warmer area.

"How long will they be fermenting for?" Gillian asked after they walked out of the cellar.

"It depends on the grape, starts at two weeks and can go

longer from there," Aiden said. "With the red, we pump it off into tanks and press the skins to get the press wine. Then we'll combine them later."

"I still can't believe you know how to do all of this."

"I'm lucky to have good help," he said. "But it has been fun to learn."

On fermentation day, they took a 2016 bottle of pinot noir and a lunch of kimchi, pickles, salami, and sourdough bread and headed to Aiden's secret picnic spot—the site of their second date. After the sandwiches were made and the pickles and kimchi doled out, they snuggled together and sipped their wine.

"I know we're not supposed to talk about Kent," Gillian said. "But you've been so focused on it. Can you give me, like, the short headlines of what's going on?"

Aiden sighed. She knew that she was breaking the bubble between them about the proceedings, but she couldn't help it.

"Basically," he explained, "it started small. Gloria didn't even pick up on it for a long time. He paid for a painting for the residence with school money and nobody noticed. And after that, he and his wife used a little bit of school money for one thing or another. They loved to buy art, and they could swing it mostly with their own money until his wife lost her inheritance in the Bernie Madoff Ponzi scheme. And all of a sudden, they were just paying for everything with school money and hiding that fact by taking it from the scholarship fund, which disperses big chunks of money on a predictable basis."

"So he blamed his wife?"

"Not exactly, but he didn't not blame her," he said.

"What a desperate dick," she said.

"I mean, that's the least of his offenses," Aiden said.

"Okay," she said. "Good point."

"In any case, it's all proceeding. Gloria will be fine."

"That's my main worry," she said. She made a mental note to follow up with Gloria to see how she was doing.

"The worst thing that will happen is that she'll be asked to retire but will retain her full pension. But the new headmaster could decide to keep her. The board is basically staying out of it."

"What a crazy thing," she said. "I can't believe I was here for it. I mean, it feels like he's been the headmaster for essentially our whole lives."

"Well, you were the one who helped make it happen. We should all be grateful that you came back to Glen Ellen," he said. "Especially the future students."

Gillian took a deep breath. It felt good to have done the right thing—so much better than it felt to get a celebrity out of a social media jam. Maybe that was what being an adult was—it was having a sense of satisfaction about doing the right thing. "It feels good to do something meaningful," she said.

"It does," he said. "I'm proud of you and proud to be with you."

Gillian loved this new version of Aiden so much—it was what she had hoped he would be but hadn't been when they were younger. And now it had somehow manifested itself in his late-thirties self. It was annoying but true that he was her dream man. Her high school self had had good taste; if only she weren't constantly paranoid that he was going to break her heart. She comforted herself with the thought that even if she didn't have love, she did have a friend in Lila.

TWENTY

....

December 2018

With two weeks left in the term, everyone was losing their minds. Exams were one week away, term papers were due, early admission decisions were imminent, and Christmas vacation was on the horizon. Gillian was holding her study breaks in the lounge, where she provided cookies and juice for energy, as well as emotional support for stressed-out students. She put signs on the wall that said, YOU CAN DO IT and KEEP CALM AND STUDY HARD. Plus her personal favorite: a picture of an owl that said, OWL STUDY HARD AND DO MY BEST. It made all the kids groan, although she heard them saying it to one another in the halls, so even if they were kind of making fun of it, she knew it was okay. Exams were one thing, but early admission was really what was making everyone crazy. The twins had applied to NYU and were worried that they wouldn't both get in. "Do you think there's a special twin statute?" Farrah asked one night when the decisions were a few days away.

Their new song, "Trust Me," had gone viral as soon as it had been released, partially, Gillian believed, due to her publicity plan. Even Bunny had admitted that it was a good song and worthy of being popular.

"I feel like they accept one twin pop group per year," Freddy joked. "Maybe this year we can be it."

Farrah just made a fretful face.

"We both got 1540 on our SATs," Freddy said. "We wrote good essays about becoming famous on the internet. We have recommendations. Why wouldn't they take us? I think you need to stop worrying."

"Even if you don't get in early," Gillian said, "there's plenty of time to get in later. And then the schools can have a bidding war for you. You're the complete package. But it'll be okay either way, I promise."

"I just won't be able to handle it if one of us gets in and the other doesn't," Freddy said. "But since you want it more, if one of us has to, I hope it's you, Farrah."

"It won't be the same if I have to go alone," Farrah said.

"If you get in and I don't, I'll go to the New School or Juilliard and we'll just get an apartment together somewhere between the two schools."

Farrah smiled, but Gillian could tell that she didn't like that solution. "You'd go to the New School for me?" Farrah asked.

"I want to live in the same city as my beloved sister," he said, as earnestly as a sentence like that could possibly be said by a teenager.

"You two are the cutest," Gillian said. The exchange reminded her of this time when she was in high school—she had applied early to Yale and Miranda had applied early to Michigan's Honors Program. It was way more likely that

Gillian would be deferred and Miranda would get in. After all, what were the odds of getting into Yale early? Slim to none. Michigan was much bigger, even though the Honors Program was very competitive. So Gillian had already completed the narrative in her mind that Miranda—who got everything she wanted—would get in early and she, Gillian, would have to wait until spring. And then somehow, through some act of God that she still couldn't quite fathom, the reverse happened. Gillian got a big fat envelope from Yale and Miranda got deferred from Michigan.

Gillian was thrilled, but they were roommates and she basically needed to completely contain her joy because of how sad Miranda was. She never got to enjoy getting in early except in one phone call with her mother, who was so proud. It would have been better, she felt, if she hadn't gotten in and Miranda had. Would Miranda have comforted her? Yes, but Gillian had expected not to get in, so the disappointment wouldn't have been so sharp. Whenever college came up, Miranda would be defensive, saying, "But you already have that all settled." And Gillian would try to soften the blow—she still wouldn't know if she could even go until the financial aid package came through. It was an early lesson in interpersonal relationships—how sometimes personal success comes with a cost. For that reason, she hoped that Farrah and Freddy either succeeded or failed together. She hoped NYU understood that too.

Gillian knew that Julia was also waiting on an early application, to Yale. But Julia seemed less worried about it than the twins—maybe she, too, understood that it was such a long shot that it wasn't worth even thinking about. Despite many conversations about it, Gillian hadn't been able to convince Rainbow and Bunny to apply outside of the U.C. system. Bunny said that her parents would love to brag about her going to a fancy college, so she was going to defy them and go happily to a state school. And Aiden was happy with Rainbow's decision as well. He wanted his daughter within driving distance—she was hoping for UCLA but willing to go to Davis. Gillian couldn't imagine the Three Musketeers (as she had started thinking of them) at three different colleges, although maybe it was time for them to set out on their own—for them to develop some individuality.

By December, it was confirmed that everyone knew about Aiden and Gillian's relationship. Bunny and Julia teased Rainbow that she would have to start calling Gillian "mom" soon, instead of "dorm mom." But Rainbow never took that bait, and nor did Gillian; they both knew that Aiden wasn't the marrying kind.

The night that Gillian tried to calm Freddy and Farrah down about their college dreams, Julia, Bunny, and Rainbow also wandered into the study break—Bunny wearing her volleyball clothes, Julia in head-to-toe Lululemon, and Rainbow in a linen jumpsuit. The threesome came over as Farrah and Freddy faded away, engulfed in their own anxiety. They truly had nothing to worry about, so Gillian tried not to take their nervousness too seriously.

"We need to get out of here," Bunny said to Gillian, cookie in hand.

"You only have two more weeks," Gillian said. The students were not allowed off campus unless they were with their parents or another adult with whom they had parental permission to leave. Rainbow got to go home to get a break from campus every few weeks, but Bunny and Julia had to obtain permission even to leave with her and neither one relished asking their parents for such a favor.

"Ugh, I have to spend the vacation in Chamonix," Bunny said.

"I can't believe you are complaining about that," Gillian said.

"I hate skiing and I hate my parents' dumb friends. And their spoiled kids. Ugh. Even worse."

"I'll go with you," Julia said.

"I wish," Bunny said.

"I'll pay my way—my parents don't care about the money. And I'd rather not see them. They'll just ask me how much I weigh and what my grades are and why didn't I get into Yale. It's healthier not to see them anyway."

"You don't know yet about Yale," Gillian said. "And even if you don't get in, you'll have another chance in the spring. You really don't want to see them?" Gillian asked.

"I'd rather be with Bunny and help keep her from being miserable," Julia said. "I'll just put the ticket on their credit card. I can't believe you didn't already ask me, Bun."

"I didn't want you to have to experience my misery."

"We'll have fun. The French won't care if we get drunk in the lodge."

"Neither will my parents," Bunny said. "They would be disappointed if we didn't, really."

"Will you be spending family Christmas with Rainbow and your boyfriend, Gillian?" Bunny asked.

"It hasn't been discussed yet," Gillian said. "Plus, I haven't seen my mom in a few years and she lives in Sacramento."

"Too bad," Bunny said. "It would have been a cute Instagram."

"You know I would never do that," Gillian said. "It's inappropriate."

"Pics or it didn't happen," Julia said.

"You girls are really incorrigible," Gillian said.

"I hope you do spend Christmas with us," Rainbow said. "But I know it's up to you and my dad."

"That's nice of you," Gillian said. "But we honestly haven't talked about it. And I really do want to see my mom."

"You haven't seen her since you've lived here?" Rainbow asked.

"I guess I just haven't had time," Gillian said. All she wanted was for her mom to understand her a little bit and it felt like ever since she'd left home to go to the Gem, her mom had never even tried. True, Gillian didn't spend enough time with her mom to remind her that she was a real person, but she wished her mom would just understand innately without having to be shown.

After the study break, Gillian shooed all the children back to their rooms, reminding the seniors that this was their last chance to make a good impression on colleges and pointing out to the younger girls that if they did well now, they could relax a little more in their final year. Then Gillian went back to her room and called her mother.

"I was wondering when you were going to call me" was her mother's opening salvo. Not a good sign.

"It's been a busy few months," Gillian said.

"Well, when my Google Alert for you stopped updating me every day, I figured maybe you would call. But you seem to have gone into hiding."

"You have a Google Alert for me?" Weirdly, this warmed Gillian's heart. It meant her mother cared about what was going on in her life.

"I'm actually in California," Gillian said.

"Oh, that's a surprise," her mother said.

"I'm working at Glen Ellen Academy. I did call when I first got here, or texted at least, and you didn't respond."

"Oh," her mother said. "I'm sorry. How could I have missed that? What a twist of fate to be back there. You have such a complicated relationship with that place." Her mother paused. "How is it?"

"Basically the same as when I went here, just with cell phones. I'm even dating Aiden Lloyd, if you can believe it. He lives nearby and owns a winery. Remember him?"

"Well, that's different from when you went there, because he was dating Miranda then."

"I'm well aware of that, Mom."

"I remember how he betrayed you and made you cry every day for a month."

"It's different now," Gillian said, feeling increasingly like a teenager. How was it that it took only moments to revert back to the teen-parent dynamic?

"Well, since it took you months to call me, why are you calling now?"

"I was wondering if you wanted to spend Christmas together."

"Do you have time to spend it with me?" her mother asked.

"Of course," Gillian said. "I'm living here now, and I was hoping we could reconnect."

Her mother sighed. "Of course, love, I just . . . I'd reconciled myself with you not really being in my life."

"I've been through a lot, Mom, and I'm trying to change. To come to terms with what I've done wrong and try to fix it. And try to make other people's lives better too."

"Do you think my life would be better if you were in it?"

"I do," Gillian said. "And I think you should think so too."

"I guess if you can trust Aiden Lloyd again, I can trust you again."

Gillian nodded. Sometimes her mother did act like a teenager, but now she was used to that behavior. "Okay, so I'll come by on Christmas. Write it on your calendar, so you don't forget."

"Okay, love, and be careful of Aiden—I still have a bad feeling about him after all these years."

"Thanks for looking out for me, Mom," Gillian said.

After they hung up, Gillian sat down on her couch. She and her mom had been through a lot together, but they had also been through a lot apart. There were so many things they didn't know about each other's lives. And now that Gillian was back in Northern California, she needed to try to make things right, to reconnect. Even if it was awkward. It was her mom, after all.

She took a deep breath and texted Aiden: "Ok if I come over?"

"See you soon," he wrote back.

TWENTY-ONE

....

Aiden was standing at the open door of his house when she arrived, something he hadn't done since the beginning of their relationship. It made her nervous. She hopped out of her Lyft and walked quickly up to the door, gave him a quick kiss on the lips, and followed him inside. "What's going on?" she asked. "You seem stressed."

He was drinking a coffee, which was just a deeply odd thing for him to be doing at eleven o'clock at night. He never had coffee after noon. He pointed at the newspaper sitting on the kitchen counter. "Look. This is tomorrow's *Sonoma Index-Tribune*. I got an early copy."

She picked it up. The headline on the top read, GLEN ELLEN ACADEMY FIRES EMBEZZLING HEADMASTER.

"Wow," she said, scanning the article.

"The board has met three times over this," he said. "Twice after your testimony. It's a difficult problem. He's been the headmaster for so long. But he's been doing this for so long too. The independent accountant found all sorts of ways that he had stolen money from the school, beyond what

Gloria initially discovered. It totaled up to over a million dollars."

"That's messed up. Does anyone on campus know that this article is running tomorrow?"

"It's just the local paper. The school parents don't necessarily read that." He collapsed on the sofa in front of the fire.

"This could very quickly become a big story," she said. "Especially with Farrah and Freddy being famous. This school is on the national radar now." She went over and sat next to him, but he kept his distance.

"Ugh," he groaned.

"Well, you should direct all media requests to me," she said. "And you should lock down the gates of the campus. At least to keep the vans outside."

"What a mess," he said. He started making notes on his phone.

"You did the right thing," she said.

He shook his head. "There's no good answer. I just wish it all could just go away."

"Now's your chance to get more progressive leadership at the school, after all these years."

"He's been good at it," Aiden said.

"You should be happy he's gone," Gillian said. She was getting a little outraged at Aiden's complacency. She could feel her voice rising to a louder pitch. "He's been stealing from your daughter."

"You're right," Aiden said. "I'm just overwhelmed by all of the cascading problems this creates." He looked defeated. He put down his phone. There were no more notes to take.

"I know," Gillian said.

"And I feel like it complicates our relationship," he said, his voice breaking a little bit.

"You feel that way now?" she asked. "Now that the whole thing is over?"

"It's not over yet," he said. "He's just leaving today. It's just becoming public. It could come out that you were the one who brought the scandal to the board's attention."

"What does that matter?" she asked.

"If the head of the Parents' Association and the whistle-blower are found to be in a relationship, that could compromise things more."

"We discussed this months ago and you didn't think it was a problem," she said.

"I know, but now I'm worried," he said. "Now that it's going to be public."

Tears welled up in her eyes. This was exactly what she had been hoping would not happen. It was why she had discussed the situation with him back in October when she had testified before the board. She had pointed out the potential conflict of interest then, but it hadn't mattered to either of them at the time.

"I'm sorry," he said.

"I'm just frustrated because you had the chance to stop this before, and now . . . now it hurts more."

"It would have hurt at any time," he said. But he was scrunching his face a little—to keep from crying, she could tell.

"Things were just getting really good," she said. "And it is almost the holidays. I will have a break from the kids and my nightly door check."

"I know," he said. "I'm sad, too."

"Then don't let this happen," she said. "It doesn't have to be this way."

"I think right now it does," he said. Now she could really see tears in his eyes, but he was gritting his teeth like he was trying not to break down.

"You said you wouldn't betray me again, and here you are, doing it. For no reason. The board isn't asking you to break up with me. The Parents' Association isn't asking for it. And your part in all of this is over. It doesn't make any sense."

"Let's just take a break while this news becomes public, Gillian. I think it's for the best."

"Your sense of honor is deeply frustrating," she said. She wiped her eyes with her sleeve and stood up. She wished he would let himself break down, or at least show some remorse. But he didn't. "I guess I should go home." She took her phone out of her pocket and called for a Lyft.

"You should really get a car," he said.

"I'm a New Yorker," she said.

"You seem to live in California now," he said.

She looked around the cabin, taking it all in: the smells, the fireplace, his floppy hair. It didn't make sense to her that it was all over. Up until now, it had been working so well, and she had been having fun. She had found someone who could be a friend and a boyfriend. As Lila had predicted, she liked having an outlet outside of school. But also, as Lila had predicted, he wasn't ready for a commitment. But if she could commit to a car, anyone could commit to anything.

"You're right. I should get one. A car. I'm committed. Let me know if you change your mind," she said as she stood at the front door, waiting for the cab to arrive. As the words came out of her mouth, she regretted them. They put her in a weaker position. Made her seem desperate. That was the last thing she wanted to seem. She wanted to be strong and independent, a woman who didn't need a man.

"I will," he said. Although as he said it, he was the one who looked weak.

The driver who picked her up was the same one who'd dropped her off. "Didn't think I'd be back so fast," he said.

"Things didn't go as planned," she said.

"They often don't," he said.

Then they were quiet for the rest of the ride.

The gates hadn't been closed, she noticed when the cab pulled up. She got out where she was supposed to—at the campus gates. As she walked to the dorm, she saw the telltale signs of a scandal: the news trucks were back. A few had circled the quad. With the headmaster fired, she wasn't even sure who to call to fix this. So she just texted Aiden. What could she do? He was her connection to this scandal. "I don't know who to tell, but whoever's in charge of those gates should close them right now. There are already trucks here. Tomorrow's going to be a day. A message should also go out to the students and faculty explaining what happened and recommending that they not talk to the media."

"Can you draft the message?" he wrote back.

"Ugh. Fine," she responded. It was literally the last thing she wanted to do, especially for him. But she was also the most qualified person to do it.

She went back up to her room, opened her laptop, and started writing. As she wrote, she reflected that it was a good thing she'd come back to campus; otherwise, it would have filled up with vans before the morning. Was her love life more important than defending the rights of the members of the Gem community? It certainly felt that way, even though she knew the feeling was irrational. She mourned her own wound, but she had to focus on what was going on. The statement had to be vague enough not to implicate anyone yet specific enough to get people to take it seriously.

To All Faculty, Staff, and Students of Glen Ellen Academy:

Effective immediately, Headmaster Kent will be removed from his position. After a lengthy and thorough investigation, we have found that Headmaster Kent has embezzled a large amount of money from this institution.

   As a result, Headmaster Kent will be replaced. "The search will begin in earnest after the holidays," said Board of Directors President Helene Waxman.

   There will likely be media attention surrounding this story, as well as reporters on campus. We recommend that faculty, staff, and students not comment on this situation. A spokesperson for the school will be handling official requests and interviews. Please forward any inquiries you might receive to me. Gillian.Brodie@glenellenacademy.edu

When she was done, she emailed it to Aiden and noted to him that he should get approval from Helene Waxman for the quote she had drafted for her. Then she got into bed and looked at her phone for the first time in an hour or so. She already had voice mails and texts from many of the producers she had talked to about Farrah and Freddy, asking about the headmaster situation. She shook her head. Tomorrow was not going to be a fun day. Before she closed her eyes for the night, she texted Aiden one more time, telling him about the requests. "You also need to designate someone who will talk to the media," she wrote. "And tell me who she or he is, so this situation can be handled."

It felt good to school Aiden. It was his job, after all; it wasn't hers. Or at the very least, it was his job to figure out whose job it was. She was just a dorm mom, a former publicist, and an ex-girlfriend. But, of course, even though she was mad at him, a small part of her wanted to help him.

She expected to fall asleep immediately—it had, in the end, been an exhausting day. The call with her mother, the news about Kent, the breakup with Aiden, and this publicity situation. It had all happened so fast. Only there were so many feelings running around inside her brain, it was hard to isolate any given problem. And so she just lay there with her eyes open, watching the texts pour in from producers and reporters.

She figured they must have had alerts set up about Glen Ellen Academy after Farrah and Freddy broke out. She wished the board had consulted her about the timing of letting Kent go. If they had just waited another week and a half, until the holidays were in full swing, it could have gotten buried. But now, in that sweet spot between Thanksgiving and Christmas when nothing really big happens and reporters are dying for a juicy story, there it was: GLEN ELLEN ACADEMY FIRES EMBEZZLING HEADMASTER. Maybe at the end of the day it would be good for the school—it showed, at the very least, that they were committed to their own policy. She had tried to tell Aiden the upsides. But they were going to have to suffer through another week or so of national attention, something no school really wanted.

In any case, she was equipped to help them swim through the attention. All she could hope was that on the other side, Aiden would reconsider their relationship. She had wanted it for so long and had been so happy that it was finally happening. For it to be ruined by politics felt wrong. Of course, politics was the reason it hadn't worked out in high school as well—or at least that was what he had said. He had gone back to Miranda after she came back from her grandmother's funeral out of duty as much as out of peacekeeping. He'd known that it would blow up their lives for him to be with Gillian, just like Gillian getting into Yale a few months earlier had blown up their lives.

As she thought about this, it made her mad—they had both spent so much time and effort and sacrificed their own happiness for Miranda's. Gillian had never celebrated getting into Yale because it upset Miranda, and if she was totally honest with herself, she had never really fully appreciated it because it had tainted their friendship. The same thing had happened with Aiden a few months later even though they had (she liked to think) fallen for each other while Miranda was away—they had not been able to be together when she was back because it would have hurt her. And then when it went public, Miranda had, as Gillian had predicted, joined the Deltas and turned against her only friend. Yes, Gillian had done something wrong with Aiden, but she hadn't done anything wrong in getting into Yale.

The more she thought about the Yale thing, the madder she got. Why were Miranda's feelings more important than her own? Why was Miranda allowed to be sensitive but Gillian had to be stoic? Why was the preservation of their triad so important? Aiden got everything he wanted—his beautiful rich girlfriend and Gillian as a pining friend. He enjoyed having Gillian around until it tarnished his image. And he was doing it again now—breaking up with her to save his own face politically. Keeping himself separate from her in case it should come out that she was the accuser. But she was proud of being the accuser. It was the right thing to do. It shouldn't have anything to do with his role on the Parents' Association. And if he had a problem with it, he should have spoken up about it in October, when she'd originally made the presentation.

The tears that had been rolling down Gillian's face were turning to rage. All this time (well, except when she kissed her friend's boyfriend, but she was truly sorry about that) she had been in the right. She had acted nobly; she had done what everyone else wanted her to do. She had been the "good girl," protecting everyone else's feelings. She gritted her teeth. Her time of being the good girl was over. It never got her what she wanted. It only led to her having to compromise. Miranda got what she wanted. Aiden got what he wanted. And she, Gillian, had just waited in the wings, watching. She had let life happen to her. Accepted the conventional wisdom. Well, that approach was bullshit as far as she was concerned. She didn't need anyone else's approval. All she needed to be was proud of herself. And she was proud of herself for reporting Kent, and she was proud of herself for helping these kids navigate their lives, and she would be proud of herself for how she would handle the coverage of Kent leaving. She had taken responsibility for the mistakes she had made in her past. She was taking charge. Growing up. A better Gillian Brodie would emerge from all of this, that she was sure of.

Sun started filtering into her room a little before seven. She bolted out of bed. She had meant to get up earlier, but she had slept so hard it just hadn't happened. On her phone, she had fifty-seven unread texts and seventeen voice mails. The statement had been sent out to GEM-ALL, a rarely used email distribution list, as well as sent via text so the students would actually read it. Her phone was full of texts and emails from producers and reporters asking to talk to someone about the story. The one thing she didn't know was: Who was the face of this story? Was it Helene Waxman? Was it Aiden? Was it her? She quickly texted Aiden to find out who should be commenting to the press, if anyone. Then she texted a link to Lila, saying, "Well, I guess it's official. The news about Kent is out."

Then she waited to hear back from Aiden about who should be speaking to this crisis. She needed to know that before she went outside and was bombarded by the reporters. As she waited, Lila called.

"How did this happen?" she asked.

"I guess the board of directors made it official and an article went up on the *Sonoma Index-Tribune*'s website last night and now it's a national story."

"Ugh. I mean, at least he's out. But I wish all the trucks weren't here again."

"What can we do? The school is famous now because of Farrah and Freddy. But the worst part is that Aiden broke up with me last night."

"WHAT?" Lila exclaimed.

"He said it was a conflict of interest now that it's public."

"But didn't you give him the chance to do that months ago, when this all started?"

"Yes, exactly," Gillian said. "But now I still have to deal with him because somehow I've become the de facto publicist on this. While my heart is broken. I haven't even really had time to reflect because so much has been happening."

"Well, he's broken your heart too many times, in my opinion," Lila said.

"I will say that this all made me realize that I'm done playing by the rules. Being a 'good girl.' That's over. I'm living life my way. And I have to admit that you told me this would happen. Lila, you were right."

"I hate being right in this situation," Lila said. "I really did want you two to be happy. Honestly."

"Thank you," Gillian said. "But I don't need him. I'm different now. And all these years I spent wanting him, I was really wanting the one thing I didn't have when I was young. He was like a totem for the regret I felt at how I spent my high school years—pining for him instead of trying to branch out. Miranda got him, but so what? And now I can do better."

"You can," Lila said. "Whenever my friends decide to completely change their approach to life, that's when they find the right match. Maybe Aiden wasn't right for you. You just needed to get him out of your system."

"Maybe," Gillian said. "It just feels weird because I've loved him for so long."

"What was your favorite song in high school? The one you loved more than anything?"

"'Ice Cream' by Sarah McLachlan," she said without hesitating; then she hummed the chorus.

"Can you even bear to listen to it now?"

"I hadn't thought about it in ages," Gillian said. "But it's so cheesy."

"Right, so if you can't even bear your favorite song from high school, why should you love the same person you loved then?"

"Okay, okay, you've got a point," Gillian said.

"Think of all the things you loved then. Your favorite outfit, best friend, even what you thought you would do with your life. All of those things have changed."

"I know," Gillian said. "But it was also nice to have my dream come true."

"Maybe not all dreams are supposed to come true," Lila said. "I mean, I had one last night about all my teeth crumbling while I ate a salad and I really hope that doesn't happen."

"Me too," Gillian said, laughing. "I do have one dream that I think you can help come true."

"What?" Lila asked.

"Can you come with me to buy a car?"

"I thought you'd never ask," Lila said. "This is a big step for you."

"I know," Gillian said. "But I think I'm ready."

As they hung up, she felt her phone buzz. Aiden texted, "Can you be the spokesperson? Thanks!" She groaned. So flippant, just putting the hardest assignment of all onto her. Not even asking. With anyone else, he would have had to phrase it as a great favor—to butter that person up, to ask permission. Anger bubbled to the surface. She grumbled to herself. Being the spokesperson for this scandal was literally the last thing she wanted to do. And weren't there people at this school whose job it was to speak to the press? She took a deep breath. It was frustrating and rude, but there weren't many options, and in some ways she was the best person for the job. Time was moving quickly and she started to feel like she had no choice. She had to do it. And if there was anyone who was equipped to do it, it was her.

The question was: Should she admit that she was the person who had started the investigation or should she act just as a spokesperson? The pros and cons ran through her mind as she showered and put on her television-friendly makeup, which was thicker than the daily BB cream she used just to smooth out her complexion. She also made sure to put powder over the top. It sealed the foundation and also offered a layer of protection against sweat. Television lights made everyone sweat; powder was the secret weapon. She took her normal publicist uniform out of the closet, then decided that she needed a little more flair as a spokesperson. She grabbed a white silk T-shirt and a cropped pin-striped blazer that showed the bottom of the T-shirt under it. She paired the top and blazer with black cigarette pants. Instead of her normal wedge, she put on a kitten heel that showed off her ankles. For jewelry, she wore a three-inch rainbow Bakelite bracelet and a chunky gold necklace that drew the eye up to her face. Then she grabbed her phone, slipped a powder compact into her back pocket, and went outside.

In the shower, she had decided that the only way to make this go away was to issue a statement in a little impromptu news conference. She couldn't handle this the way she had Farrah and Freddy's situation because she didn't want there to be a sit-down interview. The facts were the facts and there was no need to delve into them more deeply. As she walked across campus, she had a quick call with Helene Waxman.

"What should I tell the press?" Gillian asked. "Only tell me what I need to know."

"Well, Ken is gone, as is his wife. They'll be moved out of the headmaster's house and we'll begin a search for a new administrator."

"And what will happen in the interim?" Gillian asked.

"You know Barbara Dudley?"

"Of course," Gillian said. "She's a good assistant head-master. She'll do a good job."

"Yes," Helene said. "I think that's basically all you need to know. You know how to say all the right things. Talk to Alma Hamilton about getting the press conference set up."

"Okay," Gillian said. "Talk to you later."

When she got to where all the trucks were parked, she started going around telling each of the producers that she would be making a statement about the removal of Stuart Kent from the headmaster role in an hour on the steps of the clock tower. Then she called Alma Hamilton, the concierge, to tell her what was happening and that she needed a po-dium. After they hung up, she went into the clock tower building and headed up to the headmaster's office. Gloria was sitting at her desk, looking shocked. Gloria's white hel-met of hair around her head made her face appear even more pale.

"Gloria," Gillian said as she walked into the office. "Are you okay?"

"I just can't believe it," she said. "He's gone. After all this time."

"Well," Gillian said. "You did the right thing. Did you know that they found even more embezzlement that he had hidden even from you?"

"I'm not surprised," Gloria said. "But I am sad. He was a good boss. He always encouraged me to take vacations and told me to go home at five o'clock."

"You can be a good boss and also a corrupt person," Gillian said. "Did you ever find out why he did it?"

"I don't like to think it was malice," Gloria said. "I think he just got caught up in something that he couldn't control."

"That's kind of you," Gillian said.

"I try," Gloria said. "How can I help you? It looks like for the moment I don't have a boss to help."

"I need to revise and print out a statement that I'm going to read to the press," Gillian said. "I got a little more information from Helene."

"Well, the headmaster's computer has been seized, so the only one here is mine. Do you want to use it? I can go take a break. I could use some time to clear my head."

"Sure," Gillian said. "Can you also just cut and paste the GEM-ALL message that went out this morning, so that I can expand on it?"

"Of course," Gloria said. She quickly hit a few keys on her machine and pasted the message into a Word file; then she pushed back from her computer. "I haven't been answering the phone. I've just let everything go to voice mail."

"That's the right approach," Gillian said. "If somehow someone does get ahold of you, just send them to me." She scribbled her cell phone number down on a Post-it for Gloria and then sat down at her desk.

"Thanks, Gillian," Gloria said. She took her purse, a large

white triangle with rattan handles, and headed toward the door. "When you were in high school, you were so sweet, but so meek. The world seemed bigger than you. And now look at you. Taking charge. I'm impressed."

"I've turned over a new leaf," Gillian said. Glad that someone else had noticed.

"I'm proud of you," Gloria said. "And thank you for helping and defending me. I really do appreciate it." Gloria looked around mournfully and walked out of the office.

Gillian sat down at Gloria's computer and studied the statement she had already made. She wasn't exactly sure what else to add to it. It was succinct and to the point. Any additions would invite more questions, the sort she didn't want to answer. She decided instead to focus on the harm embezzlement did to the school. She figured that would look better than admitting that this had been going on for years without anyone doing anything about it. As she typed, she shook her head. A publicist's job was often unglamorous. And this was the hard part. But she had dealt with enough scandals in her time that she felt like she was following the proper protocol, that she knew how to handle such things. She hoped she was right.

TWENTY-TWO

....

Gillian walked out of the clock tower building to a circle of about a dozen reporters holding microphones along with photographers holding cameras. The concierge had placed the podium in the exact center of the steps, so that the shot would include the ivy that grew up around the front door of the building. It was a perfect location for a press conference.

She looked around at the eager faces waiting for her to make a mistake. Though her stomach was fluttering with butterflies, she tried to calm herself so that she wouldn't sweat. She took a deep breath, then began.

"Hello, I'm Gillian Brodie. A member of the faculty here at Glen Ellen Academy. I'm here to tell you just a few things and I won't be answering any questions. Stuart Kent, who was the headmaster here for over twenty years, has been removed from his position. He was accused of embezzlement. After further investigation it was revealed that he had stolen over a million dollars from the institution he led. This type of crime hurts the entire community, especially those who could have been given opportunities to change their fortunes in life via scholarships or other funded programs. As a result of this discovery, the headmaster will be replaced and will be asked to repay the money he has stolen. We will begin our search for a new headmaster after the holidays. In the interim, Assistant Headmistress Barbara Dudley will be stepping into the role. Thank you for coming today. Please do not question the students or faculty on campus about this. In fact, we ask that you leave the premises immediately. This is a school, not a circus. Thank you."

The reporters started shouting questions about Kent, but also about Farrah and Freddy. She smiled as genuinely as she could and then walked back into the building. She took the rear exit and skirted the far perimeter of campus to get back to her room. When she got inside, she closed the door, went into the bathroom, sat on the cool tile floor, and cried for a good long time.

That evening, Lila came over with a pizza and a bottle of wine. "Did the kids see you?" Gillian asked.

"Who cares," Lila said. "You had a hard day." Lila put the pizza down on the table and gave Gillian a big hug. She tried not to cry again.

"It's been a hard week," Gillian said. "I've just been thinking so much about the past and also the last year and how I've changed. Plus, I'm kind of in shock about Aiden. I mean, I guess I knew that one day he would choose the winery or the school or something over me. But . . . it's just surprising. Things were going well."

"Maybe he'll regret it," Lila said. "They often come back."

"I don't even know if I want him to. Although I do think his reason for breaking up with me was kind of bogus."

"Well, hopefully this whole thing is over now and it won't be a conflict of interest anymore. Maybe wait a few days and see what happens." As she said that, Bunny, Julia, and Rainbow burst through Gillian's door.

"Wait a few days for what?" Bunny asked.

"Don't you guys knock?" Gillian asked.

"The door was open and we saw you on TV and we want to know what happened," Julia said.

"Just boring legal things," Gillian said. "And now you'll get a new headmaster."

"Maybe they'll get someone cool," Julia said. "Who doesn't have a weird fancy stuck-up wife who always wears pearls and expensive scarves. This scandal actually explains why she looked like that. Our money was buying her fancy scarves. How rude."

"I'm sure they will want someone forward-thinking," Gillian said.

"And what's going on with you and my dad," Rainbow said. "He's all mopey."

Lila winked at Gillian.

"I'm not discussing that," Gillian said. Like a true publicist, she said it as definitively as possible so they wouldn't ask follow-up questions.

"Okay, fine," Rainbow said.

"Anyway, we came to tell you my news," Julia said.

"I don't even know what that means anymore," Gillian said.

"I didn't get into Yale," Julia said.

"I'm sorry," Gillian said, meaning it. "But honestly, I know you can find a better fit, I promise."

"Yeah," Julia said. "Since I got all of those Instagram followers, I've been doing more creative things—taking more artistic photos and also writing longer messages. Showing my clothes. I even made a dress for someone who paid me five hundred dollars, plus materials. I don't know, made me think maybe I should take some time to focus on that. On art."

"You're an influencer!" Rainbow exclaimed.

"And an artist," Gillian said.

"Farrah and Freddy both got into NYU," Bunny said. "I figured you would want to know because they're your favorites."

Gillian smiled. She was glad; this was such a hard time of year. "I don't have favorites. But that's also great news. They were so worried they would be separated. I'm glad they'll be together."

"So now you can stop worrying about all of us," Bunny said.

"I am proud of each and every one of you," Gillian said.

As she said that, her phone rang. It was Helene Waxman. Gillian hoped she wasn't calling to yell at her about the press conference. She didn't think she had done anything wrong.

"Gillian, this is Helene Waxman."

"Hello, Helene," Gillian said, stepping into her bedroom to take the call. She sat down on her bed and held her pillow in her lap. It was dark out and the moon was perfectly positioned next to the clock tower, framed by her window. She was lucky to live in such a beautiful place. It was important to appreciate the little things when the big things were so . . . big.

"Thank you for everything you've done for us in the past few months," Helene said. "Between handling the Farrah and Freddy situation and now this. You did a great job today. Handled it exactly right. I'm so glad we hired you."

"Even after the past few months?" Gillian said.

"If you hadn't brought it to our attention, someone would have. And this way we were able to deal with it as quietly as possible."

"True," Gillian said.

"And you've done great things with the Vallejo dorm. The kids there just adore you."

"I have fun with them," Gillian said.

"That's why I've called," Helene said. "Because you've done so well. We're thinking that the school is missing a head of communications. We realized this year that we really need one. And we think you would be perfect."

"I don't know," Gillian said, flabbergasted. "I wasn't necessarily planning on staying here . . ."

"You've basically been doing the job all year, so really we'll just be paying you to do something you're already doing."

"Who would be the dorm mother to Vallejo?"

"You could continue to live there if you wanted. Dorm parents often do other things for the school and technically you haven't been doing that. Or you could move off campus and just go to work like a regular faculty member."

"Wow," Gillian said. "I guess I need to think about it."

"The school's never had a head of communications before, so you wouldn't have any legacy to live up to. You could make the job your own."

"I appreciate your confidence in me," Gillian said, remembering to be gracious. "I'll get back to you soon."

"Thank you, Gillian. Regardless of what you decide, we really appreciate you."

Lila was still there, although the girls had left, so Gillian went out and told her what Helene Waxman had proposed to her.

"Wow," Lila said. "Do you want to do it?"

"I don't know," Gillian said. "I wasn't sure I would stay here. But now I've committed to buying a car, so I must want to stay. And she said I was kind of already doing it."

"You're the perfect person for it and she's right. You've totally been doing it the past few months. I think you'd be great."

"I will say that dealing with Farrah and Freddy, and now this, it made me realize that I'm really good at being a publicist. And I like being good at what I do."

"Me too," Lila said. "The cool thing about this is that you can apply what you're good at to a place that you've learned to love."

"It feels hard to start a whole new chapter of your life at thirty-eight," Gillian said.

"You have more than half your life ahead of you," Lila said. "Why not spend a few years of it here, in a beautiful place?"

"I guess that's true," Gillian said.

"The school is lucky to have you," Lila said. "And selfishly, I don't want you to leave. But also it would be nice if you didn't live in the dorm."

Gillian nodded. As much as she loved the girls, especially spending that liminal time with them after classes were over and before they did their homework—those were the times when she learned the most from them and felt like they got the most from her—it would be nice not to have to do a hall check at ten o'clock every night and sneak around so the kids didn't see her coming or going. It would be nice to have a beautiful California deck and a wine refrigerator and a driveway with a little hybrid car in it. She smiled. "Yeah, there are things that could be good."

"And you could see how it goes," Lila said.

"The Aiden part is the worst though," Gillian said.

"Maybe he'll come around. Or maybe you'll meet someone better. I'm rooting for the latter. I think you can do better than him."

Gillian sighed. It was so hard to see outside of her current situation, to imagine how things could be different. So much had changed in the past few months. Could it all change again? She hugged Lila good-bye and took her glass of wine into her bedroom. She crawled into bed with her glass and looked out the window, trying to process. Everything was happening at the same time and she just didn't like it. She wondered how she would have felt if Aiden hadn't broken up with her. If they were still comfortably ambling toward a long-term love, would any of this be a question? If they were in love, she would be doing everything in her power to stay in Glen Ellen, to continue their relationship, the one thing she had wanted for her entire life. And yet, she had also made this great friend, one she really trusted and counted on. And that was a gift she hadn't expected.

Maybe Lila was right: maybe this love was outdated, was based more on a romanticized version of the past than on the present. Maybe she needed a fresh start when it came to love. She had just given her life a fresh start by moving to California and now it already felt like she needed another one. Was she going to be restarting forever? When did she get to up-grade? Maybe the secret of it all was that you actually never stopped restarting. That everything was always changing, and you had to be ready to adapt. If that was true, it was a frustrating realization: that you are never done growing and changing. But maybe having that knowledge would better prepare her to face what lay ahead. There was only one way to find out.

TWENTY-THREE

....

"Can I please come by to see you?" was the text she woke up to. From Aiden. She sighed. She had decided the night before that she didn't need him, didn't want him. But she should hear him out, she told herself.

"OK," she wrote back. Then she dragged herself into the shower and put on a pair of shorts and an old T-shirt from high school. To show that she wasn't trying to impress him. When he got to the security desk downstairs, she went down to meet him. She expected that they would take a walk.

"Can I come up?" he asked. "I don't want anyone to overhear us."

She sighed. "Fine." She signed him into the building and they took the elevator back up to her room. It was early on a Saturday morning; the kids were all sleeping in.

He came inside and sat at her little dining table. She offered him some cold pizza and sat with him while he ate eagerly. Before he broke up with her, they'd had plans to go out to dinner. She wondered if he had eaten. But that wasn't her job now—to make sure that he was fed.

"What do you think of Helene's offer?" he asked.

"Oh, so you know about that?" she asked.

"I will admit that I had something to do with it."

"It's hard to decide," she said. "I don't know anything about working at a school in a real job. I'm totally wrong for it except that I'm here and I know the kids."

"That makes you great for it," he said.

"I was trying to think of what I would have done if you hadn't broken up with me."

"And?"

"I would have taken it without hesitation," she said. "Because I would have felt like I was building a life here. But now . . . it all just feels wrong."

"You are building a life here," he said. "You have friends, a great job, respect."

She shrugged. "I'm good at being a publicist. I don't know how to be a school administrator."

"I think you know better than you think. It's a perfect job for you." He got up and looked out the window. His back was to her. "You know exactly how to help these kids, and these parents."

She stayed on the couch. "Right now I feel like I don't know anything."

"What if I made a mistake?" he asked, turning around.

"What kind of mistake?"

"What if instead of breaking up with you, I stepped down from the Parents' Association. I'm about to have to leave anyway, since Rainbow is graduating. They need to be able to run it without me."

"I don't know," she said. "I don't want you to make that

kind of sacrifice for me. You have a few more months on the association."

"Not being with you is more of a sacrifice," he said.

She paused. It wasn't what she'd expected him to say at all. She was a bit speechless.

"I mean it," he said. He came over and sat next to her and touched her cheek.

"It's just hard for me to trust you," she said.

"You can trust me, I promise, if you give me one more chance," he said. She stared ahead at the framed picture of the New York skyline on her wall, a place that felt so far away. Should she give him another chance? Or was it time to move on? She sighed. It was too hard to think of a different way right now. She had already changed things so much. And she did love being with him, she did love him. Probably Lila was right that he was the past, not the future. But Gillian did feel a present-day connection with Aiden. It wasn't like she was getting back together with her high school boyfriend. She was falling in love with her high school friend. Somehow that was different. It was a step forward, or at the very least a step sideways. Not a step back. Being alone, that was a step back, and that had been her situation for so many years. Even if it wasn't forever with Aiden, it was for now and it was good.

"Okay," she said, turning to him and smiling. "This time if anyone breaks anyone's heart, it has to be me." She could see a hint of a tear glisten in his eye.

"Thank you," he said, pulling her toward him into a hug.

She closed her eyes and envisioned the two of them standing next to each other at a party celebrating her appointment as the head of communications. She would wear her white Albert Nipon jacket and dress set, the one with a kind of shawl collar and gold buttons. He would wear some sort of pin-striped suit; actually, she didn't know if he had a suit, but he had to somewhere, right? You never knew with these California types. He kissed her neck and then slid his hand up her back and she stopped thinking about parties and more about the moment at hand. He took it slower than usual, removing her clothes one article at a time, taking a moment to luxuriate in skin against skin. He kissed her shoulder, then her arm, then wrapped around to her stomach. She wrapped her legs around him and closed her eyes, leaned back and into him almost simultaneously. Everything felt right, almost choreographed, like a dance they hadn't quite gotten right before, but now it was really working. She led him into the bedroom and the rest of their clothes fell onto the floor. She smiled at him. "Hi," she said.

"Hi." He smiled and then they fell onto the bed together, enraptured.

Later, under the covers, as they were chatting about nothing, her phone rang. It was an unknown number and it looked international. She let it go to voice mail. She waited for a message to come through. "It's Bunny's mom," she said to Aiden.

"Call her back," he said.

She was already dialing.

"Gillian Brodie?" said a breathy voice on the other end of the line.

"Yes?" she asked.

"This is Alice Winthrop, Bunny's mother."

"Oh hi," Gillian said.

"I wonder if you have a few minutes to talk. I'm a little worried about Bunny."

"Sure," Gillian said, surprised. Everything Bunny had told her about her mother had indicated that she mostly didn't even know that Bunny was alive. She pulled her T-shirt over her head and walked over to the window seat. Aiden started scrolling through his phone, still shirtless in bed.

"I am just worried," Alice said. "Because I know Julia didn't get into Yale and Bunny didn't even apply early anywhere. She seems to be fixated on UCLA, but I don't know, I feel like she needs a backup plan. She trusts you so much. You are her hero, really. I wonder if maybe you can talk to her?"

"I don't know about that," Gillian said, feeling a little embarrassed.

"You're all she talks about. We talk about three times a week. I'm sure she's told you that I neglect her, but that's a story she likes to tell. She has every advantage in the world and she likes people to feel bad for her. But I get it—she likes drama and she doesn't really have any, so she makes it up. We're actually very close. I know every grade she gets, every conversation she has with her friends, I know about all the stuff with the twins. But mostly she tells me about you. How you got the dorm under control. How the kids all love you. How you got rid of Headmaster Kent."

"How does she know that?" Gillian asked. "I never told her that."

"She has her ways," Alice said. "Don't worry, she won't tell anyone. Anyway, you inspire them. And her especially.

So if you could talk to her and make sure she's doing these college applications the right way. It's okay that she didn't apply early, but I don't want her to mess up because she's proud. She's just a teenager. And you know they get dumb ideas in their heads sometimes and they can't get past them. I'm sure you remember."

"I do," Gillian said. "I don't envy them, really."

"She has a good head on her shoulders," Alice said. "But she needs some guidance. I really appreciate you helping her. All you've done for her. All the parents do. We talk to each other too, in case you wondered."

"I had no idea," Gillian said.

"Well, now you know, and you're our favorite topic. All the girls have a Gillian story."

Gillian felt a little bit embarrassed that she was being discussed and observed in such detail. But it helped give her some more confidence in the head of communications opportunity, and it also kind of explained why they'd offered it to her in the first place. Who knew that there was a parent back channel?

"I'll do my best," Gillian said. "But she's an independent girl."

"I know it," Alice said. "It's a good quality in the long run, but frustrating now."

"Thanks for the call, Alice," Gillian said. "I really appreciate it."

"You make this school a better place," Alice said. "Have a great afternoon, and thank you."

Gillian smiled as she put the phone down on the cushion. Bunny had told her that her mother was such a monster, but she was a lovely person. Gillian had always known that

Bunny wanted attention. Still, she hadn't thought that she would lie about her mother so convincingly all year. Based on what Alice had said, they seemed to have a great relationship. Gillian knew better than to take what kids said about their parents at face value. Even so, she wondered why Bunny played the victim so much when she actually had a fun and perceptive mother. Maybe it was just some jealousy at feeling left behind. Her cool mom was off partying and having a great time and she'd left her daughter behind. Gillian felt a little guilty that she had believed Bunny wholeheartedly.

"What was that all about?" Aiden asked.

"It was Bunny's mom. Calling to tell me how great I am. How much the kids love me and asking if I can help get Bunny to have a backup plan to UCLA."

He smiled. "Sounds like it was a good call then."

"Did someone put her up to that?" she asked.

"Absolutely not," he said. "She's totally out of the loop of Parents' Association stuff."

"She told me there's a back channel of parent gossip and I'm their favorite topic."

"I'm not in that back channel," he said. "But it's entirely possible she's friends with other parents here."

"Anyway," she said, crawling back into bed and putting her head on his chest. "She did make me feel a little better about the head of communications job."

"You honestly would be great at it," he said, beaming.

"I need to take some alone time to think about it." She narrowed her eyes as if to indicate thinking.

"Does that mean we need to get up?" he asked.

"I can take my alone time later," she said.

"Great," he said, kissing her shoulder. "Take all the time you need. Later."

She giggled and kissed him. She finally had a modicum of control and power. She was wanted. She was (dare she admit it?) happy.

EPILOGUE

....

April 2019

The introductory party for the new headmistress was a totally different experience from her first party at the headmaster's house as an employee. The new headmaster was to be introduced today, but Gillian was already acquainted with her. Gillian had been on the faculty interviewing committee, so she had met each of the candidates. Just one of her many new responsibilities as the head of communications.

Although there had been three finalists, Jasmine Reade had stood out above and beyond all of the other applicants. She had attended Exeter as a scholarship day student back in the mid-1990s, she had a PhD in education from Columbia's Teachers College, and she had been the dean of students at Simon's Rock and the acting headmistress of the Piney Woods School in Mississippi—but before the Piney Woods administrators could make her the permanent headmistress there, Helene Waxman had recruited her for Glen Ellen Academy.

Gillian had a real admiration for Helene Waxman; she was a great board president. Gillian had never met Helene in person—she lived in Washington, D.C., and conducted all the board meetings and interviews remotely—but she felt close to her even so. She was also so happy that Headmistress Reade was joining the school. Jasmine had already redecorated the house with colorful sofas and art created by her former students—no Picassos to be found. Gillian had heard that the school had repossessed what they could of Kent's excesses and planned to put it toward the betterment of the school—the scholarship fund and the endowment. It felt like Glen Ellen Academy was finally catching up with the times.

Gillian hung up her purple coat in the front hall of the headmistress's house and walked into the living room to join Aiden and Lila in front of a poster from a Basquiat exhibit at the Brooklyn Museum. She looked around the room and took a moment to appreciate that she was a part of something. It was a welcoming and happy something, not a competitive and backstabbing something, like her publicity business had been. Glen Ellen Academy really felt like a family.

The new headmaster had wanted to include the students in the welcome party, but the house was too small for all of them to be there at once, so they had created a rotational schedule. Fifteen students rotating in every twenty minutes. The kids were all adhering to the schedule, which amazed Gillian; they must have really wanted to impress their new leader. She saw Bunny and Rainbow and Julia come in together, wearing matching belt bags; Gillian had made the mistake of calling them fanny packs when they first debuted them and had been resoundingly laughed out of the room. Their arms were linked and they made a beeline for Gillian when they saw her.

"We haven't seen you since before Christmas break!" Julia said.

"Well, I have," Rainbow said, giggling.

"Well, we have news for you," Bunny said, rummaging through her bag for her phone. "Now that you're not our dorm mom anymore."

"What?" Gillian asked, truly curious.

"I got into UCLA, Irvine, Tufts, *and* Bennington."

"Congratulations," Gillian said. "Those are all great choices. You know, I chatted with your mom. She seems really great."

"Well," Bunny said. "She can be. That's the thing about her. She knows how to charm people."

"But according to her, you guys have a great relationship."

"Ugh, I'm sorry I didn't tell you the whole truth, Gillian."

"And you love her," Gillian said.

"I do. I'm sorry to say. I wish I hated her. It would be a better story."

"I just don't really get why you lie about her," Gillian said. "You're lucky."

"I don't know," Bunny said. "One thing I have realized this year is that what you say can have repercussions beyond your own life, so maybe I'll talk about her differently when I go to college. Anyway, all these acceptances prove that it was a waste to fill out all those applications and write that extra essay for Bennington, but I won't hold it against you."

"It's nice to have options," Gillian said.

"I got into UCLA too," Rainbow said. "And also Davis."

"What do you think you'll do?" Gillian asked. She already knew about Rainbow's acceptances from Aiden.

"We're going to room together at UCLA, of course," Bunny said.

"Yeah," Rainbow said.

Gillian wondered if maybe Rainbow wanted to be a little closer to home at Davis. But she felt it was the wrong time to ask.

"I went to Davis," Lila said. "And I really liked it. It's the reason I'm here, really."

"I've lived here my whole life," Rainbow said.

Lila nodded. "Good point."

"And I'm going to go to FIT," Julia said. "My parents are losing their minds. A fashion school. But it's what I want to do."

"I think that's great," Gillian said.

"I'm so proud of all of you," Aiden said.

"*Dad,*" Rainbow groaned.

"I know, I know," he said. "It's my job to say that."

"Dads aren't supposed to be at boarding school parties with their kids," Rainbow said.

He took Gillian's hand. "Good point," he said. "You're allowed to stop talking to me now."

"Let's go meet our new headmistress," Bunny said. "At least for a few more months."

Gillian smiled as they walked away. "They're good kids," she said.

"They are," Aiden agreed.

After the meet and greet in the house, everyone gathered outside. Gillian and Aiden stood off to the side with Rainbow, Bunny, and Julia while Farrah and Freddy got set up on the porch, he with his guitar, she behind the keyboard. They smiled at each other and then out at the crowd.

"We're proud to be here today," Farrah said into the

microphone. "To welcome Headmistress Reade. She's already changed our school for the better by redecorating this fussy old house. I can't wait to see how she redecorates the rest of our beloved school. We're on our way out of here, but we'll always remember our time here fondly. We're going to do a cover for our new headmistress. But we request that nobody record it or post it on the internet. We haven't cleared the rights to sing it. But it's an old favorite of ours."

Gillian punched Julia lightly on the upper arm.

"We've all learned from our mistakes," Julia said.

"We can just enjoy the song," Gillian said.

"Thank God," Bunny said.

"It's called 'Dayton, Ohio—1903.' It's sort of a mournful song, but it's about coming together and spending time. I hope you like it."

She started the rhythmic beat of the keyboard that opened the song. As she began playing, Gillian realized that she knew the song. It was one that her mother had sung to her as a child. It was a sweet song about community, about visiting, spending time together. They had played it, actually, when Gillian was home with her mother over Christmas. It had been a good reunion—Gillian had been solicitous and her mother had been honestly happy to see her. They had talked about the misunderstandings between them of the past few years and Gillian had told her about her job offer. Her mother had been excited about having her nearby and Gillian had realized that one of the things that had made her relationship with her mother difficult was distance. Not seeing each other all the time had made it so they didn't understand each other. But a few hours in each other's presence had brought them back to their old pre-Gem relationship. Their inside jokes, their joy.

After the visit, Gillian had called Helene and accepted the job. Now the song reminded her of her mom, of her childhood, when it was just the two of them, and of those days when they had reconnected. Farrah and Freddy had updated Randy Newman's version, jazzed up the chords with Freddy's guitar, added a harmony.

Gillian leaned against Aiden as they finished singing, tears on her cheeks.

"That was beautiful," he said.

"I love that song," she said.

"You're crying," he said.

"Happy tears." She smiled.

Headmistress Reade then got up from the porch swing, still clapping for the duo. "What a lucky school we are," she said. "To have this talent among us. Thank you, Farrah and Freddy. I feel lucky to be here also."

She was holding cards in one hand, but she didn't consult them. "I'm a product of boarding schools," she said. "I went to Exeter for high school, as a scholarship student. My parents didn't know a lot about private school, but they had heard of Exeter, and they found a scholarship and they got me in. It changed my life. Granted, it was hard. I was the first person in my family to go to boarding school, and unlike most of my classmates, my family wasn't a wealthy one. That said, I was mostly welcomed and learned a lot. The most important thing for me, though, was that I made lifelong friends—both with some of the teachers and with some of the students. I still email with my high school English teacher and I have three friends that I meet every year in New Hampshire in a little house by a lake—we call it the GLOE weekend, the Gorgeous Ladies of Exeter. I wish you students many GLOG or GMOG weekends in your future. And I hope to facilitate a school that makes those types of ongoing friendships happen. My vision for this school is to take what we have and make it better—more inclusive, more cohesive, more immersive. All the -*ive*'s. I'd love to hear from all of you, but especially the outgoing seniors, for you to tell me what could be better. And also what's already good. That's important too. I'm sure you'll be hearing a lot from me in the next few weeks and months and years, but I want to say to everyone that I'm really happy to be here and also so glad that we're having this day-long party. I think Farrah and Freddy are going to play us another song and then we can all go on our way. Thank you for welcoming me already and I can't wait for us all to learn together."

Gillian smiled and leaned over to Aiden. "She's so great."

"All of this was worth it," he said.

"Totally," she said.

Then Farrah and Freddy started playing "We Are Family" and everyone started dancing.

Later that night, Gillian, Aiden, Lila, and Barbara Dudley sat at the dinner table with Jasmine and her partner, Rose, eating steak and corn they had grilled together on the headmistress's back porch.

"It was a long road to get here," Gillian said. "But I'm glad we all ended up at this table." She raised her glass of rosé to toast.

"Me too," Jasmine said.

Gillian looked around at her friends—old and new—and her school, which she had come full circle with. She thought about the new business cards in her pocket, which also brought together her old life as a publicist with her new one as a school employee. She thought about the room filled with shopping bags and the framed Picasso in the living room and the budget that Gloria had shown her that didn't balance. And her mom, happily aging with her third husband in Sacramento, now fully reintegrated into Gillian's life—texting her photos of flower arrangements for house showings. All of those things had brought her to this moment. She held up her glass and clinked with everyone around the table.

Gillian smiled and slung her arm over the back of Aiden's chair. Good food, new job, new friends. It was so rare that things felt right all at once, but for this very moment, they did. And for once she knew to savor it. She sipped her wine, which was crisp and acidic, with a hint of sweetness. She closed her eyes and said to herself, "Peace."

ACKNOWLEDGMENTS

....

I want to thank my amazing editorial team, led by the inimitable Maya Ziv. Maya, your thoughtfulness and support are unending and amazing and I could not have done this without you. Thanks also to Lexy Cassola, who gave me a letter I really needed and made this book infinitely better. And Natalie Edwards, whose notes were extremely thoughtful and helpful. I could not have done this without my amazing agent, Allison Hunter, who also read and commented on so many drafts with such insightful wisdom. To my delightful and brilliant copyeditor Bonnie Thompson—you made me laugh, taught me things I didn't know, and noticed so many things I had missed. My marketing and publicity team at Dutton, who are second to none—Katie Taylor, Isabel Dasilva, Becky Odell, and Jamie Knapp—thank you for all you've done and are doing to spread the word about my book. To John Parsley and Christine Ball and the wider Dutton team and sales force, thank you for your support.

I also have to thank everyone at Ecco, past and present, for their understanding and support in this process: Helen Atsma,

Dan Halpern, Meghan Deans, Sonya Cheuse, Martin Wilson, Caitlin Mulrooney-Lyski, Ashlyn Edwards, Jin Soo Chun, Rachel Sargent, Sara Birmingham, Gabriella Doob, Sarah Murphy, Norma Barksdale, and TJ Calhoun.

I must also thank my dearest friends, Alafair Burke, Renee Daley, Natalie Sandoval, and Megan Heuer, for bearing with me and supporting me during all of this.

I couldn't have done this without the ongoing support of my parents, David and Elaine, and my sister, Beth. And my gratitude to Luke Epplin, for being a person who can understand my complaining better than anyone. As well as my in-laws, Steven and Pam Olson, and my brothers-in-law, Simon and Nat. All have been instrumental in getting moments of this book revised.

The true hero of the writing of this book, though, is Ben Olson, who has seen me through *so* many drafts of it. My first book was basically finished when we met, so I don't know that he understood exactly what he was getting into when he agreed to marry a writer, but he has been so kind and generous to me during the writing of this book and I couldn't be a luckier person to spend every day with him. I should also acknowledge our daughter, Nora, whose due date was looming during the first draft; the maternity leave she gave me allowed me to finish that draft. (I gave myself a month and a half to get my brain back—and then started in. I am not here to say that brand-new mothers can or should write books. They very much shouldn't. But if you have a book seventy-five percent written and a maternity leave, well, that's what you have to do.) And since then her regular nap schedule has been the saving grace of the revision process. To Ben, who enjoys a long walk, to Nora, who goes along for the ride, and to Nora's naps. I couldn't do it without you three—husband, daughter, naps.

I wouldn't be me if I didn't acknowledge my dog, Leopold Bloom, who snoozed through it all but did so with the most love. There's nothing like the love of a dog, and there's certainly nothing like the love of my dog.